Praise for
The Medic's Wife

The Medic's Wife is a story of altruism, bravery, and leadership in the face of unimaginable adversity. Set against the backdrop of WWII, this gripping story follows the lives of Mary and her husband Edmund, a combat medic in the U.S. army, before, during and after the war.

The writing is raw and honest, capturing the complexities of military life and the toll that war takes on the brave soldiers who have "borne the battle" and the families who have sacrificed along with them. But at its core, *The Medic's Wife* is a testament to the strength of the human spirit and the power of love to heal even the deepest of wounds.

This book is a must read for anyone who wants to draw inspiration from a generation of Americans who put the country's needs ahead of their own. With its compelling characters, evocative settings, and powerful message, *The Medic's Wife* is a story that will stay with you long after you turn the last page.

Robert A McDonald, West Point Distinguished Graduate and Chairman of the Board of the West Point Association of Graduates. Retired Chairman, President & CEO of the Procter & Gamble Company. Eighth Secretary of the Department of Veteran Affairs.

We, a group of armed forces veterans, have come together to write about a man who lived in our hometown and was a silent war hero many years ago. As young kids growing up alongside him, we simply knew him as "Mr. K" a quiet dad and kind neighbor who never spoke of his military service. It wasn't until a decade after his passing that we began to learn the true extent of his service to our country.

During WWII S/Sgt Kruszynski led a platoon of army medics and took part in some of the most dangerous missions of the war. Despite the danger and hardship he faced, this silent war hero remained committed to his fellow soldiers and the missions he was given.

Through our own service to our country, we have come to understand the immeasurable debt of gratitude we owe to those who have served before us. We are privileged to share the story of our neighbor "Mr. K" and his wife Mary, for whom this book is named.

In an age where heroism is often celebrated with fanfare and publicity, *The Medic's Wife* is a must-read and a powerful reminder that true heroism often goes unnoticed.

Michael Good	**Kirk Shawhan**	**Ralph W. Lunt**	**Mark Louis**
Col (ret) USAF	LtCol (ret) USMC	Col (ret) USAF	Cpt USAF
Astronaut	Marine Pilot	Senior Navigator	Instructor Pilot

All United States Armed Forces (ret)

The Medic's Wife is a powerful and deeply moving account of an American medic's experience as he bore witness to the horrors of the Holocaust. The story is retold through Mary, the medic's wife, and we are given a stark and unflinching view of the atrocities committed by the Nazis, and the unimaginable suffering endured by those who were imprisoned in the concentration camps.

The story's vivid and haunting descriptions of what was seen and heard within the camp walls are a testament to the strength and resilience of the human spirit in the face of the unimaginable. The author's commitment to retelling the truth about what happened in these camps is a powerful reminder of the importance of bearing witness to history.

This book is a must read for anyone interested in the history of the Holocaust, and for those who seek to understand the depths of human depravity and the power of human compassion. It is a powerful reminder that we must never forget the atrocities committed during the darkest chapter of our history, and that we must always strive to ensure that such horrors never happen again.

The Nancy & David Wolf Holocaust and Humanity Center,
Cincinnati, Ohio

As a Maj. General in the U.S. Army, I have encountered numerous stories of bravery, sacrifice, and unwavering commitment. *The Medic's Wife* delves deep into the heart and soul of an army combat medic, shedding light on the trials and tribulations they face while tending to wounded soldiers on the front lines. The author's meticulous research and attention to detail transport readers to the battlefields, allowing us to witness the horror and courage that permeated every moment of those trying times.

I have seen firsthand the toll that war takes on the families of our servicemen and women. The author expertly captures the emotional rollercoaster experienced by those left at home, portraying the fortitude required to carry on in the face of unimaginable adversity. It is a beautifully written story that will transport readers to a pivotal era in our nation's history, and showcases how unbreakable bonds are forged during times of trial.

Maj. General John A. Yingling, United States Army (ret)

Being a military wife and mother, I found *The Medic's Wife* to be a powerful and deeply moving memoir of love, sacrifice, and resilience in the face of the unimaginable horrors of war. The story brought to memory my time with the U.S. Army Wounded Warrior Program whose mission was to advocate for the most seriously injured soldiers returning from the Gulf Wars and beyond. Unlike the WWII times, I am relieved to report that there are now many programs in place to help with all types of service-related disabilities.

Like Staff Sergeant Kruszynski and his friends, there continues to be dedicated and courageous men and women serving our country today. And like Mary, the military spouse continues to be a hero, keeping the "home fires burning" while supporting loved ones who serve our country all around the world.

The Medic's Wife is a must-read for anyone who has ever loved someone in uniform and for those who want to be inspired by the indomitable spirit of military spouses, and their families.

Mrs. Ann Yingling, former U.S. Army Wounded Warriors Advocate. Wife of Maj. General John A. Yingling U.S. Army (Ret). Mother of Maj. Scott Yingling, currently serving on active duty in the U.S. Army.

THE MEDIC'S WIFE

Edmund A. Kruszynski

Published by Hellgate Press
(An imprint of L&R Publishing, LLC)
email: sales@hellgatepress.com

Cover design and photo restoration by Brigid Krane
and Evan Ecklund of Artists Eleven LLC
Book design: Michael Campbell

Cataloging In Publication Data is available
from the publisher upon request.
ISBN: 978-1-954163-74-4

Printed and bound in the United States of America

THE MEDIC'S WIFE

EDMUND A. KRUSZYNSKI

The Medic's Wife is dedicated to the gallant

medics of the 648th Medical Clearing Company.

They are the unsung heroes of this story.

CONTENTS

PROLOGUE

S/SGT KRUSZYNSKI JOURNAL ENTRY
SOMEWHERE NEAR BASTOGNE, BELGIUM
DECEMBER 29th 1944

The American tank took a direct hit from German 88s. The men trapped inside were burned to a crisp, except for one unlucky soul. How he slithered out of the inferno no one knows. But he wouldn't make it either. He knew it, and I knew it.

His face was badly disfigured, and he couldn't speak. When we made eye contact, I knew what he wanted me to do. Still, I asked him the question to be sure. Blink once for yes, or twice for no. He blinked once.

Two syrettes of morphine were all it took. Out here it's called mercy, back home it's called something else.

I closed his eyes, took his tags, and left his body there. Smoldering.

PART I

CHAPTER 1:
BRECKSVILLE, OHIO
JUNE 2006

*A "once in 100 years" flood devasted portions
of the town of Brecksville, Ohio.*

MARY WATCHED in horror as the murky water reached her ankles. Her condo had turned into an obstacle course of floating furniture, and water was shooting through the drywall like whirlpool jets. Mary steadily, carefully inched her way toward the front door as fast as her 87-year-old bones could carry her. Stopping to catch her breath, she glanced out the back slider and gasped. The deck was ripped from its foundation, and a three-foot wall of roaring river water pressed against the glass. Knowing at any moment the glass door could rupture, Mary forced herself to move faster. But by the time she reached the hallway, the raging flood water had already reached her kneecaps. Her face turned a deeper shade of red with each labored step.

The front door stood less than four feet away, yet each step was a vicious struggle. It felt like a victory when she grabbed onto the door-knob with her right hand. Holding it for balance, Mary breathed a sigh of relief when she managed to unlock the deadbolt. But when she tried to pull the door open, it wouldn't budge. With remarkable determina-tion and grit, she anchored her legs to the floor and gave it another try. This time, she succeeded in wresting the door open just enough to whip one leg around the door and use it as leverage to press it far enough open for her to slip through.

"Oh, My God!" she cried. The front porch, lawn, sidewalk and cul-de-sac had turned into a three-foot deep swimming pool as far as she could see through the hammering rain. She braced herself by press-ing her arms and legs against the door frame. She was secure for the moment, though she couldn't spy a single soul outside.

Mary knew if she moved away from the door she could be caught in the current and whisked away to God only knew where. Only one option remained. Bracing herself, she screamed at the top of her lungs. "Help! Please someone, help me!" Tears mixed with the driving rain-drops when nobody responded to her calls for help. *Is this how it's going to end?*

Mary's life flashed before her eyes and a carousel of memories clicked rapid fire through her brain. But one memory served as the catalyst for the decision she would make next. Mary thought about her husband and his brave group of medics who had launched themselves into the churning water off the coast in Normandy on D-Day.

If Ed could be so brave in the face of such insurmountable odds, so can I! I need to be brave and try to swim to the other side where I'll be more visible.

Holding the sides of the door with her hands, Mary moved her feet away from the corners of the door. Immediately, her lower body became unstable and instinctively, she jammed her feet back into the door jamb to regain some stability. She wailed as she pinched the sides of her bare feet into the 90-degree door cracks. Now she was truly stuck. She hung there, arms shaking with exhaustion, wondering if she might see Ed in heaven sooner than she planned.

CHAPTER 2:
BRECKSVILLE, OHIO
JUNE 2006

JUST AS Mary was ready to give up, she thought she heard a voice. Was she hallucinating? Or was someone coming to her rescue? To her great relief, she heard it again. And this time, the voice clearly yelled, "Hold on!"

Mary cocked her head in the direction of the voice and gasped when she saw a young man wading toward her, the water level up to his belt. Through the pelting rain, he looked almost like a mirage. But she could make out his determined expression, so much like the faces of the heroic young men she met while she visited Ed at Fort Oglethorpe GA in the early 1940s, before the war changed all their lives forever.

Suddenly, the young man disappeared under the water. Terrified for his safety and for hers, Mary watched intently until he reappeared. When he shook the wet hair off his face, grinned, and waved, Mary breathed a huge sigh of relief to know he was unhurt. It took a few minutes, but at last, he reached Mary's side and latched onto a porch column to steady himself against the onslaught.

"I'm so happy to see you! I didn't know if anyone could hear me," Mary gushed.

"How long have you been out here?" he shouted over the driving rain.

"About twenty minutes, I think."

"I'm Paul. Take my hand." He reached out, but Mary couldn't grasp his fingers and was afraid to let go.

"I don't think I'm strong enough, and I'm not wearing shoes," she said, tears starting up again.

"Don't give up," Paul said. "How do your arms feel? Think you're up for a piggyback ride?"

Mary's face brightened as she remembered Ed carrying her that way during his Army training. He claimed it was good practice for his 25-mile marches. "Yes, I'm up for that."

"Great," Paul said with obvious relief. "I'll crouch down, and on the count of three, grab on with your arms and legs. Once you're secure, I'll carry you across the parking lot." Paul got into position and began the count. "One, two, three!"

Mary furrowed her brow and bent her knees. She attempted to spring up, but her legs were too fatigued from bracing her body between the door posts; she fell backward and submerged under the water. Luckily, Paul spun around and pulled her back to the surface.

"Are you alright?" he screamed.

Mary coughed up water and shook her head to unclog her ears. "My legs felt like two lead pipes." She wiped her forehead with her shirt sleeve and sensed something was missing. *My wig!* She pivoted and scanned the water, only to see it floating downstream like silvery rat.

Paul's gaze took in the rising water level. "Let's try it one more time."

Mary gritted her teeth. "I'll do it this time if it's the last thing I ever do."

"One, two, three!" he yelled, and without delay, Mary grabbed onto Paul's shoulders and pulled off a perfect bunny hop. As promised, he grabbed her legs and locked them around his waist. Mary circled her arms around his chest like vice grips on a pipe, and they were on the move.

"It's clear from here to the mailbox. You can stop there to steady yourself before you cross the parking lot," Mary yelled over several claps of thunder.

As Paul trudged toward the mailbox, Mary shot a quick look back at her garage. The hood of her car barely poked above the flood waters. They managed to avoid a wheelbarrow and other debris that rushed past them before reaching the mailbox. She gave Paul an extra tight squeeze for moral support as they paused.

Mary raised her voice so she could be heard over the din. "Ten paces from here you'll feel a gradual slope downward. Try to avoid the middle of the parking lot. There's a gully there, so it will likely be the deepest point."

"Aye, Aye, Captain, thanks for letting me know" Paul brushed the water from his eyes. "I think that's where I ran into trouble on my way to you," he said sheepishly.

Mary realized that she'd never told him her name. "I'm Mary, but Captain will do just fine."

Mary held on for dear life as Paul pressed onward. It was a madhouse of sirens blaring, firefighters on bullhorns, condo residents yelling out of windows, and rescue boats entering the parking lot. When dry ground was within sight Mary couldn't stop fresh tears from flowing, she'd never been happier to be in the midst of chaos and confusion in her life.

Paul sat Mary down on the high ground and plopped on the grass next to her, breathing heavily. Other than having a few lacerations on her feet and being cold and shaken, Mary could hardly believe she'd emerged from this ordeal in one piece.

She placed a hand on her savior's shoulder. "Paul?"

"Yes?"

"You're an angel," she said softly.

CHAPTER 3:
BRECKSVILLE, OHIO
JUNE 2006

"GRAM!" MARY'S 24-year-old granddaughter Peach called out as she approached Mary's place of refuge in the shelter. "I was so worried about you."

Mary, wrapped in a blanket and clutching a cup of steaming coffee, managed a weak smile. She was grateful to see Peach but felt like she had aged ten years from the ordeal. She and other flood survivors had been conveyed here in official-looking trucks, while Paul, bless his soul, had stayed outside to continue helping with the rescue effort.

"What happened? Are you okay?" Peach rattled off questions like a gatling gun.

With a sigh, Mary retold the highlights of her story.

Peach gasped. "That must have been so scary! How did you end up here?"

"God sent a guardian angel named Paul to save me," Mary said, "I don't know how much longer I could have held out if he hadn't come along." Mary's fingers trembled, making the coffee slosh in her cup. She barely managed to place it on the table, and her eyes began to water.

Peach retrieved a packet of facial tissues from her purse and passed it over. "Gram, you must be exhausted. You can stay at my place for as long as you want. Tomorrow, we can sort out our next steps. Let's get going." Peach reached out her hand.

Mary motioned for Peach to come closer. She cupped her granddaughter's ear with her hand and whispered, "I lost my wig."

Peach smiled. "I'll take you shopping once the rain stops. We can get you a new one along with some fresh clothes and anything else you need."

Mary nodded her head in relief. "But we have to go back to my condo as soon as possible."

"Why?" Peach asked, eyebrows furrowed.

Mary shook her head, fighting internally about what to tell her granddaughter. "I just need to."

Peach sighed. "It's impossible to go back there now. Let's go to my house so you can get some rest."

Finally, after three days of monsoon-like rain, the fourth day dawned with sunshine. There were still standing pools of water in the streets, and yellow tape and orange barrels prevented drivers from entering the condo complex. In the meantime, Peach took Mary shopping and purchased toiletries, clothes, and of course, a new wig. In the evening, the family convened at Peach's house.

Kory, Peach's mom, was the elder of Mary and Ed's children. She and Peach's dad, Stan, also lived in Brecksville. Their house had survived the flood, but their cellar was filled with standing water. Mary's son—Peach's Uncle Dean—lived a few towns away and missed the full brunt of the storm. Over sandwiches and beer, the five of them discussed what to do next.

"I have to get back to my condo," Mary said, interrupting the conversation.

"Are you going to tell us why?" Peach blurted.

Mary looked at the expectant faces of her children and grandchildren. She realized she owed it to them to share general information about what she'd been hiding for so many years. "On the floor of my closet, I kept a cardboard box containing all my important papers, and I pray the box is safe. I can't rest until I find out."

"Wouldn't your bank or lawyer have copies of your important documents?" Kory asked.

Mary lowered her head and stared at her hands. "This box contains other items which are extremely valuable to me, including some cash."

Dean paused, his sandwich mere inches from his mouth. "How much money? A hundred?"

Mary blushed. "Well, it's a little more than that."

Dean put the sandwich down. "A thousand?"

Mary pointed her thumb at the ceiling.

Stan spit out a mouthful of beer, "Five thousand?"

Mary's thumb went higher.

Dean leaned forward in his chair. "Ten thousand?"

Mary nodded.

Kory stood abruptly. "You tossed a box on your bed with $10,000 in it? Are you crazy?"

Stan broke into hysterical laughter, while Dean kept repeating, "$10,000, I don't believe it!"

"Mom, why in the world do you have so much cash hidden in your house? You should have kept it in the bank!" Kory said, her cheeks turning bright red.

Mary shrugged. "After living through the depression and watching the banks fail and savings become worthless, I've always kept some cash stashed at home for peace of mind. My parents did it, and it worked out fine for them. Up until now, it worked for me, too."

"These days, banks have FDIC insurance, and your savings could have grown with interest," Kory said, breathing heavily. "It galls me to think all that money might have been sucked down the storm drains."

Mary met Kory's eyes. "Some things are more valuable to me than all the money in the world."

"Like what?" Kory's voice softened.

Mary had tucked away Ed's love letters, countless wartime photos, many of which showed the two of them together in happier times before the war. The box also contained his war journal, which was full of atrocities too hard to imagine.

"The box contains correspondences and pictures of your father and I during the war years. If those keepsakes are lost or ruined, I don't know if I can bear it."

Mary furrowed her brow and made eye contact with each family member around the table. The implied message was clear: *no more questions.*

After an uncomfortable few seconds, Stan leaned forward and rubbed his hands together. "Who wants some *Peach Cobbler* for dessert?"

Peach burst out laughing, "Way to change the subject, Dad!"

Stan winked, and the discomfort around the table evaporated.

CHAPTER 4:
BRECKSVILLE, OHIO
JUNE 2006

A FEW days later, the phone rang while Mary and Peach were enjoying their morning coffee. It was the Fire Department notifying residents it was safe to go back to Mary's condo complex.

Mary's eyes lit up. "Let's go now! I've been on pins and needles waiting for the green light."

Peach grinned. "Sure thing, Gram." They slipped on the rubber galoshes and hopped into Peach's car.

When they arrived, firemen were using high-pressure hoses to clear muck from the parking lot. Mary was amazed that the pavement was visible, as were the flower beds and grassy areas. Piles of debris were pushed off to one side, creating a safe pathway for the residents to get back into their units. But as soon as they walked into the condo, her heart sunk: a five-inch-thick layer of muddy sludge covered the floor, and the drywall in the hallway was torn away, exposing the wall joists. Still, Mary was determined to learn the full extent of the damage, and most importantly, to discover if the box had miraculously survived unscathed. Peach followed, their boots sinking ankle deep into the gooey brown muck as they trudged down the hall. Reaching the kitchen, they stopped to look around. Spoiled food mixed with overturned trash and muddy sludge produced a nose curling odor.

Peach pinched her nostrils and tried not to gag. "Oh, that's awful." Mary agreed, though luckily, her sense of smell wasn't as strong as Peach's.

The living room was also a disaster, the sofa and love seat flipped over and saturated. Every few steps, Peach had to move an end table or basket out of the way to clear a pathway to the bedroom.

Mary felt something crunch beneath her foot. She bent down to pick it up and discovered it was a picture of Ed dressed in his military uniform, ruined beyond repair. The realization that her most sacred keepsakes might all be destroyed hit Mary like a ton of bricks. She hunched over and rested her hands on her thighs, overcome with grief. The last few years had been challenging times for her and Ed. They had sold their family home and moved into the condo, then Ed got sick, and Mary became his primary caretaker. He passed away only six months after the move, turning 60 years of marriage into a memory.

Mary felt a hand tenderly caressing her back. "I know this is hard, but I promise you don't have to face this alone."

Mary stood and rested her head on Peach's shoulder, her emotions still raw. After composing herself, she lifted her head and took Peach's hands. "I've lived a full life. The only things I really care about are my family and the special keepsakes I've saved throughout the years." She let go and lifted what was left of the framed photo from the floor.

"This was a picture of your grandfather, so handsome in his uniform. I've looked at this picture every day for the past 60 years, and now it's ruined. It sat on top of two beautiful handmade white doilies your grandfather sent to me from Belgium during the war. Now the doilies are gone as well as so many other things I'll never be able to replace."

"I'm so sorry, Gram," Peach said, blinking back tears.

Mary shook her head to banish her melancholy. "Let's try to find the box and get out of here."

Moving toward the bedroom, they peeked inside the hall bathroom. The tub and toilet were filled with muddy water. "Gross," Peach uttered.

Across the hall lay the master bedroom. When they peered inside, both Mary and Peach gasped. The bed frame rested at a crooked angle. From the dark line on the wall, it was clear the water had reached the same height as the headboard. The mattress and comforter were completely waterlogged.

Peach's lips formed a grim line. "There's something on the floor." She bent down to pick it up.

"What is it?" Mary asked breathlessly.

Peach stood; a muddy $100 bill clutched in her fingers. "Finders-keepers!"

"Very funny, smarty pants!" Mary said. "The smell and mess are starting to get to me, so please keep looking."

Peach bent down again, her hands deep in the muck. "There's another $100 bill! And another! It looks like it's forming a trail toward the closet."

Heart pounding, Mary followed Peach to the open closet door. There it was, laying on its side with the lid off. Mary couldn't believe it survived, and she let out a sound somewhere between a laugh and a sob. Mary was so transfixed, she barely noticed when Peach lifted a discolored envelop and counted out six wet $100 bills. "Is all the money loose like this?"

"That's my mad money for shopping and playing bingo with the girls. The rest of the money is on the bottom of the box, double wrapped inside two plastic shopping bags," Mary said. "But please, I need to see what else survived."

Peach tossed the shredded cardboard off to the side, and everything inside the box sat on the floor of the closet. Piled beneath two books was a plastic grocery bag filled with bundles of one-hundred-dollar bills. "Yay! We found the money!"

Mary didn't share Peach's enthusiasm. "Can you hand me the two albums which were on top of the money bags?"

The photo albums were caked in mud, waterlogged, and heavy. Mary put them both on the nearby dresser and sighed. It had been nearly six decades since she had laid eyes upon these albums. She held her breath and cracked open the book on top.

Mary choked back tears to discover that muddy water had seeped between the plastic inserts and damaged the old photographs. As she turned each page, every picture was soiled and discolored. The second album was no better than the first. These pictures had captured the most magical, romantic, and harrowing times of Mary's younger life in the 1940s, and now they appeared to be ruined and lost forever.

Mary closed the second scrapbook, her tears making the cover even muddier. "It might have been easier if I'd destroyed them after all," she whispered to herself.

CHAPTER 5:
BRECKSVILLE, OHIO
JUNE 2006

AFTER PEACH and Mary left the condo, they drove straight to the bank and deposited Mary's cash. Later in the evening, the family met at Peach's house for dinner. Their mealtime discussion centered around how best to tackle the mess at Mary's condo.

"I think we need to videotape the inside for insurance purposes." Dean paused to take a bite out of his cheeseburger. "We'll haul out the waterlogged furniture and appliances and put them out on the curb."

"I'd like you to bag my clothes and shoes and bring everything back here so I can look over what to keep and what to throw away," Mary said.

Dean wiped his mouth. "Okay, Mom, you got it."

After everyone left, Mary and Peach washed and dried the last of the dishes. Peach paused, a dish towel in her hands. "Gram, you don't have to bear the burden of keeping Grandpa's wartime memories to yourself."

Mary took in Peach's earnest expression. "Honey, I appreciate your willingness to listen. But I haven't spoken about all this in so many years, and it's such a long, difficult story."

Peach took the glass from Mary's hand and put it in the cupboard. "I don't care if the story is long and difficult. I hardly know anything about what you and Pops went through during the war, and I've wanted to learn more for a really long time."

Peach ushered Mary into a chair and sat next to her. "If this flood taught us anything, it's that none of us know how much time we have left. We have to take advantage of the time we have now."

Mary rubbed her chin as she thought about what Peach had said. After Ed returned from the service, they both agreed to move forward and let the past stay in the past. *Perhaps Peach is right. If I don't share the story now, soon, it will be gone forever.*

Mary herself was a bit of a family historian and reveled in hearing her own mother's story of immigrating to a new country. From time to time when family history questions popped up, she wished her mother was still alive to tell the back story. Mary decided she would answer some of Peach's questions as honestly and truthfully as she could. "Where did you put those photo albums?"

"I wiped off the covers and left them in the garage," Peach answered.

"Is there a place we can lay out the photos so they can dry? I'm anxious to see if they can be saved."

Peach turned off the faucet and grinned. "Sure. I can put a bed sheet over our ping pong table in the basement."

For the next few hours, they carefully removed the photos from the saturated albums and laid them on the table. Most of the pictures were water damaged, had mud on them and were faded. A few were stuck together and when they were separated, Mary noticed something peculiar. "Look, these two pictures got superimposed onto each other, making the people look like ghosts!" On cue, a light over the table flickered like a firefly and burned out.

Peach shivered. "That's a little eerie!" She walked to the workbench, retrieved a new light bulb, and replaced the old one. "Much better. Do you have any ideas about how we might clean the mud off these photos?"

"Fill a small bowl halfway with soapy water. And bring some cotton swabs and paper towels."

Mary dragged a folding chair over to the ping-pong table. She hoped the soap and water wouldn't inadvertently damage the photos any further.

When Peach placed the requested items on the table, Mary dipped an end of the swab into the soapy water and applied it to a picture. When a few delicate dabs didn't cause any more harm, Mary expanded her dabbing technique to the rest of the photo. A few minutes later, she was satisfied with the result. The image in the crinkly photograph wasn't perfect but it was recognizable.

She turned to Peach, who was hovering over her shoulder. "What do you think?"

Peach placed another folding chair next to Mary's. "Still faded, but better. Mind if I try?"

Mary waved her hand across the table. Dozens of photos remained. "Help yourself!"

Peach selected one and copied Mary's dabbing technique. After ten minutes of gentle cleaning, a 1940s version of Mary and Ed amidst a group of other couples materialized. "Look at you two! So handsome and young! It looks like this picture was taken at an Army base. Were you single or married at the time?" Peach slid the photo over to her grandmother.

Mary perched her bi-focal glasses on her nose and peered at the picture. "We weren't married yet, but we were going steady. The Army base was Ft. Oglethorpe, where Ed was sent for basic training. Later, he was transferred to Camp Forrest in Tennessee, and I visited him there too.

"Who were the other people?" Peach asked, peering closely.

"That's Dean Cooper, Scott Rollins, and Robert Louis. They stuck together for the entire war. I became great friends with Dean's and Scott's wives, Marie and Janice. Robert Louis was single.

Peach squinted at some other photos. "You and the other women were such fashionistas. Why so dressy?"

Mary smiled. "The Army required that men be smartly dressed at all times as a reflection of the United States Military. All these young men were in tip-top shape and looked so handsome in their uniforms."

Mary's eyes unfocused as a memory took hold. "When I was sixteen, I had a side job as a seamstress and learned how to make my own dresses. When I got a chance to visit your grandfather, I wanted to look my very best."

Peach scooched her chair closer to Mary's. "Tell me more! What were your visits like?"

Mary's eyes lit up. "It was a magical time. Never before or since have I been around so many young people our age, and the youthful energy was infectious. The Army base housed thousands of soldiers, and the entire facility was like a self-contained city. The base was centered on war training, but when the soldiers weren't practicing for war-related activities, the camp offered lots of entertainment to keep the boys and their guests occupied. There were movie houses, dance clubs, a sports arena, bowling alleys, a library, and even a golf course."

Peach picked up another blurry picture. "Is this you on Pops' back?"

Mary laughed. "Your grandfather pretended carrying me piggyback was part of his training regime."

Peach bumped Mary's shoulder. "It sounds romantic."

Mary laughed. "I suppose it was."

Peach leaned over the table and pointed at another photo. "Is that Pops boxing with another guy?"

"It sure is" Mary answered. Seeing a younger Ed with his shirt off brought up so many steamy memories, which made Mary blush.

Peach laughed. "Whoa, how did he get so mean and lean?"

Mary fanned herself. "Ed told me his muscles came from working with his father at a local brick factory."

"Wow! Tell me more! This is the first time you've mentioned my Great Grandfather."

Ed's father worked in the Cleveland Brickyards for over 30 years. His name was Michal, but his nickname was Big Hand because his hands were twice the size of a normal man's and his fingers were thick as sausages. Rumor was that Big Hand Mike earned more money from arm-wrestling bets than from his weekly paycheck."

"What a funny nickname!" Peach said with a chuckle. "How did Pops do in his boxing matches?"

Mary scrunched her nose while she recovered the memory. "He wrote me that he won his first two matches. I sent a letter back urging him to quit before someone broke his nose. A few weeks later, the postman dropped off a letter at my parents' house. Ed wrote that my advice came a day too late. I'll never forget what the letter said: *I drew a semi-pro fighter in my third match, and it took only one round for my nose to run into his fist, breaking my beak.*

Peach shook her head. "Pops sure liked sports."

He really did. Mary pulled out a plastic bag filled with old newspapers clippings. "Ed was so proud when he made the Camp Forrest Company "A" fast-pitch softball team. Over a hundred players tried out for each position." Mary removed several pamphlets. "I'm so relieved the plastic bag kept the papers from being damaged." She handed them to Peach. "Read the headlines."

COMPANY "A" WINS CAMP FORREST SOFTBALL TOURNAMENT.

COMPANY "A" SOFTBALL TEAM TO PLAY
IN ARMY STATE CHAMPIONSHIP.

COMPANY "A" TO PLAY THE CADETS OF CHATTANOOGA
IN ROUND ONE OF THE STATE CHAMPIONSHIPS

A smile creased Mary's face as she watched Peach read the storylines. During the summer of 1943, Company "A" had a record of 11 wins and no losses. As the headline suggested, the team made it all the way to the Army state tournament in Chattanooga. Mary enjoyed watching their games whenever she visited. She fondly remembered the frenzy surrounding the team's winning streak.

Caught up in the memory, Mary used her fist as a microphone. "Ladies and gentlemen. Welcome to The Camp Forrest Coca Cola Fast Pitch Softball Classic! Batting in the #5 spot, Staff Sergeant and catcher, Ed Krow-zin-skeeee!"

Peach clapped. "Whoa, Gram! You could be the next Harry Carey!!"

Mary grinned. "We were in the prime of our lives and enjoying every minute of it. And I was introduced to so many new friends who came from all over the country. It was exhilarating and such a wonderful time in my life. Everything was great until…" Mary stopped herself.

Peach blinked. "Until what?"

Mary wrung her hands. "Pearl Harbor."

CHAPTER 6:
BRECKSVILLE, OHIO
JUNE 2006

"I'LL NEVER in my life forget how all radio programs were interrupted to report news of the vicious attack on our Navy." Mary's chest heaved as her memory was assaulted. She paused to collect herself before she could speak of the horror. "I remember seeing the pictures of the burning ships in the newspapers, and the faces of the poor sailors who drowned. They never had a chance; there was no warning signal. The news called it a "sneak attack." Pearl Harbor changed everything."

Peach placed a hand on her grandmother's shoulder. "I know this is difficult for you, but can you tell me more?"

Mary drew a deep, steadying breath. "Pearl Harbor gave the men a renewed sense of purpose, and patriotism throughout the entire country rose dramatically. The base was eager to avenge the attack, and training intensified. The men knew they were heading to war, and success and survival would depend on being as prepared as possible in the classroom as well as in the field. I'm proud to say your grandfather excelled in both. He was smart, led by example, and other men seemed to gravitate toward him.

Peach brought water for them both, which Mary drank gratefully. "Your grandfather lived in a neighborhood with immigrants from all over eastern Europe and besides being fluent in Polish, the language of his parents, he also learned Russian and Czech. Later, when he was training at Camp Forrest, he enrolled in a class to learn basic German so he could be an interpreter. He sometimes thought of becoming a career Army man."

Peach's eyebrows raised. "He did?"

"Yes, as an interpreter, he thought he could move up to Captain and perhaps beyond. Of course, his attitude changed when he experienced live combat and witnessed the atrocities of war."

"So how did he become an Army medic?" Peach asked.

Mary's eyes sparkled. "Well, that's a funny story. Do you want Ed's version or mine?"

Peach grinned. "How about both?"

Mary leaned back in her chair. "I'll start with your grandfather's version. Ed was given two exams at the Army Induction Center, physical and psychological. Since there were thousands of inductees in the camp, it was impossible for the Army Psychologist to conduct a full assessment. He only asked each inductee one question."

"Was it a comprehensive question to help the psychologists quickly identify a personality disorder?" Peach asked.

Mary shook her head. "You would think that, but according to your grandfather the Army Psychologist asked, "What are your future plans after serving in the military?" And Ed replied, "I want to become a butcher just like my brother and own my own meat market." Mary let out a funny little chuckle.

"What's so funny?" Peach asked, hanging on every word.

"When your grandfather told this story, he would pound his fist on the table and bellow, 'I said BUTCHER but the Army shrink heard MEDIC!'"

Peach's mouth flew open. "That's how he became a medic? That's crazy!"

"Of course not," Mary said, shaking her head. "Your grandfather wasn't one to toot his own horn. The truth was that Ed knew the Army had a special need for advanced medics; he studied for the placement test and passed it with flying colors. Afterward, he was transferred to Camp Forrest in Tennessee and joined the 65th Army Medical Battalion stationed there. His primary role would be evacuating the wounded and transporting them safely to a mobile field hospital where surgical care could be given. Ed took two years of medical and evacuation training at Camp Forrest before he deployed to Europe."

Peach's eyes remained glued on Mary as she listened to the story. "Did Pops ever perform surgery?"

Mary grimaced. "No, sweetheart. The Army had surgeons for that, but your grandfather had more training than the average medic. He could set broken bones, operate x-ray machines, and administer blood plasma through arteries. In a pinch, he could assist a doctor during surgery."

Peach rubbed her chin. "It sounds like he was an EMT."[1]

"Yes, I guess you could think of it that way," Mary replied, nodding.

Peach stood and grabbed two more bottles of water. "I'm amazed I never heard this story before. Are you up to sharing more or do you need a break?"

Mary unscrewed the cap and took a swig. "It feels good to share stories of your grandfather's war experiences after keeping them bottled up for all this time. Let's clean some more photos."

A half hour later, a particular photo caught Peach's interest. She held it up and showed it to Mary. "Where was this taken? It looks like a group of soldiers camping in the woods. Some of them have smiles on their faces."

Mary leaned over the table to examine the photo. "That wasn't a fun camping trip; those men were on maneuvers."

"What are maneuvers?" Peach asked.

"Maneuvers gave the soldiers the opportunity to practice real life situations they would face in actual combat. Your grandfather participated in three sets of maneuvers before being deployed."

Peach straightened. "Did he ever talk to you about what happened during maneuvers?"

"Yes, he sure did," Mary said with a chuckle. "He told me he would never eat pork again, and he hated *fucking* chiggers." Mary's eyes bulged and she instantly covered her mouth. "I can't believe I said that!"

---

1   EMT: Emergency Medical Technician.

CHAPTER 7:
BRECKSVILLE, OHIO
JUNE 2006

PEACH LAUGHED so hard; she could barely catch her breath. Soon, both Mary and Peach were giggling and snorting, their eyes leaking joyful tears. Peach ran to the nearby bathroom and came back with a roll of toilet paper. "Here use this!" She tore off a clump for herself and gave the roll to her grandmother.

Mary blotted her eyes. "Oh boy, I haven't had a good laugh like that in a long time. Where were we?" Mary set down the toilet paper and drained half the water bottle.

"You were talking about maneuvers," Peach said, her eyes sparkling.

"Many of the enlisted men, your grandfather included, had never traveled outside their state of birth. When Ed went to Louisiana for maneuvers, he wrote me the funniest letter."

"What about?" Peach asked.

"About a pack of wild boars called razorbacks that infiltrated the camp. Apparently, those gnarly beasts could sniff the food from the mess tent. Worse, if the men had any food in their own tents, the boars would root through bags and bedding and tear everything apart. Ed said the camp was "attacked" regularly until the men finally came up with a solution."

Peach's eyebrows lifted. "Did they shoot them?

Mary shook her head. "They probably wanted to shoot every one of those critters but instead, the men decided to bury their leftover food deep inside a hole after every meal so the boars couldn't smell it. Still, the razorbacks were never far away, and followed his unit as they moved from location to location."

"And what about the effing chiggers?" Peach used air quotes. "I've never heard of those either."

"Count yourself lucky! They're nasty insects, and there's even a funny poem about them." As Mary recited the verses, she swooped her hand in the air like an orchestra conductor.

Oh chigger, chigger, you little mite,
Why must you give me such a plight,
Your bite is small, but oh so mean,
Leaving me scratching like a fiend!

I rub and scratch and itch some more,
Until my skin is red and sore,
I've tried lotions and creams,
Nothing works, I scream!

So here I am, a sorry sight,
Thanks to little chigger bite!

Peach burst out laughing. "Chiggers sound like little devils!"

"They are little devils," Mary said. "When the soldiers were on maneuvers, they had to crawl on their stomachs through the woods. Chiggers are attracted to all the hot and sweaty parts of the body: the back of the knee, the crease of elbows, armpits, and especially in the crotch area. With all those sweaty men, I'm sure the chiggers had a field day."

Peach rubbed her hands up and down her arms. "Yuck!"

"Right!" Mary said. "Their bite itches like hell itself."

Peach scrunched her nose. "I don't like camping because of mosquitoes buzzing around my head and bees flying over our food and having to use a community outhouse. By the time Sunday rolls around, I'm itching for a hot shower and a good meal."

"Imagine having to live that way for months or years at a time," Mary said softly "There weren't any nice hotel rooms with comfy beds or hot showers. The guys had to rough it."

Peach stood and stretched. "Gram, these stories are fascinating. Why did you keep all this hidden?"

Mary put her hands on her knees and turned away. "When Ed was discharged from the Army, he had trouble getting the war out of his head. Whenever he caught me looking at these photos, he got agitated and asked me to get rid of them. The doctors have a name for it now: post-traumatic stress disorder—PTSD for short."

Peach stared at her grandmother. "Everyone looks so happy in these pictures. I don't understand."

Mary grimaced. "These pictures were taken *before* the war. Some of our friends in those photos never made it back home."

"But you didn't throw any of them away, did you?"

"I couldn't bring myself to get rid of any of it," Mary admitted. "These albums contain my most cherished memories: love letters, poems, journals, and of course, these photos. I packed it all in this box and stashed it out of sight for all these years. In fact, I might never have remembered the box if not for the flood and fear of losing my mementos forever."

Mary eased herself out of the chair and rolled her shoulders. "That's enough reminiscing for tonight. Let's clean this up and get to bed."

Peach looked at her watch and gasped. "Wow, it's after midnight already. I hope you get a good night's rest. I won't push you, but whenever you're ready to share more about the war years, I'll happily listen."

Mary nodded. *If only all the stories were this happy.*

CHAPTER 8:
CLEVELAND, OHIO
NOVEMBER 2011

DURING THE months it took for her condo to be rebuilt, Mary used the time to visit old friends who lived out of town. When she was given the okay to move back home, she resumed hosting people for lunch and playing cards. She also restarted her keyboard lessons and enjoyed reading library books in her new recliner chair. Though many damaged pictures remained, she diligently kept chipping away at them each week.

As the years marched forward, Mary celebrated her 90th, 91st, and 92nd birthdays. Each birthday was celebrated with big family fanfare with birthday cakes, candles, and singing. When friends asked her what it was like to grow older, Mary would say, "Getting old ain't for wimps." She put aside her age-related aches and pains and never let them get in the way of leading a fulfilling and happy life.

Eventually though, time catches up with everyone. Even someone as vibrant and upbeat as Mary.

Shortly after her 93rd birthday, the family made the difficult decision that their mother could no longer live independently. While Mary had previously toured a few assisted living centers and reluctantly picked one she liked best, she emphasized many times that she only went on these visits "to get Kory off my back." She had no intention of ever moving into *one of those places*.

But then Mary fell in her condo and broke her hip. After her hospital stay, she was transferred to a rehabilitation center for convalescence. At the urging of her doctor, Mary grudgingly agreed she could no longer take care of herself at home.

✦ ✦ ✦

"This place smells like a rotten egg," Mary complained as she was wheeled into the Shady Acres Senior Center. Wrinkling her nose, she took note of her surroundings. Old people were holed up in every corner, flanked by bored-looking family members. The air inside was dry, stuffy, and smelled like mothballs. When she heard raspy coughing, Mary was ready to insist her family remove her immediately. But before she could speak, a woman in a white coat approached her wheelchair and bent down to look her right in the eye.

"You must be Mary," she gushed. "I've been looking forward to meeting you. Welcome to your new home!"

Mary frowned. Moving to a strange, stinky place wasn't part of her life plan. If she could, she would run out the door and never come back. Now wheelchair bound, she couldn't run anywhere. She remained silent, feeling totally trapped.

Kory tried to ease the situation. "Mom, this is Stephanie, she's the manager and is here to help you."

Mary tightened her grip on the handlebars of her wheelchair. "I hope my room is far enough away from here, so I don't have to put up with this dreadful stench all day long."

"Mom!" Kory's eyes shot lasers at Mary. "Stephanie, I'm so sorry."

"It's ok, sometimes I feel the same way your mom does," the manager said without registering any dismay. "We do our best to keep our facility safe, clean, and fresh. Occasionally mother nature takes over and unexpected accidents do happen. We do the best we can to discreetly handle those situations as soon as possible."

Recently, Mary had experienced a few accidents herself. Her voice softened. "Can you take me to my room, please?"

"Follow me!" Stephanie spun around and led the family down a long corridor.

It was close to dinner hour by the time Kory and Mary finished organizing her room. Privately, Stephanie instructed Kory to go home and let Mary dine with her preassigned tablemates. "Dining with the same people each day facilitates making friends more quickly," she assured her.

Mary wasn't left alone in her room for long before a healthcare worker knocked on her door.

"Hello Mary, my name is Virginia. I'm the aide who will help you get ready for dinner tonight." Virginia gave Mary a brief orientation of the process, and shortly afterward, wheeled Mary into the dining hall. Large windows and skylights brought in the late afternoon sunlight. Mary was rolled to a round table in the middle of the room, #14.

"This is your supper table," Virginia said. Mary looked around the table and took note of each person. *Oxygen man single. Husband and wife, cute. Two widows, and a widower, still wearing their wedding rings.*

Some of the seniors at her table sat in their wheelchairs like she did, and others had walkers or canes next to their seats. All were smartly dressed and seemed to be enjoying themselves.

"I'll let these nice people introduce themselves to you." Virginia smiled at Mary and excused herself from the table. The seat next to Mary was unoccupied. But not for long.

A woman strode into the dining hall on her own steam, and Mary couldn't tear her eyes away. Between her red hair, fair skin, and shamrock green vest, it seemed clear the woman was of Celtic heritage. She made a beeline to table #14 and took the chair next to Mary's.

"My name is Margaret, but I go by Maggie. This is my first day here," she said in a thick Irish brogue. Mary couldn't help but notice a few small beads of sweat dotting the woman's forehead.

Oxygen man facilitated the table's introduction process. It eventually got to Mary's turn. "I'm Mary, and it's my first day, too."

Maggie's blue eyes lit up, and she clasped her hands together. "I'm relieved I'm not the only new person here! Perhaps we can figure out this confusing place together!"

The stress of the day and the anxiety of trying to fit in with a group of strangers all washed away. A true smile graced Mary's face. "Yep, I'll be your partner in crime!" she laughed.

CHAPTER 9:
CLEVELAND, OHIO
2011–2013

MARY AND Maggie became fast friends. Best of all, they discovered their rooms were next door to each other, which allowed the two "newbies" to spend a lot of time getting to know each other. Maggie was a self-achiever; she didn't consider herself old like *those people*. Mary was like-minded.

They were similar in many ways. Both were in their nineties and had been happily married to good men for over 50 years. Each raised well-adjusted hardworking children. And they shared a wonderful sense of humor, with Maggie "the baby" at 91 and Mary "older than dirt" at 93.

Mary and Maggie tried to make each day count. "*One never knows*" became their motto, and they made a game out of introducing each other to visitors and newcomers at the facility. The pair became known for their "partying ways." Any holiday was an excuse to dress in an outfit befitting the occasion. Ugly sweaters for Christmas, red blouses for Valentine's Day, and of course, Maggie celebrated St. Patrick's Day like it was the Super Bowl. The friends signed up for almost every off-campus excursion, like movie nights and lunches at the nearby shopping mall. A special treat was going to Cleveland Indians baseball games.

As the women began to share details of their past lives, Mary learned Maggie was a first-generation Irish immigrant who came to the United States with her husband shortly after World War II. She hailed from a small village near Donhagadee, Ireland.

Occasionally, Mary would haul out her photo albums and share pictures of Ed's time in the UK. Maggie used a paddle-sized magnifying glass to see the finer details in each photograph taken in Ireland, while Mary peered over her shoulder with the aid of her walker.

"My father operated a small laundry business that catered to the American military in Donhagadee," Maggie told Mary. "He cleaned and pressed uniforms seven days a week. It was exhausting but steady pay during tough times." Later, Maggie shared the devastating news of losing an older brother in the war. "My mum never stopped grieving his death."

The ladies were both voracious readers and joined a book club at the local library. The library was only a few blocks from the assisted living center, so the two became regular visitors. During one of their trips, Maggie noticed a sign next to the check-out center.

WHAT: World War II Veteran Story Project

WHO: Looking for WWII Veterans to share their personal stories

HOW: A moderator will videotape the Veteran's testimony

WHY: Preserving our Military History honors those veterans who served our country

DETAILS: Phone number and website below

Maggie took a pen and piece of paper from her purse and scratched down all the details. During the short ride home, Maggie handed Mary the information. "You should give them a call. You have all those pictures from the war years. I bet they'd be interested in hearing Ed's stories." Initially, Mary liked the idea, but quickly began to have second thoughts.

Maggie grinned. "So, what do you think?"

Mary sighed. "Ed was in the war, not me. I'm not sure they want to hear from a widow."

Maggie whipped around to level Mary with a stare. "Where else would they get the information if not for us? Our loved ones were among the millions of brave civilians who fought to save our world from oppression. Ed saved countless lives and my brother gave his life for our country. In this age of overindulgence, young people need to hear about the selflessness, sacrifice, and the bravery of our loved ones from those of us who remember them." As she spoke, Maggie's fingers wound tightly around her seatbelt. Mary was about to affirm Maggie's point when the bus driver made an announcement on the intercom.

"Home sweet home! Let's get you folks off this van so you don't miss supper!" The back doors swung open, and the wheeze of the electronic winches and ramps signaled it was time to debark the seniors who were wheelchair bound.

Once wheeled inside, Mary and Maggie made their way to their rooms and spruced themselves up for dinner. In perfect synchronicity, they opened their doors at 4:55PM sharp and stepped into the hallway. Immediately, they were absorbed into the senior stampede. The staff used the term to describe all the residents and the plethora of mobile equipment moving at a glacier's pace toward the dining hall.

Mary didn't offer much conversation during dinner and left most of the food on her plate. However, she couldn't resist taking a few bites of the apple pie. After a cup of herbal tea, she excused herself and went to her room.

Mary sat on the couch with a heating pad laid over her abdomen; she had been enduring frequent bouts of stomach pains over the past few weeks. The TV was on, but she was too distracted both by pain and whether to contact the Veteran's Story people to pay any attention. After an hour, Mary clicked off the heating pad and TV and began preparing for bed. She was about to turn off the lights when she heard a familiar rap on her door. With a grunt, she hauled herself out of bed and opened the door. Maggie stood in her silky green pajamas and matching robe, worry etched on her freckled face.

"Are you mad at me? You were awfully quiet at dinner tonight," Maggie said, her words coming out in a rush.

Mary's lower lip trembled, upset that she'd given her dear friend cause to worry. "Heaven's no. C'mon in and take a seat." There was a two-person breakfast table just outside the kitchen, and Maggie plunked down in her customary chair. Mary flipped on the kitchen light and grabbed two coffee cups from the cabinet over the sink. "The usual?" she asked, though she already knew the answer. There was a secret ingredient they liked to add when having coffee in the evening. And it wasn't sugar.

Maggie smiled. "Make sure you mix in two full tablespoons for me!" She rubbed her hands together in anticipation.

Mary put the coffee pods in the machine and turned toward Maggie. "I was thinking about the Veteran's project and what you said in the van."

Maggie leaned a forward, elbows propped on the table. "Are you going to call them?"

Mary retrieved the secret ingredient from the refrigerator and carefully measured one tablespoon for each cup, ignoring Maggie's request for more. After putting the cups on the table, she returned the bottle to the refrigerator and eased herself into the chair opposite Maggie.

"Ed and his war buddies were so young, and the complex decisions those poor boys were forced to make in the heat of battle haunted them all their lives." Mary stirred in the elixir, which turned the coffee from jet black to chocolatey brown. "I feel like sharing his private memories would be a betrayal."

Maggie sniffed her steaming cup, took a sip, and savored the sweet flavor. "Nothing like a good Irish Crème coffee to warm the soul! I think telling his stories would be a way to honor him."

Mary fiddled with a book of matches and lit the candle in the middle of the table. The wick sizzled and melted the wax, unleashing the candle's lavender scent. She inhaled deeply and began. "When Ed came home from the service, he had trouble getting the war out of his head. One night I'll never forget, he had a terrifying nightmare. In the throes of it, he mistook me for an enemy soldier. He climbed on top of me, pinned my arms to my sides, and started to choke me, yelling 'Kill the Krauts.'"

Maggie's face went slack jawed as she hung on Mary's shocking words.

Mary stared at the flame. "We were living with my parents at the time. Thankfully, my father heard the commotion and came running into the room. After pulling Ed off me, he shook him awake. I'm not sure what would have happened to me if my father hadn't intervened." Mary twisted her wedding ring around her finger as she spoke. "Ed was devastated, embarrassed, and a mess for days afterward. He repeatedly apologized and begged for my forgiveness. He appeared strong on the outside, but on the inside, he was a tormented, angry, and fragile soul."

Maggie took a swig. "That must have been terrifying,"

"It finally came to a head between us. I told him I couldn't go on living that way unless he told me what was bothering him. The next morning, I found him waiting for me at the kitchen table." Mary closed her eyes, reliving the moment. "That's when he told me the worst of what he experienced during the war. It was difficult for him, but he didn't hold back. He opened his heart to me, and it was the deepest conversation we ever had." Mary's chest heaved and she gazed at the overhead light, unable to meet Maggie's intense stare.

Maggie reached over and laid her hand over Mary's. "You don't have to say anything else. I shouldn't have pried but…"

Mary cut her off. "It's okay, Maggie. It's a huge weight off my shoulders. I never told anyone this story, out of respect for Ed. I didn't want them to think the war made him a raving lunatic, because he wasn't like that at all. I promised him that what he shared would always stay between the two of us. I guess I just violated that trust."

Maggie gently squeezed Mary's hand. "Your story is safe with me. I swear."

Mary smiled. "I know it is and I want you to know that after our intense conversation, things improved greatly between Ed and me." Seeing her dear friend so quiet and troubled, Mary decided to lighten the mood. "There's one more thing."

Maggie furrowed her brow and leaned forward.

Mary chuckled. "I must confess when I slept with Ed, I always kept one eye open in case that nasty German soldier ever showed up in our bedroom again!"

Maggie rolled her eyes and exhaled mightily. "Geez, you had me thinking the other shoe was about to drop." And just like that, the spell was broken. Maggie glanced at the kitchen clock. "It's already 11PM, way past our bedtimes." She couldn't suppress a large yawn. "So, what are you going to do?"

"My brain is swirling; I'll sleep on it and give you my answer in the morning." Mary hugged Maggie extra-tight and watched her friend shuffle to her room. She took in every detail of Maggie's appearance, wanting to commit it to memory. Even at this late hour, Maggie was so well put together, from her ponytail to her housecoat to her fluffy slippers. She watched until Maggie opened her door and disappeared.

Clicking her own door closed, Mary kept her hand on the handle and pressed her forehead against the wood. At her ripe old age, she never imagined she'd meet such a dear friend. Mary didn't know how much time she had left, but she intended to savor every moment of Maggie's friendship.

CHAPTER 10:
CLEVELAND, OHIO
MARCH 2013

WHEN MARY woke the next morning, her decision was made. *Why did Ed compile all this information if he didn't intend to share it some day? If we forget our history, how do we prevent repeating our mistakes?*

Mary dialed the phone number Maggie gave her and spoke to Roger from the WWII History team. Mary explained how Ed had kept letters, maps, journals, and photos that served to document his war experiences. "I'm willing to share his stories in a videotape session," she offered.

Roger's voice was flat, as if he was on autopilot. "I would like to thank you for your husband's service and your willingness to provide his testimony in memorandum. Regrettably, the project is only funded to conduct interviews with WWII veterans who are still living. I'm sorry."

Mary's blood pressure rose. She should have listened to her first instinct. "But what about the men and women who gave the best years of their lives to protect our freedom and are no longer with us? Who will provide their testimony if not their loved ones?" Mary asked, her voice becoming shrill.

"I understand your point," Roger replied. "My father served in the war, and he too died before this project started. From time to time, he confided certain things to my mother, though he shared nothing with us kids. After he passed away, my mother wrote a family diary of sorts. Maybe you could consider doing the same thing; it could be a way to honor your husband and preserve his experiences for your children and grandchildren."

Mary squeezed the phone handle and barked into to the receiver. "I'm 94 years old, and I might keel over any day now. There's not enough time left to write a memoir." Mary slammed the receiver down, her blood boiling. She really didn't have much time left, if her increasing stomach pains was any indication.

Mary looked at the clock and couldn't believe she'd had such a distressing conversation at 8:30 AM. After swilling her morning coffee, she rapped on the Maggie's door. On the way to the dining hall, Mary shared her disappointment.

"There has to be some other way to get them to accept your testimony," Maggie said firmly.

"Not according to Roger," Mary said with a sigh. "They're only accepting actual veterans, just as I originally assumed."

Maggie pursed her lips. "I'm sorry I got your hopes up."

After they finished breakfast and were heading back to their rooms, Maggie stopped abruptly. She tapped her cane on the side of Mary's walker to slow her down.

"Why did you stop?" Mary asked.

Maggie danced an Irish jig around her cane, then plopped in the nearest chair. "I have an idea." She dug into her purse and pulled out her smartphone. "Do you own one of these?"

"Yes," Mary said, sitting in the chair opposite Maggie. "But I hardly use it."

Maggie tapped on the camera icon and pointed the phone in Mary's direction. "Say cheese!"

Mary and Maggie took the next hour to formulate their game plan. It was agreed that Mary would write down a list of questions. Maggie would film Mary and ask the questions. They agreed to take their dinners to-go style and meet in Mary's room at 6PM to begin their videotaping session.

Right on schedule Maggie walked into Mary's room lugging a plastic bag with her. She didn't spot Mary right away, so she put the bag on the kitchen table, careful not to disturb some props Mary had laid out to use in the interview and sat down on her usual chair. From her vantage point, Maggie spotted the light emanating from underneath the bathroom door. She crinkled her nose and took a few dog sniffs of the air. "Are you using perfume for an interview?" she snarked loudly, announcing her presence.

"Pipe down! I'm almost done primping; I'll be out in a second." After checking herself in the mirror one last time, Mary opened the bathroom door and stepped out. Bobbing a little curtsey and stepping into her walker, she said, "Ta-da"

Maggie's jaw dropped. "I'm speechless, you look stunning. Truly. The lavender blouse, and matching blazer look very professional. You're even wearing makeup and jewelry!" Mary blushed at the compliment.

"What's in the bag?" Mary asked as she made her way to the kitchen table.

Maggie grinned as she rummaged through the sack. "I brought two bottles of water and this!" Maggie thrust a bottle of Irish Whiskey high into the air.

Mary chuckled. "What's that for?"

"Liquid Courage!" Maggie pulled out two shot glasses and filled them with booze.

Mary shook her head. "I need to keep my head on straight if I'm going to do this right. I'll take water now and save the hootch for later."

Maggie took one of the shot glasses in her hand and slid a bottle of water to Mary. "Cheers!" After draining her whiskey, Maggie smacked her lips and announced, "Let's get started."

They decided the video should be recorded on Mary's phone, so Mary handed it over. It was the same model as Maggie's, so she clicked on the camera icon and pointed the phone at her friend.

"Wait!" Mary said, nervously patting down her hair. "I'm not ready."

"Stop fussing," Maggie admonished. "You look great. I'm starting to record."

"Okay, okay. Go ahead and ask me a question," Mary said, sitting up ramrod straight.

An evil grin lit Maggie's face. "What size are your boobs?"

"Bigger than your old saggy sandbags!" Mary shot back. "C'mon, let's get serious."

"Turns out my hands are too shaky to hold the phone," Maggie admitted, lowering it into her lap.

"Do you have a hardcover book I could use to prop it up?"

"There's a craft book on the coffee table that should work," Mary said. While Maggie retrieved the book and fiddled to get the best set up, Mary used the delay to gather her thoughts.

"Are you ready?" Maggie asked.

Mary folded her hands primly on her lap and took three deep breaths to calm her mounting nerves. "Yes, I'm ready now. Promise me you'll be serious this time."

"I promise," Maggie said and clicked record. "State your full name."

"My name is Mary Kruszynski."

"What's today's date?"

"March 10th, 2013."

"What's your age?" Maggie said, trying and failing to keep from smirking.

Mary lifted her chin. "I'm ninety-four and six-months old."

Maggie snuck another sip of whisky. "Are you of sound mind, and do you pledge that everything you say will be truthful?"

"Yes," Mary said. "Everything I say will be as truthful and accurate as I can remember it."

Maggie nodded. "Excellent. Please state the purpose of this video."

Mary didn't pause as she knew precisely why she was doing the interview. "The purpose of this video is for me to share the oral testimony of my husband's service in WWII. He passed away twelve years ago and was unable to share his military experiences as part of the WWII Veterans Testimonial Project, so it falls upon me to tell his story. I may not have been deployed myself, but I learned a great deal from letters Ed wrote to me during the war years, pictures he sent, the European map he marked with his unit's movements, and the personal journal he kept during the war. I also have newspaper articles in which his name appears."

Maggie grinned. "Very good. What was your husband's name, military branch, specialization, rank, unit, and years of service?"

"My husband's name was Edmund D. Kruszynski. He served as a U.S. Army infantry medic. His outfit was the 648th Medical Clearing

Company, which was part of the 65th Medical Regiment. He ascended to the rank of Staff Sergeant, and he led a platoon of 40 medics. He served in the Army for four years from 1941–1945."

"What military campaigns did he participate in while in service of his country?" Maggie asked.

"He participated in five major combat battles in the European Theater: Normandy, Northern France, Rhineland, Central Europe, and the Ardennes," Mary answered.

"Did he receive any medals for meritorious service while in the military?" Maggie asked.

"Staff Sergeant Edmund D. Kruszynski received the Good Conduct Medal, the American Defense Service Medal, and the European African Middle Eastern Service medal with a silver star. He also earned five bronze combat stars for each battle campaign in which he participated." Mary held up all Ed's medals and combat stars so they could be captured in the video.

"Very impressive; is there anything else you'd like to share?" Maggie asked.

"Ed's platoon and the balance of the 648th Medical Clearing Company received the Army's award for Meritorious Unit Commendation." Mary held up a gold patch which represented the uniform decoration for this prestigious Army accolade.

"Can you explain this award?" Maggie asked.

Mary lifted her reading glasses from the table and scanned the official letter which accompanied the commendation. Clearing her throat, she read, "The Meritorious Unit Commendation is awarded to units for exceptional conduct in performance of services rendered in combat situations. The unit must display such outstanding devotion and superior performance of exceptionally difficult tasks as to set it apart and above other units with similar missions."

Mary laid the script on the table and took a few seconds to regroup. She fidgeted with her reading glasses, and she blinked hard several times to clear the swell of droplets blurring her vision. Then she reached for her water and drained it.

Maggie spoke softly. "You're doing great. Keep going."

Mary rolled her shoulders back and fought through her emotions. "The degree of achievement for a group to receive the Meritorious Unit Commendation is equivalent to receiving the Legion of Merit award as an individual."

"Would you like to take a break?" Maggie asked tenderly.

Mary shook her head. "Let's keep going."

"Excellent," Maggie said. "Let's start from the beginning, back when you and Ed first met."

Mary closed her eyes and her mind drifted back in time. A smile lit her face as she relived these precious memories from 60 years earlier.

PART II: THE WAR YEARS

CHAPTER 11:
CLEVELAND, OHIO
SUMMER 1940

EVERY SATURDAY morning, the summer after she graduated high school, Mary met her best friend Evelyn at her friend's house. The pair walked together to their part time job at a print shop in downtown Cleveland owned by Evelyn's brother.

Across the street from the print shop was Camela's furniture and home decorating store. The owner sponsored a local men's baseball team called the "C." The "C" won the industrial league several times and was considered the team to beat.

As the team gathered for pictures in their blue and white wool-blend jerseys, Mary and Evelyn sashayed past them on their way to the print shop, heels clicking on the concrete sidewalk. Some of the players catcalled and wolf whistled to try to get their attention, though the girls acted as if the men were invisible. Reaching the print shop, Evelyn unlocked the door and the two of them entered without a telltale backward glance.

Evelyn closed the door behind her. "Did you see all of those huuunky boys on that baseball team?"

"Did you hear the crude comments as we walked past them? They must all be dirty-minded pigs!" Mary fired back.

"I agree, but I know you loved it as much as I did!" Evelyn squealed.

Mary laughed. "Yes, I sure did."

Evelyn fanned herself. "What should we do now? Should we go over and meet them?"

Mary shook her head. "We have work to do, and besides, it's not ladylike to make the first move."

"You're right," Evelyn said, pouting. "We'll play hard to get. But what if we never see those boys again?"

Mary slipped behind the front counter and began pulling manila folders from the inbox. The files contained the work orders to be completed before noon. "If those boys want to get to know us, they'll just have to walk in here and introduce themselves like gentlemen instead of barnyard animals."

Evelyn removed the dust covers from the machines. "Are you sure you don't want to walk past them one more time?"

"Evelyn!" Mary admonished as she handed her the first work order of the day. "We have to get to work." A few hours later, the metal doorbell jingled and two young men in double-breasted suits came into the shop.

Mary noticed this tall, strong, and incredibly handsome man, but did her best to look occupied and uninterested, though her heart thumped wildly. She was nearly certain these young men were members of the baseball team and couldn't help but feel as if she'd conjured them.

"I'm here to pick up the thank you cards for my sister's wedding," the more handsome one said.

"Name?" Evelyn asked, trying to keep a straight face. She had been setting type in place for a newspaper advertisement but abandoned it.

"Helen" he said.

"I'm sorry. Could you repeat that?" She looked him right in the eye.

"The order is for Helen. I'm her brother Ed, and this is my friend Frank. Are the cards ready?"

Evelyn's hands fumbled as she searched for the order, betraying her nerves and excitement.

"Who's your friend?" Ed directed his question to Evelyn but gazed at Mary.

Mary felt the heat of his stare and was stunned speechless. Evelyn kicked her leg under the counter. "Her name is Mary."

"Nice to meet you, Mary," Ed said with a winning smile.

Before Mary could respond, Evelyn blurted, "Do you boys have dates for this wedding?"

It was Mary's turn to kick Evelyn's leg. Hard.

Here's the order for Helen," Evelyn said, and somehow managed to keep her cool while handing Ed the box and accepting his payment. She remained cool until the young men were almost out the door, then she exploded.

"My name is Evelyn! Evelyn Kowalcek! Phone number Garfield One 6551. That's Evelyn Kowalcek with a K."

Frank pretended to write her phone number on his hand, Ed grinned and waved goodbye. Mary's face was flaming, and she was about to give Evelyn the business when Ed popped back inside.

"Hey, I wanted to apologize for the guys being disrespectful when you walked past us earlier. I talked to them about their behavior, and I promise you won't be bothered again. We're actually nice guys, not a gang of cement heads."

"You play for Camela's?" Evelyn asked, fanning her face with a folder.

"Yes, I'm the catcher. All my teammates call me "Krow.""

"Why Krow?" Mary asked, unable to stop herself.

Ed chuckled. "It's a helluva lot easier to say Krow than my last name!" With a bow, he walked out.

After a few seconds, the girls ran to the front window to enjoy the view.

✦ ✦ ✦

Six months later...

Mary took a job as a parts inspector in a factory called Schoemberger's that produced stoves and ovens. In those days, it was unusual for women to hold those types of factory jobs, but Mary's cousin Sue worked at the factory and when she and her husband decided to start a family, Sue recommended Mary to be her replacement. The pay was good, plus it was closer to home.

The United States Defense Department issued incentives for businesses to produce war-related materials. The government terms were so lucrative that Schoemberger's converted their factory from making consumer goods to manufacturing military equipment. When the company ramped up their hiring for the new shifts, Mary encouraged her friend Evelyn to apply for one of the entry level inspection roles. Evelyn passed her interview, and the two of them were reunited.

The west wing of the facility manufactured the new military equipment. After the parts were produced, they were shuttled via a conveyor system to the east wing of the factory where Mary and Evelyn worked as parts inspectors. The factory was a cacophony of sound, with metal clanking against metal, rivets beings drilled, equipment rattling, and whistles blowing to signal shift changes. The good news was that workers in proximity could talk about whatever they wanted without being overheard by their co-workers.

"Why do we get stuck working with all the new guys?" Evelyn asked Mary.

"Because women are superior to men in every way. Isn't it obvious that the two of us are the *BEST* parts inspectors in this building? Our role is to bring the inferior gender up to our superior female standards!"

Evelyn laughed. "You crack me up."

A whistle blared, indicating break time. "Let's hit the breakroom and catch the latest factory gossip," Evelyn said.

They had barely finished coffee and a particularly juicy story when the whistle blared again, causing the sea of workers to herd their way toward the exit. But one worker pushed against the tide, colliding with Mary. In turn, she knocked into Evelyn, who had been standing behind her, and they fell like a pair of dominoes.

"Sorry!" the guy said breathlessly as he helped them up. "I got lost on my way here, and I was in a hurry to grab a coffee. Are you okay?"

Evelyn let out an angry screech. "Watch where you're going! You made me bite my lip."

"Geez, I'm sorry," the young man said. "I didn't see you. I just got hired as a screw machine operator and I'm not having a good first day on the job!"

An older man pointed a half-eaten cinnamon roll in their direction. "C'mon, you lovebirds, you're blocking the door."

As they shuffled past him, Evelyn thrust her finger at the new guy's chest. "You're off the hook this time around, buddy. But we have our eyes on you from now on!"

The new guy smiled, and instantly, Mary knew who it was even before his eyes lit with recognition. "I swear it won't happen again, Evelyn with a 'K' and Mary."

✦ ✦ ✦

Mary tossed and turned all night, unable to stop thinking about Ed. Later she would learn that Ed couldn't sleep either, his mind filled with how to ask her for a date without seeming too forward.

It was a long day, made worse because Evelyn was absent; Mary was grateful when the shift-ending whistle blew at exactly 4PM. As she moved into the clock-out line, she felt someone breathing down her neck. Mary squared her shoulders and slid her timecard into the slot, relieved when the stamping machine made the familiar *cha-chunk* sound, and she could make her escape.

She hastened out the door and across the parking lot but couldn't shake the feeling she was being followed. At last, while Mary was still amidst other workers, she whipped around. Her irritation and worry bubbled out. "Why are you sneaking up on me?" As soon as she realized who it was, her anger dissipated. Still, she couldn't resist making him squirm and kept her face stern.

Ed stepped back and began to stammer. "Um, I w-was w-wondering if I could w-walk you home?" Mary shook her head and playfully tried to sidestep past him.

Undeterred, Ed kept pace, even though Mary kept up the hard-to-get routine. "Stop following me!" she gushed.

Ed wrung his hands together. "I just…just want to know if you're going steady with someone else."

Mary's resolve faltered when she saw the pathetic look on his admittedly handsome face. "No, I'm not. And yes, I guess you can walk me home after all." The conversation was pleasant and surprisingly effortless. When they arrived at Mary's house, Ed handed her a business envelope with the Schoemberger's logo on it. "What's this?" she asked.

"It's official work business. It's important you read it," Ed said with feigned seriousness.

"Uh-Ok. Thanks," Mary said. They shook hands clumsily before Ed turned and walked away.

Mary entered her house and immediately opened the envelope. As she read the letter, her body started to convulse. By the end, she was laughing hysterically.

MY DAY AT WORK

7:00AM: Punch timecard and clock into work.

7:30AM: Tell security guard a funny joke. He tells me one too. Har, Har.

8:00AM: Electric sander not working. Call to get it fixed.

8:30AM: Repairman comes. Plugs it in. It works!

8:31AM: I tell repairman. "You fixed it!"

9:00AM: Go to water cooler. No cups. Take shoe off and fill it with water. Take drink.

9:30AM: Slip and fall on floor due to wet shoe. Talk to God about it for a while.

10:00AM: Late for break.

10:12AM: Bump into nice looking girl in the breakroom. She adores me, I can tell.

10:13AM: Her friend pokes me in the chest. Not intimidated. Sorry for fat lip.

10:14AM: Large man waving danish yells for me and nice-looking girl to get moving.

10:15AM: Back at workstation. Drop power drill on foot. Go to dispensary.

10:30AM: Nurse asks why foot wet? I say, "my foot sweats a lot." Nurse gives me aspirin.

11:00AM: Stop at vending machine. Lose 5 cents.

11:30AM: Walk to accounts payable. Report losing 10 cents.

12:00PM: Lunch. Notice nice looking girl making eyes at me from across cafeteria.

1:00PM: Back at workstation. Supervisor coming, I start hammering something.

1:30PM: Hit thumb with hammer. Resume previous discussion with God.

2:00PM: Put mercurochrome on thumb. Watch thumb turn red.

2:30PM: See foreman coming, I start moving things around.

3:00PM: Bad stomachache. Aspirin, probably.

3:30PM: Let supervisor know I don't feel well. Want job where I can sit down.

3:45PM: Back to water cooler. Still no cups. Girl staring at me (again). I keep shoe on my foot.

4:00PM: Back on job. Starting to clean and put tools away.

4:30PM: Supervisor coming. Asks me why I didn't get much done today.

4:35PM: Told him girl keeps staring at me. Distracting me from my duties.

4:36PM: Supervisor says, "She probably wants you to ask her out for a date."

4:37PM: Tell Supervisor "I will consider it."

4:38PM: Shine supervisor's nose. "Thank you for being such a smart boss."

4:39PM: Supervisor slaps me on back. Says I'm his best worker.

4:45PM: Lock up tools. Leave workstation.

5:00PM: Punch out timecard. I'm exhausted.

NEXT DAY: Almost the same, only asked for a raise. And, have new girlfriend.

CHAPTER 12:
CLEVELAND, OHIO
FEBRUARY 1941

INDEED, MARY and Ed had begun dating and by this point had been together for about a year. During the summer, they hung out at Edgewater Park and enjoyed swimming and picnics with their friends. They went on double dates to Cleveland Indians baseball games, and they loved to go dancing at the local Polish American club, bouncing to polka and swing music.

Mary and Ed were both athletic, and especially enjoyed competitive games they could play with others. Bowling and horseshoes were popular, but ping pong was their favorite. They played as a team against their friends and played as singles against one another. They created a scorecard to keep track of the number of games each of them won during the previous week. On Fridays after work, the loser was required to buy the winner a coke float at Rudy's Five and Dime store.

On Friday, Ed was walking Mary home from work when she dug into her purse and pulled out a small index card. She waved the card in front of his face. "I beat you 10 games to 8 this week. You owe me a creamy coke float!"

They stopped at Rudy's and Ed ordered a float for each of them. Mary stirred the long spoon around in the tall glass to blend the coke and vanilla ice cream together. She smiled and took the first sip.

"How does it taste?" Ed asked as he prepared to scoop out the ice cream with a spoon.

"It tastes like victory," Mary said with a grin.

"I'll get you back next week," Ed promised, eyes gleaming.

When they finished their drinks, Ed escorted Mary home. "I'll be back in exactly one hour to collect you for our dancing date at the PA Club." He pecked her on the cheek and jogged away.

One hour later, Mary was sitting on her front porch swing, all dolled up. But for the first time since they started dating, Ed was a no show.

Two hours passed, and Mary had long since ripped off her heels and fancy dress and changed into comfortable clothes. While Ed had never shown her up before, she kept waffling between being terrified he'd been in an accident and upset that he'd somehow managed to replace her with someone else. She worried if she didn't hear from him soon, she might not have any nails left from picking at them. When the doorbell buzzed at last, she was in the middle of an anger jag. But when she opened the door, she gasped, her anger dissipating into shock. Ed hadn't showered or removed his grimy blue machine operator jumpsuit from work. In short, he was a gritty, sweaty mess and instantly, Mary knew something was very wrong.

"What happened?" she cried.

"I hardly know where to start," Ed said as Mary joined him on the stoop. "When I got home, I found my mother and father waiting in the living room. Mother was dabbing her eyes with a handkerchief and Big Hand was wearing a hole in the carpet from pacing so much. At first, I thought someone must have died. Then my father held up letter addressed to me from the local draft board."

"Were you drafted?" Mary whispered, afraid if she spoke any louder it would turn out to be true.

Ed glanced away recalling the notice. "Yes, my draft number came up. I'll be going to Basic Training and after I finish, I'll be sent back home as an Army reservist. The idea is that if the country is dragged into the fracas in Europe, the U.S. will have a trained civilian army to augment regular military personnel."

Mary shivered, and not from the blustery March temperature. "How long will Basic Training take?" After a tense moment, she added, "Did any of your older brothers get drafted?"

Ed sighed. "18 months. And no, thankfully, none of my brothers qualify. One of the reasons I was so late is that I had to track down each one to find out. Then I had to call my boss at Schoemberger's to let him know."

"Will they hold your job?" Mary asked, arms wrapped around her waist.

Ed shook his weary head. "Turns out I'm the first to get drafted, and they don't have a policy in place. He said he'd have to discuss it with the owners and get back with me."

"It goes without saying, but I really hope they save your job for you. You may be the first, but doubt you'll be the last." Mary took Ed's hand. "Let's go inside and have a warm drink."

Ed and Mary spent the rest of the evening discussing their future. "It's only 18 months. It will go by fast and when I get back home everything will go back to normal."

Sadly, Ed's prophecy didn't come true.

CHAPTER 13:
COLUMBUS, OHIO
MARCH 1941

ED WAS instructed to report to the Army Induction Center at Fort
Hayes, which was near Columbus, Ohio. The primary role of Fort
Hayes was to induct recent draftees into the Army. Like all others, Ed
received a physical and took a psychiatric exam. After passing those
with flying colors, lots of paperwork came next, including selection of
a beneficiary for the $5,000 veteran life insurance policy. Ed had less
than two minutes to make one of the most important decisions in his
life, and he began to sweat.

Ed thought about the people who would most benefit from having
this money. *Maybe my sisters, but how do I pick one over the other?* Next,
he considered his mother, father, and ultimately, Mary. He was head
over heels for her, but they weren't yet engaged.

There was a long line of recruits behind him, so he felt enormous
pressure to decide fast. Ed made the split-second decision to name
Stella, his mother, as his primary insurance beneficiary. He signed the
document to make it official and binding. Ed didn't know it at the time,
but his decision would lead to a major rift between Mary and Stella in
the coming year.

The rest of the day was spent gathering all the equipment he would
need for basic training: barrack's bag, military clothing, and boots. At
the conclusion of the jam-packed day, Ed boarded a bus and returned
home to Cleveland. The Army had given him two weeks to get his
personal affairs squared away before reporting to Fort Oglethorpe,
Georgia for boot camp.

✛   ✛   ✛

When Ed arrived home, he discovered Big Hand had marched to the local draft board and tried to enlist in the United States Army without telling Stella. Apparently, the military didn't buy his assertion that he was 45 years old and in good enough shape to take on the Nazis, plus the Russians after the Nazis were defeated.

Ed knew Big Hand felt a huge sense of guilt and regret about staying in America during the First World War, while many of his family and friends in Poland sacrificed their lives for their country's independence. It didn't matter that he was married with four small children to support; his Polish relatives never forgave him for abandoning them in their time of crisis and cut all ties. It went without saying, however, that Stella and his children were immensely grateful he stayed with the family then as well as now.

"I can't believe it," Mr. Camela said when Ed broke the news that he wouldn't be coming back to play baseball for the upcoming season. "When you finish your Army "sabbatical," rest assured, you'll be welcomed back."

All too soon, it was the day before he was required to ship out to boot camp. He went to tender his official resignation at Schoemberger's and was surprised when his co-workers threw him a going away party. Ed roared with laughter when he saw the clever words written on the sheet cake: "Good luck Eddie. Put the screws to the enemy!"

That night, his last in Ohio, he and Mary went to dinner. Though they weren't engaged, they were committed, and Ed knew he would miss her like crazy. "I promise I'll write to you as much as I can," he said.

His heart warmed when she replied, "I'll write to you, too. We'll stay together through thick and thin. I brought a little keepsake you can take with you to remember me while you're away." Mary reached into her purse and surprised him with a wallet-sized picture of herself and a handwritten note.

"Holy smokes, you look like a movie star in this picture!" Ed cooed. He looked at Mary's handwriting on the paper. "And it looks like I am down one to zero on letter writing!" Ed laughed.

Mary smiled. "It's not a letter, silly. It's a poem that goes with my picture, and I'd like to read it to you. She put the paper down in front of her and out of the corner of her eye, she could see Ed reaching for something in his back pocket.

He held up a handkerchief. "Just in case I need it," he explained.

Mary leaned forward in her chair. "The poem is called *Return to Me*."

I'll keep a picture of you in my heart,
As you venture far from home,
Across the seas and distant lands,
Wherever you may roam.

Though war may rage,
And danger near,
I'll hold you tight within my thoughts,
And banish all my fear.

For as I gaze upon your face,
And see your loving smile,
I know that you'll return to me,
And make my life worthwhile.

When Mary paused to take a breath, she saw Ed dabbing his eyes. When he noticed her watching him, he said, "It's beautiful, sweetheart, keep reading." Mary nodded and continued.

And so I'll keep your picture close,
Through every night and day,
And pray that God will keep you safe,
Until your home to stay.

For though you're far away from me,
You're always in my heart,
And nothing can ever change the love,
That we have from the start.

Mary clasped her hands over her heart and leaned back in her chair. "Did you like it?"

Ed lifted a soggy hankie. "If I'd have known you were going to read such a tear-jerker to me, I would have brought two of these," he stammered. "I loved it, honey, every word, truly." He walked to the other side of the table and gave Mary a heartfelt hug.

"I'll keep these with me always," he said, his voice rich with emotion. He knew he'd look at them every single day.

The next morning, after saying teary goodbyes to both Mary and his mother, Ed arrived at the Cleveland train station dressed in a suit and tie. His father came along to see him off and took Ed's barrack's bag as they approached the train. Before Ed embarked, Big Hand laid the bag on the ground and gave his son a guilty look. "I'm sorry you're the one who was forced to do this. It should have been me instead of you."

"Pop," Ed said with a reassuring smile, "I'm glad you'll be home to take care of mom. I also want you to know how much we all appreciated having you around all these years."

Big Hand beckoned him closer. "I want to tell you something important."

"What is it?" Ed asked, glancing toward the train.

Big Hand's chest heaved. "If you talk to soldiers wearing a German uniform, ask them about their home countries. If they're Russian Polska, German Polska, or Czech, you'll be able to trust them better. In these regions, many citizens are forced to fight for Germany against their will. You ask them this, understand? It could save your life."

Ed was taken aback by his father's intense and detailed warning. "I'll only be gone for 18 months. I'm only going as far away as Georgia, and there won't be any Germans there. I swear, I'll be back home before we know it." Ed glanced at his watch; it was time to board.

Big Hand maintained steady eye contact, his eyes misty with unshed tears. "I know, I know. Just promise me, if the conflict escalates and you get sent overseas, you'll remember my advice."

Ed hoisted his bag over his shoulder. "Okay, Pop, I'll remember. I promise."

Big Hand opened his arms for one last hug. As Ed boarded the train, he could feel his father's lingering presence. Seeing his father so rattled unsettled him. But he told himself he had nothing to worry about.

He never expected he would have to act upon Big Hand's advice.

CHAPTER 14:
FORT OGLETHROPE, GEORGIA APRIL 1941

UPON ARRIVAL for basic training in Fort Oglethorpe, Ed and the other draftees learned the program would be centered on drilling the recruits on the rules and regulations of being in the Army, whipping them into fighting shape, and receiving weapons training.

The first phase of their training translated to daily calisthenics, timed obstacle courses, grueling marches in formation, and instruction on military commands. The second phase was weapons training, which included learning how to aim and accurately fire rifles, pistols, bazookas, and how to properly lob grenades. They were also taught to fight with bayonets and were drilled on hand-to-hand combat.

During basic training, Ed became friends with Dean Cooper, Scott Rollins and Robert Louis. Inevitably, the question of Ed's long last name came up. "My friends call me Krow for short," he told them. The nickname stuck, and most everyone in the Army simply called him "Krow".

After completing their training, the four young men were assigned to the 65th Medical Regiment and relocated to Camp Forrest, TN. There, they began specialized training as Army medics.

✦ ✦ ✦

The entire 65th medical battalion shipped out for field exercises in the steamy, sticky backwoods of Louisiana. Four months straight, Ed and the other medic trainees slept in pup tents, endured wretched weather, and traversed through treacherous terrain. If it weren't for the camaraderie and support from his friends, Ed didn't know how he would have managed the relentless hardship. The purpose, their drill sergeant often reminded them, was to expose the men to combat-like conditions, evaluate their preparedness, and identify areas of weakness which needed to be addressed.

The trainees learned how to treat common ailments they would face while living outside. Things like poison ivy, spider bites, snake venom, and hornet stings, all of which they did their best to avoid. They also got creative at fending off wild animals who tried to steal their food. Somehow, Ed and the others got used to roughing it outside, eating Army rations, and keeping up with the bare minimum of hygiene requirements.

Each day, the unit was faced with situations designed to test their problem-solving skills. During a hasty evacuation, patient safety and transportation were in a constant state of flux. They learned the importance of developing a safe withdrawal plan while avoiding enemy capture.

The Army used burlap sacks filled with rocks or other materials to simulate the body weight of a patient. Each day, the total number of "patients" would change, as well as the number of transport vehicles available. When the number of simulated casualties exceeded jeeps available to move them, the men learned that anything with wheels was fair game. Ed and others also learned what to do if the enemy broke through the lines and transportation of any kind was unavailable. In those situations, a two-man foxhole might be the only option. In fact, any existing foxhole could be dug into a two-man hole, which the medics could use to dodge artillery fire and/or conceal themselves from any enemy tanks in the area.

Some of the men thought it was a joke when they were told to dig deep enough to squeeze two-deep into the hole, but not so wide so that tanks fell in instead of rolling over the surface.

To simulate this exercise, the medics were split into two groups and each man was given 30 minutes to dig a two-person foxhole. Dean Cooper, who went by Coop, was digging his two-man foxhole next to Ed. "Do you think they'll use *real* tanks to roll over our foxholes?" Coop asked.

Before Ed could answer, a loud creaking sound could be heard coming out of the woods about two football fields away. The sound was like that of a roller coaster slowly clacking its way up to the top of the tracks.

The drill sergeant grabbed a megaphone. "Group #1, drop to the ground. You are now the wounded. Group #2, each of you take a wounded man from group #1 and pull him to the safety of your two-man foxhole!" Ed was in group #2, and he quickly looped his arms under the nearest 'wounded' soldier and dragged him into the foxhole. He piled on top and prayed he dug the hole deep enough so that he and Coop, the wounded soldier under him, wouldn't get flattened. As they were digging the holes, Ed and his friends treated this as a joke. He certainly didn't feel that way anymore as the tank drew ever closer.

The drill sergeant climbed on top of the tank so he could spot the men in their holes. The tank rolled over several of the foxholes without incident. But at one of the holes, the sergeant signaled the tank to stop. He jumped from the tank with a handful of small red flags and measuring tape and proceeded to measure the width and depth of the hole. After plunging a red flag in the ground next to the trench, he climbed back onto the tank.

Pointing to the offending foxhole from his perch, he shouted loud and clear, "These men are dead! Their hole wasn't deep enough, and the tank crushed them. Alright boys, get on up and finish the job right."

The two "dead men" got out of the hole and resumed digging until the hole was deep enough. When they climbed back in, the tank rolled over them toward the remaining foxholes. The tank clacked and hissed as it approached. Ed could hear the soldiers next to him reciting the Lord's prayer. "Coop, let's move sideways so we can make sure we're deep enough." They shimmied their bodies into a spooning position, with Coop behind Ed. "The tank is getting really close to our position," Coop said, his voice muffled.

"I got an idea," Ed said. "Are you able to grab one of the sticky bombs from my backpack?"

"I'm one step ahead of you," Coop responded. "I didn't know what to do with my hands, so I already stole one from you. I don't have much leverage, so you need to be the one to sling it." He slid the fake explosive to Ed.

A large shadow shrouded their foxhole as the tank passed overhead. Despite his eyes watering from the exhaust vapors, he chucked the sticky bomb with his free hand and yelled to Coop, "Cover your ears!"

Ed grinned as the fake explosive glued itself to the bottom of the tank, a perfect bullseye. Thirty yards past their foxhole, the bomb detonated, releasing purple smoke. Ed and Coop were the only two, as part of their live drill, to be resourceful enough to take out the tank as it rolled over the top of them.

When the exercise was finished the drill sergeant barked to the soldiers. "When faced with a complex problem, don't panic, stay level-headed, and use your resourcefulness to convert a problem into an opportunity like these men did. "If you have a red flag, grab a shovel and fill in your foxholes." When he heard a few groans he added, "For all twenty of the foxholes."

As Ed and Coop walked off, exhausted and covered in dirt, Coop whispered, "I suppose we shouldn't tell Sarge we did it as a gag."

"Absolutely not," Ed agreed. "Thank God this long, grueling training is over!"

CHAPTER 15:
CAMP FORREST, TENN.
FEBRUARY 1942

UPON THEIR return from field maneuvers, Ed and his buddies had noted the absence of the weekly camp newspaper, *The Litter Digest*. Three weeks in, Robert Louis arrived at the breakfast table waving the paper. "It's back! Let me read it to you."

> *Now that the rumble of tanks has faded, the digging of foxholes in a deluge, the drying of soggy fatigues over midnight campfires and the roar of P 51s has slipped into silence we can go to press again!*

"Keep going," Coop said, motioning with his hand.

Louis scanned the second page and scoffed. "Can you believe they created this after we spent three months enduring the dreaded scourge of the earth?"

> *NEWS FLASH. NEW SECRET WEAPON TO FIGHT CHIGGERS AND TICK BITES*

A collective groan came from the table. "I don't fucking believe it," Coop barked.

Ed scoffed. "I'm still scratching the bites I got from crawling under barbed wire. So, what's the Army's so-called "secret chigger weapon?"

Louis grinned. "The big secret weapon is… drumroll, please…insect repellent!"

"What the hell do they think we've been using?" Ed growled. "Read the damn article."

Additional insect repellent has been made available to the
Camp Quartermaster for distribution to units in this camp.
For protection from Chigger bites, draw the mouth of the bottle
along the clothing, apply a thin layer wide along all openings of
the uniform, the neck, cuffs of shirt, waist, and fly.

Louis paused to make sure he still held everyone's attention. "There's more. For additional protection, don't wipe your scrotum and rectal area for a solid week. The chiggers will then asphyxiate."

Milk shot out of Coop's nose and Ed banged his fist on the table. "Louis, you're full of it!" Rollins said between laughs.

Coop wiped his face and snatched the paper from Louis. "It's my turn to find something juicy." "Hey, get a load of this horseshit! It's an article about the next level of foxhole defense"

BLUE NOTE FROM A FOXHOLE

Next to letters from home, the most comforting thing in a
foxhole is music, preferably the music a soldier can produce
himself by whipping out a pocket instrument and launching into
a nostalgic sound. So reports Maj. Howard C. Bronson, head of
the Army's Special services.

The Army has issued several million instruments, easy to play,
tonettes, a flutelike tube, harmonicas, ocarinas, and ukuleles,
with instruction sheets that turn soldiers into musicians in ten
minutes. Learning to play these gadgets can provide relief from
tedium and battle weariness.

"What the fuck is an ocarina?" Louis bleeped out. Cooper ignored him and kept reading.

The tonette has been the big hit of the war so far. An experiment
to determine the abilities of soldiers to handle the simple
instrument was undertaken at Fort George Mead. After ten
minutes of instruction they (the soldiers) were playing "Don't
Sit Under the Apple Tree. A half hour later they played anything
they knew, and shortly, Fort George Meade became the tootenest
camp in the Army with more than sixty pocket instrument bands.

Louis took a spoon from his breakfast tray and pretended to play it like a flute. "Dear German soldier: follow my sweet melodies to this here foxhole and you'll get a big surprise." Louis then made his hands look like guns.

Ed shook his head and laughed. "I gotta run. My group has an aviation identification drill today at 0900, and I have to get them ready for it."

The men stood and grabbed their trays, except for Coop, who continued to scan the paper. "You aren't dismissed yet! One of our merry band of medics has been featured in this edition of the Litter Digest."

Louis grinned. "Who is it?"

Cooper cleared his throat.

During field training Company H's Pvt Rollins never failed to write his wife every day. It's either love or a bad conscience.

"Who wrote that bullshit?" Rollins barked, his face turning red. "What the hell does he mean by love or a bad conscience?" In an instant the conversation switched from being silly and using humor to blow off some steam to something more serious.

Coop showed Rollins the paper. "See it's right there, bottom of page four."

Rollins clenched his jaw and the veins in his neck stood out. "I'm going to kick that reporter's ass! I love my wife, and it's hard enough we can't see each other for months at a time." He dropped the tray and massaged his temples. "What if our unit gets deployed? How long will Janice and I be separated then? And what if I get maimed or killed?"

He took a deep breath and clenched his fists and continued. "Janice is pregnant with our first child and instead of jumping for joy and smoking cigars with you assholes, I'm worrying that I'll never get to meet my kid."

There was a long moment of awkward silence. Ed took a deep breath. "Scott, congratulations to you and Janice. I know I can speak for all of us when I say we'll do everything to get you back home in one piece." Coop and Louis nodded in agreement and added their congratulations as they deposited their trays.

Ed lagged the group and walked out of the mess tent like a zombie. He had big plans for Mary's upcoming weekend visit, and Rollin's worries infected him. He had made a down payment on an engagement ring and was going to ask Mary to be his wife. But now, he was rethinking that plan.

CHAPTER 16:
CAMP FORREST, TENN. FEBRUARY 1942

ED AND Mary had discussed getting married after the conclusion of his 18-month stint in the Army. Then "on a day that will live in infamy" the Japanese bombed Pearl Harbor, and Ed and Mary's plans were ruptured.

The United States declared war on Japan and Germany, and it became a forgone conclusion that Ed's unit would be deployed overseas. When that might happen and for how long, no one knew, least of all Ed. But he'd managed to ignore the likelihood until Rollins voiced his fear.

He had been excited about Mary's upcoming visit, especially as he hadn't seen her for four months. He had thought long and hard on how to make their engagement special. And now, replaying Rollins' words in his head, he was filled with self-doubt and dread.

Ed kept a notepad and a pencil in his army boot and put the boots under his cot when he slept. That way, whenever he thought of something important, even in the middle of the night, he simply reached into his boot and retrieved his pad of paper and wrote whatever was in his head. That night, knowing Mary was only hours away, he couldn't sleep a wink. So, he pulled out his trusty notepad and pencil and jotted down the following day's itinerary.

Noon: Meet Mary at Train Station.

1:00p: Drive to boarding house and check-in

2:00p: Smooch time.

3:00p: Extended Smooch time

5:00p: Meet Coop & Marie for dinner.

7:00p: Go to Camp Dance Hall (Jitterbug night)

10:30p: Walk Mary back to *Farm*

11:00p: Get Mary's opinion on getting married.

He knew Mary was the right girl, *but was this the right time to get married?* There were a million scenarios running through his brain, but it all boiled down to a few options, all of which he wrote down, hoping it would make everything clearer.

Option #1: Do nothing. Stay as a steady couple and when war ends, pick up where we left off. Pro: If I die or come back incapacitated, Mary would still be single and unattached. She would be young enough to marry someone else. Con: Stinks for me, but Mary can still make positive memories with someone else. Con: I might not be there to break his ass if he treats her badly.

Option #2: Get engaged, but not married. Pro: I come back safe and sound. We get married and live happily ever after. Con: I die. If I was another guy, I would know she loved someone else and "new guy" might believe she could not give her whole heart to him. Not fair to him or her.

Con: I come back maimed or incapacitated. Out of guilt, she might decide she has an obligation to stick with me, even if I'm a good for nothing war veteran for the next sixty years. What if I step on a mine and get my nuts blown off? Then what? No kids! What if my dick and nuts get blown off at the same time! I would cease being a man. The only silver lining for her is that there's no way I'd last 60 years like that.

Option #3: Get married before I get deployed overseas.

Pro: We can enjoy being a married couple for as long as it lasts and let the chips fall as they may. Cons: Same as above but worse. If I'm incapacitated, Mary would have to be my caregiver for the rest of her life. If she wanted to free herself of that burden, she would have to divorce me to restart her life. In our religion, divorce is unacceptable. I can't do that to her.

Option #4: The war ends tomorrow, and we all go home. Fat chance!

Ed stuffed his notepad and pencil back in his boot. Totally rattled, he kept punching his pillow to get comfortable, but it was no use. His brain refused to shut down. Despite how many times he replayed each scenario in his head, he remained unsure about the right path forward with Mary.

He jumped out of bed before sunrise, showered, and slipped into his uniform. It was still dark when he walked briskly toward Rollins' barracks. Walking into the Company "H" bunkhouse, he spotted his friend still asleep. But that didn't stop Ed from shaking his shoulder. "Rolly, you awake?" When there was no answer, Ed tapped Rollins' forehead with his finger. "Rolly, wake up. It's important."

His friend's eyes remained closed. "What?" he croaked.

"Meet me for breakfast at 0600," Ed said. "I really need to talk with you."

"Fine. But leave me alone for the next 45 minutes so I can finish my dream about how I plan to murder you for waking me this early." Rollins turned his back to Ed, illustrating his point.

"Thanks, Rolly," Ed whispered.

Despite all of Rolly's grumbling, Ed knew his friend would be prompt, showered, and shaved with no wrinkles in sight. Sure enough, Rollins dropped his loaded breakfast tray next to Ed's at 0600 on the dot looking inspection ready.

"Okay, what's so important that you barged into my barracks and interrupted my dream of hot cars and fast women?"

Ed leaned toward him. "Mary's train arrives today, and after our conversation yesterday, it got me re-thinking our marriage plans. We were supposed to get hitched when I got out of the service, but as you well know, the bombing of Pearl Harbor makes everything so uncertain. There's no telling when or if we'll ship out, or how long we'll be gone." Ed bit his lip to keep from adding, "*If we ever come back from there*," knowing Rollins' situation.

"Not to mention the uncertainty over where we'll be stationed," Rollins stated, his voice oddly flat.

"Exactly!" Ed said. "I want to know how you and Janice decided to get married, and what your thought process was with the war and the draft looming."

"We got married before Roosevelt signed the Selective Service Agreement, a full two years before the draft. We never considered it was a possibility."

Ed wasn't sure how to position his next question to his friend. Based on their conversation yesterday, it was clear Rollins was stewing about being away from Janice and his unborn baby.

"Scott, based on what you know now, would you have done anything differently?"

Rollins laid down his fork. "Different how?"

Ed hung his head. "I'm really asking about me and Mary. Do you think it makes sense to get married now? I couldn't sleep so I wrote the pros and cons of each possibility in my notepad. I can review those with you if it makes it easier for you to understand my dilemma."

Rollins chuckled. "No, keep your notes to yourself. I'd marry Janice again a heartbeat, no matter what. But what's right for you and Mary is up to the two of you. If it helps, you should know that I've always got your back."

Ed was speechless. How did he ever get so lucky, in family, friends, and in his intended life mate?

Rollins broke the ice first. "Let's finish breakfast and get you ready to meet your sweetheart."

The train chugged into the station right on time. When Mary stepped from the sidecar wearing a cashmere coat with matching heels, gloves, and handbag, he realized he'd never seen a more beautiful sight. Letting out a familiar 'whit-woo' whistle, he strode her way. Ed knew she spotted him when she smiled and waved. When they intersected, he kissed her full on the lips without caring who might see. Stepping back, he gushed, "You look and smell wonderful!"

Mary laughed. "You smell pretty good yourself, mister!"

"C'mon, let's get out of this place." Ed grabbed Mary's suitcase, looped his free arm around hers, and led her to the parking lot. "I have a great day planned for us," he said as they stepped into the jeep. Before turning the ignition, Ed took his notepad out of his shirt pocket and read the itinerary to Mary, leaving out any references to the marriage discussion.

"What's this business of extended smooch time?" Mary asked with mock surprise.

"Extended smooch time means making up for lost ground. Four months away from each other has been torture."

She locked onto his opaline green eyes. "What if we need to *extend* the extended smooch time?"

Ed grinned. "I guess Coop and Marie will need to *extend* their picnic time until we get there!"

CHAPTER 17:
CAMP FORREST, TENN.
FEBRUARY 1942

INDEED, THEY were late for their dinner picnic with Dean Cooper and his girlfriend Marie. After joining them and enjoying some playful ribbing, the four of them went to the enlisted men's club and danced the night away jitterbugging to the popular music of the day.

When the band stopped playing, Ed retrieved Mary's wrap from the coat check and escorted her out the door. On the walk back to the boarding house, Ed burned with desire to broach the topic of marriage. "Hey, Mary," he blurted out.

"Hey, what?" she replied, shaking her head.

"A lot of the enlisted guys are getting married these days. You know, while we're still here. So, I was wondering, hypothetically of course, what you thought about marrying a soldier before he deploys." Ed's hands flapped all over the place while he spoke. Now he stood as still as a statue.

Mary cocked her head. "What are you asking me?"

They were standing in front of the boarding house's steps. Ed brushed away a few leaves and they sat down next to each other. "Um...I was wondering..." Ed couldn't spit it out. This was not how a proposal should go. His head drooped, and suddenly, he thought he might throw up.

Mary shifted to face him. "Are you asking me if I'd marry any soldier? Is there some other soldier on this base who wants to marry me?" Her lips twitched between a smile and a frown. "I promise I won't bite if you tell me what's troubling you."

Ed regrouped, took a deep breath, and moved closer so their knees were touching. "I know we talked about getting married after my discharge, but that's when we assumed I'd be home in a year and a half."

"Yes, that's right," Mary said.

"Since the attack on Pearl Harbor, there's no question my unit will be sent overseas to join the war effort. I just don't know when, where, and for how long. I could be deployed tomorrow or a year from now. If we get married and I get injured or killed, that would be unfair to you, and I don't know if…"

Mary stopped him cold. She scooched away, creating separation between them. "How would you presume to know what's fair or unfair for me? All the terrible scenarios have been rolling around my brain nonstop ever since you got drafted." She leaned closer and took Ed's hand. "I don't want to waste a single second we have left together. The best option for me is to get married as soon as we can. No one has a crystal ball to tell us what's going to happen in the future. The only thing we have is the here and now." Mary squeezed his hand.

Ed stared into her eyes. "What if I come back brain-dead from poison gas?"

Mary dropped his hand. "I think you're brain-dead right now! You think I wouldn't care about you if we don't get married? Whatever might happen to you will affect the both of us regardless." Mary abruptly stood and glared at him. "What if I were killed in a machine accident or hit by car? Would you care less about me if we weren't married?"

"Of course not, "Ed said, meeting her gaze as a gust of wind tussled Mary's hair. "If our future were stolen from us, I would deeply regret missing the opportunity to enjoy our lives together when we had the chance." He took a moment to gather his courage. "So, if I asked you to marry me right this minute, what would you say?"

Mary sat down and threw her arms around him. "I would say yes and would be the happiest gal in the world! I'd quit my job, have my belongings shipped, and live here with you in newlywed bliss. We could rent an apartment off-base for however many glorious days we have left together."

Ed clutched her tighter and murmured in her ear. "Are you sure this is what you want?"

Mary whispered back, "I've never been surer in my life."

Ed disentangled himself, stood. and sank to one knee. "Mary, will you be my wife?"

Mary clasped his hands with hers and held them to her chest. "Yes! Yes! You have my heart forever!"

"And you have mine." Ed tenderly kissed her lips.

Mary and Ed talked excitedly about their wedding plans until the wee hours of the morning. They were ready to face the uncertain future as husband and wife and meet all challenges together. They were madly in love and brimming with joy and happiness.

However, not everyone would be excited about their rash decision to wed.

CHAPTER 18:
CAMP FORREST, TENN.
FEBRUARY 1942

THE NEXT morning, Mary boarded the early morning train to Cleveland. There was one important detail that Ed had to take care of before Mary arrived back home. Because their decision to get married was hasty and unplanned, Ed now had to ask the bride's father for permission to take his daughter's hand in marriage.

Ed walked to the PX where there was a telephone booth for soldiers to make calls to their family and friends. Ed had always enjoyed a great relationship with Andrew Raczyka, Mary's father. A few times on the weekends, Andrew had accompanied Mary to watch Ed play ball on team Camela. When the soldier in front of him finished his call, Ed stepped up to take his turn. He dialed the number and Mary's mother answered the phone. "Hi Mrs. Raczyka. This is Eddie. How's your morning going?"

"Eddie! How are you?" Mary's mother's greeting seemed enthusiastic to Ed, but then the tone of her voice changed to one of concern. "Is Mary alright?"

"Mary's fine, she's on the train back to Cleveland. My apologies for being so abrupt, but I only have few minutes left on this call. There's a long line of soldiers behind me waiting to use the phone, and I have a question to ask Mr. Raczyka."

"I see," she said, her enthusiasm returning. "Andrew is eating his breakfast. I'll get him to come to the phone." After some muffled words, a much deeper voice said "Hello, Eddie."

"Mr. Raczyka, I don't have a lot of time, so I'll get right to it. You know I have fallen in love with your daughter. I would like your blessing to marry her." Ed pressed the receiver to his ear.

"You seek my blessing to marry her," Andrew repeated as a statement.

"Yes, sir," Ed said, starting to sweat.

"I would be honored to call you my son-in-law," Andrew said. "I give you my blessing and more. What are your plans?"

"Well, this is all happening rather quickly. Mary is going back home to get her affairs in order, and she will be returning to Tennessee immediately. We'll be getting married within the week."

Thud.

"Mr. Raczyka? Are you still there?"

After a bit of fumbling, he replied, "Yes," in a flat voice.

"I know this seems like a quick decision, but I can assure you I will love, honor, and respect Mary for the rest of my life." Ed was unaware he had just recited a standard line from a popular wedding vow.

"Have you considered all the consequences?" Andrew asked. "Anna and I assumed you and Mary would get married after the war. This strikes me as an emotional decision, and there are too many unknowns regarding your future. We will support you if you wait until after the war to marry our daughter."

"Um," was all Ed managed to say.

"Eddie," Andrew said, his voice now commanding. "You know we hold you in the highest regard, but things have changed. You're in the Army now and there is a good chance you'll be deployed. You'll be facing life or death situations, which would place an unfair burden on both you and Mary."

He left out injured or maimed. Ed ignored the growing line of soldiers waiting to use the phone and squared his shoulders. "Sir, Mary, and I talked about all those risks. None of us can control the future. All we have is the here and now. We want the opportunity to be husband and wife while we still have this chance to be with each other, however short it might be." Andrew breathed heavily, and Ed could imagine steam pouring from his ears.

"It would be selfish of you to put Mary in this position," Andrew said. "Her love for you is clouding her judgment. Maybe she's wrapped up in the Hollywood glamour of doing her patriotic duty to marry a soldier before he goes off to war. Have you considered the long-term consequences if she should be pregnant while you are overseas? The child might never know what it's like to have a father. Surely you understand all of this, don't you?"

Some of the soldiers waiting in line tapped their boots against the floor. One guy caught Ed's attention by rotating his index finger in circles. Ed took a deep breath made his final case.

"If our roles were reversed, I might be saying the same things. I can only tell you what's inside my heart. Mary and I are getting married for one simple reason. If God grants us only a few months of being married, it would be better than failing to grasp this opportunity. We both understand full well there's a possibility I won't return home from the war." Ed's heart thumped so loudly, it drowned out the tapping of feet. "I'll ask one final time. I would like to have your blessing to marry your daughter."

He could hear a muffled conversation on the other end of the phone line. Clearly, Andrew was discussing the matter with his wife. After what seemed like an eternity, Andrew finally uncovered his hand from the phone and spoke. "Ed, I'm sorry, but at this time, Anna and I cannot give you our blessing for this marriage. I strongly urge you to reconsider, not for our sakes, but for Mary's. There is nothing more for us to discuss. This is our decision. Goodbye and good luck to you." *Click.*

Ed stood in a daze, still cradling the phone in his hand. Could he have spoken any clearer to make them understand their joint decision? He was disturbed by someone shouting behind him.

"Hey, buddy! You finally done with your phone call? Give the rest of us a chance!"

Ed put the receiver back in its cradle. "It's all yours, pal. I hope you have better luck than I did."

CHAPTER 19:
CLEVELAND, OHIO
FEBRUARY 1942

ED'S MOTHER, Stella, was walking back home from church with her daughter Lottie. Big Hand was sitting on a chair on the front porch, and he smiled and waved to get their attention. Stella caught his wave and threw a smile his way.

"Good church day?" Big Hand asked.

"Yes, you should try going some time," Stella replied. "It's good for the soul."

Big Hand folded his beefy arms across his chest. "God told me I needed to stay home to receive an important phone call. Lucky for you I listened."

Stella harrumphed. "While you were talking to God, you should have asked him for a new shirt because you have a jelly stain on your breast pocket."

"Hmm," Big Hand said, scratching his chin. "Who does the laundry in this household?" He looked at Lottie for moral support.

"Oh no! Don't get me involved." Lottie scooted past her papa and went upstairs to change.

"I made a big breakfast. Bacon, eggs, waffles, and cheese pierogis," Big Hand boomed. "Come into the kitchen. I have big somethings to share."

Stella stared at her husband. "Big somethings? What did *God* tell you on the telephone?"

He looked at Stella and shot her a toothy grin. "Eddie called this morning, with big somethings to share."

Stella clasped her hands together and put them over her heart. "I missed Edmund's call! Is everything okay with him? Spill out your *big somethings!*"

Big Hand grinned and slapped his hand against his thigh. "Our son is getting married!"

Stella's smile dimmed.

"You're not happy?" he frowned.

Stella parked her hands on her hips. "Did he *ask* you if he should get married, or did he *tell* you he's going to get married?"

"Eddie didn't ask. He told me. What does it matter? We both like Mary. She's a good girl from a fine family, no?" Big Hand relayed the entire conversation, including Ed's reasons for the rush.

Stella narrowed her eyes. "What if she's using our Edmund? He told us they would get married after he's released from the military. Now he calls and says it's next week! It smells no good to me." Stella kept rolling without seeming to take a breath. "What about having a Catholic wedding? Mary is Russian Orthodox and we're Catholic. She must convert before marriage, or the church won't recognize this union. Did you ask him about this? If a priest does not marry them, they'll be committing the sin of adultery. This wedding is happening too fast."

"What's a matter with you?" Big Hand asked, shaking his head. "I've never heard him so happy. Why do you want to take this away from him?"

"She's working her female wiles on him. His love for her is making him blind to darker intentions."

"What darker intentions? This is utter nonsense." Big Hand balled his meaty hands into fists.

Stella pointed her finger at Big Hand's head. "You are a blind fool. Why do you think she wants to get married so soon?"

"Because she loves him!"

"What if she loves money more than she loves him?" Stella yelled over her shoulder as she stomped up the staircase.

Big Hand could hear her banging drawers in the upstairs bedroom and then barking at Lottie on her way back downstairs. He could see that Stella was carrying a brown envelope as she approached him in the kitchen.

"Read this!" Stella demanded, thrusting the envelope at him.

"What is it?" Big Hand asked, looking at the envelope from every angle.

"Read it!" Stella glared bullets while she waited for Big Hand to read the contents.

Big Hand took his reading glasses from his breast pocket and read the notice. It was Ed's military life insurance policy with Stella shown as the primary beneficiary. Once finished reading it, he folded the letter and placed it back in the envelope. "You think Mary doesn't realize you're the beneficiary and wants to wed Ed so she can collect the life insurance money?"

Stella stood straight as a rolling pin. "Why else would this be happening so fast? Unless… unless she's with child."

Big Hand returned his reading glasses to his shirt pocket. "Stella, why are you working yourself up with all these negative thoughts? Eddie and Mary are in love and want to spend the rest of their lives together, however long that might be. Let's be happy for our son. He's a smart boy and would know if something wasn't right. Trust him, Stella. And, for Eddie's sake, let's hope we never, ever, see one penny of the insurance money!"

"Are you too stupid to see that once they're married, she'll get him to change the beneficiary to her? Stella face turned tomato red as she tightened her clutch on the envelope. "They MUST not get married, do you hear me? You call Edmund right now and call it off!"

"I will not do such a thing. He is a grown man," Big Hand boomed and stomped his foot on the floor. "I'm through listening to your derogatory remarks. Mary's a good girl and I support their marriage even if you don't." His eyes bored into Stella's.

Stella stumbled backward. "You're placing *her* before you own wife?"

"I'm supporting our son and urging you to do the same. You loved Mary ten minutes ago and now you believe she's the devil incarnate? This is insane."

Stella stomped to the small table where the phone was kept and pointed. "If you don't call him, I will!"

Seeing her determination, Big Hand realized Stella's anger and distrust stemmed from having grown up poor in Poland and being sent to America to "marry a wealthy husband." Michal and Stella met through mutual acquaintances and were married six months later and by 1914, they had four children with one on the way. When Big Hand immigrated to the United States, he had pledged to his family that once he found a job, he would send half his pay back to his family in Poland to help with their living conditions. He kept that promise, but with each successive child, the amount diminished. The promise he abandoned was that he would return to Poland in five to six years with enough money to purchase the family farm.

At the onset of WWI, resistance groups in Poland seized the opportunity to fight for their country's freedom and to regain its status as an independent nation. Urgent communications came from Michal's family imploring him to come home to join in the fight. He desperately wanted to return to Poland, but Stella stopped him. The result was that his relationship with his birth family was ruptured beyond repair, a fact that cut him to the bone.

He walked over to Stella and did his best to keep his voice even. "Do you remember the beginning of the Great War (WWI)?" he asked.

Stella gazed at the worn carpet. "Yes," she answered.

"Do you remember how my family blamed you as the reason we sent less and less money back home? They knew your family was poor and thought that you married me for my money. Do you remember the terrible letters we got? They accused you of making me forget about them, that you made me into a traitor and a coward." He paused to make sure she was listening. "So, tell me, Stella, did you marry me for love or for money?"

Stella turned away, her shoulders shaking.

"Please answer the question."

She whipped around, eyes overflowing. "I never cared about the little money we made. I married because I fell in love with you, and you know it to be true."

"How is it different from what you say about Mary? She doesn't care about this stupid piece of paper." He waved the policy in the air. "She loves our son. Period. Be happy for them!"

Stella wiped her eyes with a trembling hand. "It's different, Michal."

Big Hand cocked his head. "How is it different?"

Stella's voice was barely a whisper. "Because it is."

"How is it different?" Big Hand jammed his fist in his palm, expecting more of an explanation.

Stella swallowed hard and blinked a few times. Her voice was barely audible. "It's different because…I'm *his* mother."

Stella remained suspicious of Mary's marital intentions, but for now, she chose to let the situation play itself out.

CHAPTER 20:
CAMP FORREST, TENN. FEBRUARY 1942

MARRIAGE CEREMONIES conducted by a Justice of the Peace (JIP) were typically bare-bones affairs lasting only twenty to thirty minutes. Some of the army brides who had been disappointed by the unromantic nature of their own JIP weddings created small businesses to make the experience a bit more special for those involved.

One of the girls at the boarding house gave Mary a tip about Nora Wilson's bridal store. Nora had recognized there was a market for gently used wedding dresses. Once a month she would go to some of the bigger cities nearby and shop the secondhand stores to find gently used wedding dresses and shoes.

Since Nora was a seamstress, she would often bargain the shopkeepers for lower prices on slightly damaged dresses. With skill and a good sewing machine, Nora could make any garment look almost new again. Her business catered to fiancés who were engaged to military personnel stationed at Ft Oglethorpe or Camp Forrest.

Mary scheduled an appointment to go to the store to shop the available collection of dresses. She hit it off with Nora and was excited when she found a nice, modest, dress for her big day.

By way of casual conversation Mary let Nora know she took sewing lessons from a friend's mother, who was a seamstress. Mary demonstrated her skills to Nora and was hired on the spot to work at the shop on a part time basis.

One door closes. And another door opens.

✦ ✦ ✦

The next decision on the list was to ask two people to be their witnesses at the Justice of the Peace. It was too hard to pick among their Army friends, but Ed came up with a creative solution.

The 65th Medical Regiment Commander was Major Terrance Lang. Ed had caught the Commander's eye both in the classroom and in field training exercises. Major Lang acted as a mentor to him, and the two got to know each other by occasionally sharing meals together in the mess tent. Ed respected the Major greatly.

"What do you think of this idea?" Ed asked Mary, "Why don't we ask Major Lang and his wife to be our witnesses?"

Mary clapped her hands together. "That's a splendid idea! I don't think Coop or Rollins would be offended by that at all."

The Lang's seemed both surprised and flattered to be included in the ceremony, which was set for Saturday, February 21st, 1942. They agreed instantly.

✦ ✦ ✦

When Saturday dawned, it promised to be one of those picture-perfect Georgia winter days where the sun shone brightly, and the air was crisp and still. The marriage ceremony was scheduled for 4PM, and all was going according to their hastily constructed plan.

Mary completed her morning exercise routine, ate a light breakfast, and headed out to Nora's boutique to get her dress. She selected an all-natural off-white long sleeve formal dress, below the knee, elegant with soft and flowy taffeta. Of course, it was far from a traditional wedding dress with a veil and a long train, but it fit the circumstances.

"You look impeccable!" Nora gushed. "You'll take your man's breath away when he sees you in this beautiful gown!"

"I hope so!" Mary said, checking herself from every angle.

Nora retrieved a shoebox and gave it to Mary to open. "I picked out some pale pink shoes for you to complete the look."

Mary slipped them on and walked to the mirror. "I love them, Nora! Thank you!"

"I have something else for you," Nora said, a twinkle in her eye. "I'll be right back!" Nora disappeared into the back room and returned with two hands behind her back.

"Ta-da!" Nora presented Mary with a beautiful floral bouquet. The centerpiece was a combination of white and pink roses, with winter red berries, snow crusted pinecones, and a sprig of dusty miller. The perfect ensemble for a winter wedding.

Mary beamed. "Oh Nora! It's beautiful! I'd like to pay you for them."

"It's on the house! I have a friend who operates a flower shop, and she owed me a favor. I wanted to do something special for you to make your wedding day as beautiful and memorable as possible."

Mary threw her arms around Nora, being careful not to crush the flowers. "How kind of you!"

"Do a twirl before we box everything up," Nora requested.

Mary obeyed and admired how the back of the dress fit her shoulders, waist, and derriere. The entire outfit was stunning, and she truly felt like a bride in it. *In a few hours I'll be married!*

Major Lang assigned his clerk Corporal Kilag Dombrowski (Dombo) the duty of picking up Mrs. Lang and Mary at their respective homes and driving them to the ceremony. Ed and Major Lang drove together and arrived at the courthouse first. Dombo pulled up to City Hall in his covered jeep about five minutes later. Ed and Major Lang watched as the ladies were helped out of the car and escorted into the lobby of the building.

Major Lang took his wife's coat and hung it on the coat rack. Mary Anne Lang wore a navy-blue dress with matching shoes and handbag.

To prolong the element of surprise Mary kept her coat on as she caught the attention of Mr. Crane, the Justice of the Peace. She had met Crane when she scheduled the date for the wedding. He waved hello and motioned for all four to come forward.

Crane conducted all his marriage ceremonies in the City Council Meeting Room. It was a large room, with elevated desks and chairs so the council members could perch above others when town hall meetings were in session. Mary gave Crane a quick hug and did the introductions.

"Well, let's get to it." Crane announced.

Mary smiled and gave Mrs. Lang a quick nod. Mrs. Lang walked behind Mary and helped remove her coat.

Ed blinked at the vision before him. The dress molded to Mary's shape, looking like it was made just for her. He hadn't even thought about flowers, and yet, they completed the whole ensemble and made Mary look every bit the bride she deserved to be. He mouthed the words "You look so beautiful" to her.

She beamed as she took her place next to him. Crane motioned for the Major to flank Ed on his right and for Mary Ann to stand on Mary's left. As expected, the ceremony lasted about twenty minutes, but Ed and Mary treasured each moment.

"You are now joined to each other by love and respect, two qualities you must always remember, even when times are difficult. This concludes the marriage ceremony." Crane smiled at the groom. "You may now kiss the bride."

Ed didn't waste any time, he pulled Mary close and gave her a tender kiss on her lips.

Mary and Ed made love that evening. Skin on sweaty skin, two electric heartbeats racing to the finish line, both wishing the moment would last forever. Afterward, Ed fell asleep with Mary resting her head on his muscled chest.

Mary got out of bed, being careful not to disturb Ed's slumber. She smiled as she shuffled her way to the bathroom. Grabbing a robe hanging on the bathroom door, she tied it loosely around herself. Peering in the mirror, she saw with dismay that the hair she had styled so painstakingly was now a disheveled mess. But she forgot about her hair when her eyes zeroed in on the locket Ed gifted her earlier in the evening. It was still around her neck. She touched it again, and her heart nearly burst with feelings of love and contentment.

CHAPTER 21:
CAMP FORREST, TENN.
SUMMER 1942

AS THEY had hoped, Ed and Mary were able to rent an apartment a few miles off base. The owners provided a discount to soldiers and their wives. The small unit had one bedroom, a full bath, a small kitchen, and a single couch in the living room. The furnishings were basic, but the apartment met their needs.

The young couple quickly settled into a routine. Ed commuted to the base each day and Mary worked at Nora's shop during the week. They made it a point to have dinner together each night.

All told, Mary spent the next 18 months living with Ed. But as the summer drew to a close, the reality of war drew ever closer and the mood at camp became more serious and somber. There was less emphasis on entertaining the boys and increased priority on preparing them to endure the harsh reality of a prolonged conflict.

The climate at the base shifted further when a train debarked at Camp Forrest. Military Police (MPs) were positioned in full gear outside the stopped railcars, on high alert with their M1 Carbines at the ready. Nothing happened for a few minutes. Then the large door of the first rail car slid open.

MPs pointed their carbines at the rail car door. Out jumped two U.S. soldiers with four American medics. Litter bearers were next, off-loading wounded men from the compartment. Load after load of injured soldiers were lifted off the train.

The MPs directed the litter bearers to take the casualties to large transitional tents inside the camp, away from the American barracks areas. Camp Forrest was used to receiving American casualties, but something wasn't right with this group of wounded.

All this occurred as Ed and Coop were getting ready to leave for home. The exit gates were barricaded, and MPs were redirecting out bound traffic. Curious, the men parked their jeep nearby and jogged over to watch the proceedings. A crowd of American GI's already began to form at the barricades.

"What's going on?" Coop asked a GI after pushing his way toward the front.

The GI shrugged. "Not sure, lots of MPs though."

Coop rejoined Ed and they watched, rapt, as more railcars opened, and additional wounded men were whisked away. Troubled, Ed and Coop moved closer to Major Lang when they spotted him talking to an officer from the train. There were two American MPs next to the officer and an American interpreter standing next to Major Lang.

Ed pulled Coop to a stop. "That doesn't sound like English," he whispered.

Coop's eyes bulged. "It's German,"

Both men turned as another wounded soldier was ferried past. "Look at their military dress. It's not like ours at all. Some of the shirts have letters on the back," Ed said.

Coop squinted. "POWs, I reckon. I wonder where they came from?"

Ed pulled Coop back a few steps. "The guy next to Major Lang is Lieutenant Smith, our German interpreter. He teaches our language classes and the 'Know Your Enemy' lectures."

Coop grimaced. "I see it now. What in the hell are German wounded doing in Tennessee?"

Camp Forrest became a major location to house German and Italian prisoners of war. By the end of the war, the camp housed more than 20,000 enemy POWs. Healthy prisoners were put to work helping local farmers harvest their crops, as there was a local manpower shortage at the time. The jobs were menial labor, loading railcars, harvesting crops, tilling soil and enemy prisoners were paid for their work per Geneva Convention rules.

✦ ✦ ✦

Since being drafted Ed had steadily moved up the Army ranks. His first promotion was to Private, First Class, then to Corporal, then to Sergeant, and in January 1943, he became Staff Sergeant. It was one of the highest-ranking non-officer roles in the Army. He was now 25 years old and placed in command of a platoon of 40 medics.

Ed had been peers with Cooper, Rollins, and Louis but now he was promoted to the 648th Medical Clearing Company to become one of its platoon leaders. During his first few months he requested that Cooper, Rollins, and Louis be placed under his command. Ed wanted to surround himself with leaders he knew, and trusted. The four friends were eventually reunited at Camp Forrest, for which all of them were grateful.

The men in Ed's platoon were trained as infantrymen, taught to handle a Colt .45 caliber pistol and an M1 Carbine rifle. Though much of the time medics would be unarmed, there would be times when each man in the unit would be placed on guard duty or asked to scout for new locations, both of which required them to bear arms. When a medic was required to carry a firearm, he removed his Red Cross medical armband per protocol.

Ed became a stickler for training his platoon on weaponless self-defense techniques. Dirty fighting methods like eye-gouging, the throat punch, an elbow to back of neck, and the nutcracker choke hold[2] were all regularly practiced.

"This type of training is critical for us medics," Ed told his platoon after a demonstration on Coop. "One can only hope our Red Cross armbands will protect us from being openly shot at by the enemy, but there are no fair fights in war. Learning these techniques could save your life one day."

Ed's motto to motivate his men during these grueling exercises was "Every man returns home." Tragically, not everyone did.

---

2   The nutcracker choke hold involves pulling the sides of an opponent's collar together and crushing the Adam's apple with the knuckles of the index fingers. The tightened collar keeps the opponent from squirming away while the knuckles cut off the target's airflow. —US Army

CHAPTER 22:
CAMP FORREST, TENN.
FEBRUARY 1943

AFTER HIS recent promotion to Staff Sergeant, Ed became more serious, less jovial, and often distracted during his conversations with Mary. During the first months of their marriage, they would regularly go out with their friends three or four times a week. But now in the evenings, Ed sat at their small kitchen table and worked late into the night. Still, they would always share supper together and talk about the events of the day. Typically, Ed would comment on needing to eat with their hands because there was no room for utensils on their tiny kitchen table. But tonight, he was silent.

"You've hardly eaten any of your dinner," Mary said twirling spaghetti noodles around her fork.

Ed looked up, a startled expression on his face. "What? Oh, sorry, babe. I'm a little distracted is all." He lathered some butter on a piece of bread, though his hand shook.

Mary put down her fork. "What's bothering you?"

"You would make a good psychic." Ed ran his hands through his hair. He always toggled a fine line about how much information he should share with his wife. He wanted to protect her from worrying about what might never happen. "I've been working with the German POW medical team in the care of their wounded."

"Why?" Mary asked.

Ed grimaced. "I couldn't shake my memory of the German POWs who came to camp last summer. If not for wearing shirts with the letters "POW" on them, you might mistake those prisoners for Americans at first glance."

"And?" Mary prodded.

"Well, our *Know Your Enemy* classes are all lectures. So, I asked Major Lang if I could work a few days at the German POW camp. I thought it might be a good hands-on experience. He agreed and assigned me a one-week internship in their medical ward." Ed drained his glass of sweat tea.

Mary retrieved the pitcher from the refrigerator, refilled their drinks, and rejoined Ed at the table. "That strikes me as dangerous. Did any try to kill you?"

"Not at all," Ed said, staring earnestly at Mary. "It's the opposite. The majority are on their best behavior." Ed picked up his fork and laid it back down. "Today, I walked the ward with one of our American MPs who oversees security. He's fluent in German but I asked him not to translate for me. I've been learning their language and wanted to practice talking to them myself. The MP introduced me to the German officer in charge of the medical care for these patients." Ed leaned back in his chair and arched his back, stretching it. "The German officer warned me against asking his patients any type of military questions. Those topics are off limits. If he felt I was interrogating his wounded, he would request to have me removed from the premises."

Mary twirled more spaghetti around her fork. "Clearly, something has you troubled. What happened?"

"Well, the bulk of the German wounded were respectful and appreciative of the care and respect they were receiving at camp. Their doctor shared some tips on how to make the patients more comfortable during treatment. But my discussion with the last two patients was odd."

"How so?" Mary asked, abandoning the meal all together.

"Well, the first soldier we visited was recovering from a leg laceration. Gangrene had set in, and he was being treated with penicillin. That's a powerful new drug, and it was rapidly clearing the infection. I asked the wounded man how he was doing? *Viel besser* (much better) he answered."

Ed put his untouched plate on the counter and gripped the counter's edge. "I asked him about his family, thinking that was a safe topic. He showed me a photograph of his wife and two sons. Pointing to his blonde, blue eyed sons he said with pride, "*Sohne Reines deutsch*," which

I didn't understand. The German doctor noticed the quizzical look on my face, so he translated it for me. "It means, *my sons are pure German.*"

Mary stood abruptly and tossed both dinners in the trash bin. "Pure German? As opposed to impure German? That's certainly an odd thing to say. No wonder you were rattled."

"The patient was arrogant, as if his two sons were superior to other children in some way. I remember the lecture Lieutenant Smith gave us regarding how the Nazis believe they're the descendants of the Aryan race. I assumed it was all propaganda, but after speaking with the enemy patient, I sensed he was brainwashed into believing those of pure German descent are the master race."

Mary whistled. "You got all of that from a two-minute conversation?"

"Yes," he said, washing the dishes. "The second German wounded POW I spoke with confirmed my suspicions."

Mary grabbed the dish towel and began drying. "What was his story?"

"He had shell fragments removed from his chest. I asked him how he was feeling, and he replied '*Klug*,' which translates to *smart* in German. He gave me wry smile, revealing a gap between his two front teeth."

"Do you think he misunderstood?" Mary hung the dish towel and put on a pot of coffee.

"No, it was purposeful, I'm sure. He was so condescending," Ed said, reaching for two mugs.

Ed purposely left out the part about those patients being Waffen-SS soldiers which were handcuffed to their beds. They were machine gunners who'd waved a white flag only *after* they'd fired all their ammunition and killed or wounded as many American soldiers as possible.

The security MP told him that he'd caught the machine gunners boasting to their fellow POWs how the *sanft* (soft) Americans would never kill an enemy soldier waving a white flag. They were *klug* (smart) Germans for fighting until their last bullet was fired. Only then would they allow themselves to be *captured* vs surrendered.

Mary poured two cups of coffee and sat back down at the table. "How about we talk about something fun and uplifting!" She slid his cup across the table. "Do you know what's coming up next Saturday?"

Ed stretched his arms over his head and faked a yawn. "What's *sooo* special about next Saturday? It's just another day."

"You big dodo bird. Next Saturday is our one-year wedding anniversary! I arranged to get our portrait taken in a professional photography studio. We didn't take any pictures on our wedding day, and we can celebrate your promotion to sergeant." Mary rested her chin on her hands and playfully batted her eyelashes at him.

"That's a wonderful idea!" Ed said, relieved to have a change of topic. "We can frame a large photo and get some wallet sizes to give to our families. I'll keep one when I'm…." Ed flashed back to earlier in the day when the German prisoner proudly showed him the photograph of his Aryan family.

"I'll keep a photograph in my wallet and show you off to all my friends!" He couldn't resist putting his hands under his chin and batting his eyelashes back at Mary.

Mary gasped. "Are you mocking me?"

The heaviness that had been plaguing him all day evaporated. "Yes, I am!"

C H A P T E R   2 3 :
CAMP FORREST, TENN.
APRIL 1943

ED, WHO now exclusively went by his nickname Krow, perhaps to distance himself from his peacetime persona, was called into Major Lang's office. There was never a speck of dust anywhere in Lang's office, and his desk was always tidy and clear of papers. The only thing on the desk was a handmade wooden cigar box with *Major T. Lang* carved on its lid.

"Krow, I would like to introduce Capt. Charles Leibold. He'll be taking over the 648th and will be your commanding officer (CO)," Lang announced.

Dr. Charles Leibold was a 38-year-old general surgeon from Bloomington, Indiana. He left a thriving medical practice to attend officer training school. Leibold was married, had three children, and this would be his first command.

The men exchanged greetings, and Lang briefed them on an important subject. "I received a phone call from my CO this morning." He pulled the cigar box toward himself and opened the lid. He offered one each to Krow and Leibold, but both men declined. Lang took one for himself but didn't light it. "Bad habit," he joked and continued speaking.

"In two days, several American dignitaries will visit the camp to inspect our troops and weapons capability. The VIPs will travel through the camp by motorcade, and the honor detachment from the 318th infantry band will play patriotic music as they enter the camp." Lang opened his desk drawer and retrieved a cigar cutter. He clipped off one end and brushed the droppings into the waste basket beside his desk.

"The 80th Infantry Division has been selected to flank each side of the road, standing at attention in full military dress for inspection by the dignitaries. The 314th Artillery Division will fire a salute with their 35mm howitzers." He held the cigar to his nose and sniffed it. "The entire inspection will last about twenty minutes."

Leibold shifted in his chair. "What's our role?"

"I received permission for our unit to be present and view the ceremony from a distance. Have your men assemble at 0900 hours in their best military dress. Our observation point will be 50 yards away, close enough to get a good view of the vehicles."

Leibold shot a glance at Krow, then back to Lang. "That's it? That's all we're required to do?"

"Yes, that's it," Lang said with a sneaky smile. "You won't want to miss this event. It might be a once in a lifetime opportunity for your men. Also, have your wives and families meet Mary Ann outside the back gates of camp." Lang rolled the cigar back and forth between his fingers, clearly itching to smoke it.

"The MPs will position them on both sides of the street so they can get a good view of the dignitaries on their way out of camp. Make sure your family members get there early so they can move through the security measures quickly."

"Any chance you're going to tell us who's in the motorcade?" Krow asked.

"Not a one. You're dismissed." Lang stood and walked them to the door. When Krow turned to leave he heard the strike of a match.

Leibold waited until they were outside the building. "The Major was almost making love to that cigar."

Krow laughed. It wasn't the first time he had experienced Lang's mating ritual with a stogie.

"Do you know who's coming to the base?" Krow was curious if Leibold was in on the secret.

Leibold shook his head. "We'll have to wait and see, but I'll imagine it's someone we'll all recognize."

✦ ✦ ✦

Two days later, on April 17th, 1943, at 0930 hours, the motorcade full of VIP's and dignitaries arrived at Camp Forrest right on schedule. The infantry honor bands played, the troops were inspected, and the 35mm howitzers boomed their military salute.

Krow stood at attention as the motorcade drove slowly past him. There were three cars, each a convertible with the tops down. After the last car passed, he craned his neck to get a better view. In the middle car sat the main VIP, waving to the crowd of onlookers lining both sides of the street. His first thought was that it might be General Patton, but it was hard to tell from the back of the man's head. Plus, the general would likely ride in an infantry jeep, not an automobile.

Suddenly, the VIP turned in Krow's direction, his face in full view. Krow gasped as thunderous applause broke out. There was no mistaking the distinguished man riding in the center vehicle in the procession, especially with the iconic cigarette holder clenched between his teeth.

The high-level dignitary was the 32nd President of the United States. Franklin Delano Roosevelt.

CHAPTER 24:
LEAVING CAMP FORREST, TENN. SEPTEMBER 1943

THE UNDEFEATED Camp Forrest fast pitch softball team was heading to Chattanooga for the Coca Cola-sponsored Army state championship. If the team won, they would play in Detroit for the regional championship.

Detroit was an easy three-hour drive from Ed's hometown, and he suspected his sisters were already organizing a family reunion. If the team won in Chattanooga, everything would fall into place.

A week before the championship game, Ed was at Saturday morning practice warming up a pitcher in the right field bullpen when he noticed Leibold's jeep pull into ballpark. *This is a first; I wonder what's going on?*

Leibold beelined to the dugout to speak with Sergeant Leo Cate, the head coach. After a short conversation, Cate blew his whistle and the activity on the baseball diamond halted. He motioned for Krow to join them, so Krow tucked his catcher's mask under his arm and jogged off the field.

Krow knew what was up even before Leibold began to talk. He nodded grimly and took off his catcher's gear, which he neatly stacked on the players' bench. He shook hands with Cate, wondering if he'd ever play with the team again.

He faced the baseball field and shouted to his teammates. "Good luck, guys! Give 'em hell in Chattanooga!" He punched his fist in his catcher's glove and left the ballpark with Leibold.

✦ ✦ ✦

Krow put the word out for his men to fall in for an emergency meeting at 1PM. He showered on base, pulled a comb through his wet brown hair, and slipped on a clean and pressed khaki uniform.

At the meeting, Leibold delivered the orders to the entire platoon. The men were leaving camp at 2200 hours sharp that very evening. The unit would travel overnight by train to an embarkation location somewhere on the east coast. They would stay on a troopship for a few days while their equipment was being loaded, and then set sail to their debarkation location. Krow wished more information was forthcoming but understood the need for withholding it.

For the past month, the camp had been buzzing with rumors that deployment orders could come at any moment with little to no notice. Krow, like all the others, had already prepacked his duffle bags with clothes, toiletries, and gear. Krow checked his watch, *seven hours until departure. I need to tell Mary.*

There was an important detail he had to complete first, before he lost his nerve. He had noticed an area in the mess hall where soldiers who were going overseas could update or compose their last will and testament. All the men under Leibold's command felt the same sense of urgency.

Krow stood in line with Coop right behind him. A legal clerk handed them some forms and motioned for them to take a pen from a tin cup. Wordlessly, they moved to a nearby mess table to fill out the information.

They lowered their pens at the same time. Krow looked at Coop and his friend nodded. They slid their forms across the table to so they could sign on the witness line for each other. As Krow authenticated Coop's last will and testament, the reality of the situation hit hard.

Both men rose from the table and made their way to the notary desk, and the documents were stamped with the official seal.

Wordlessly, Coop handed the public train schedule to Krow, having circled the outbound trains for Cleveland and Detroit. Their wives would be going back home for the duration. Krow handed it back to Coop and said, "I'll drive."

As they headed out of the tent they found Louis sitting at a table near the exit, scanning his will. Louis pretended to be reading his document intently and waited for the perfect moment to needle his friends. He kept his head down until his pals were within earshot, then he loudly proclaimed:

"I, Robert Louis, of sound mind and body, do hereby declare this document to be my last will and testament. I hereby bequeath my tin can of brown shoe polish to Dean Cooper, the biggest nose shiner of them all."

Krow laughed out loud as they passed him, grateful to Louis for breaking the heavy mood. "Good one, Louis!"

Cooper rolled his eyes. "Why do you keep encouraging him?"

The two men arrived at the train station and prepaid for one-way tickets for their wives. They both figured it would be best to present the will and ticket together and tucked the tickets inside the will envelopes.

Krow dropped Coop at his home and then drove to Nora Wilson's shop where Mary was working that day. The gravel crunched under the jeep's tires as he pulled into the driveway. Leaving the envelope in the car, he stuffed his restless hands in his pockets as he walked toward the building. *How will Mary take the news? It was fine and dandy when we considered the possibilities, but now war is breathing down our necks. When I open the shop door, our wedded bliss will end.* Krow glanced at his watch. *Six hours until departure.*

But as he approached, the sound of drums, saxophones, and a jazz trombone burst out of an open window. He recognized the music as *In the Mood* by Glenn Miller, and the closer he came to the window, the louder it became. Was this the right house? Perhaps the shop had changed hands without his knowledge? This was a far cry from the *chuka chuka chuka chuka* sounds of sewing machines that he expected.

Krow crouched and peeked through the window, and his mouth fell open in shock. Was that Mary jitterbugging with another man, their arms interlocked? As the pair twirled around, he realized with great relief that Mary was dancing with another woman. He also realized that she was wearing his staff sergeant shirt, the one with the emblem on the sleeve. He wanted to memorize this image of Mary filled with joy and laughter, her face glowing, and her eyes twinkling. He laughed out loud when Nora attempted to jump on and slide off Mary's back but she landed on the floor, fanny first. Mary thrust her hand out, helping Nora to her feet. Then she glanced toward the window and gifted him with a heartwarming smile.

A heartbeat later, her smile fell.

She knew.

CHAPTER 25:
TROOP TRAIN
SEPTEMBER 1943

24 September 1943

My Dearest Mary,

I am writing you from a troop train. It's taking us to a seaport (our letters are being censured so I cannot tell you where we are headed). We are jam-packed in these rail cars, about twenty to a car and you should see our "beds." They are cots bolted to the ceiling at various lengths. The cots are stacked in a vertical row about five hammocks high. Visualize a tin can of sardines and put the tin lengthwise on a countertop and that represents our sleeping arrangements. I pulled rank and got one of the bottom bunks which makes it easier to hit the bathroom during the night.

Our duffle bags are with us, and I have several changes of clothes, especially socks. I made sure I included a few pens and plenty of paper so I can write you frequently. I'll write more a little later at the next stop.

My Love always and forever,
Ed

**JOURNAL ENTRY:
25 SEPTEMBER 1943**

I never expected I would be keeping a journal, but it will help me preserve the memories of my time in service.

I'm not 100% sure why I'm choosing to write but it helps me to sort out my feelings, as well as helping to pass the time. I'll have to be careful as to what material I include in these writings in case I am captured. I don't want to give the enemy any secrets to use against us.

At present, I'm aboard a troop train heading somewhere east. I'm in one of the state rooms on this train, and there's a bit more room here than in our sleeping quarters. The company clerk says we have about seven more hours before we arrive at our next destination. Many of us already know where we are going, but I hesitate to put the actual location in writing.

Some of my pals are playing cards to pass the time. These friendships have become one of my greatest sources of personal stress. I'm not one of the guys anymore. I still try to fit in and not be too heavy handed.

The fact remains I am responsible for the safe return of these men back to their wives, girlfriends, and families. Same goes for the wounded in our care. I'm keenly aware the orders I give will impact their lives one way or another. I pray I can make good decisions.

There are three men in my platoon I've worked with for over two years. I'm lucky to have these guys in my squad as highly skilled medics, but also as confidants and friends.

Dean Cooper recently got promoted to Sergeant. He leads our ambulance and litter section. He's levelheaded, smart, and is my closest confidant in the unit. He's a long-distance swimmer and a good baseball player, too.

Before the war, he was a foreman in a steel factory in Detroit. Coop wed Marie shortly after Mary and I got married.

Scott Rollins is our medical supply chain leader and head trainer for all new medics who come into the platoon. In the states, he's a surveyor for a large construction company. He's a few years older than the rest of us. He's married, with a kid on the way.

Robert Louis works underneath Rollins as his gopher. He's the funniest guy in the outfit (also a smartass.) He keeps everyone loose or on edge, depending on his mood each day. Louis is smallish but super strong for a person who only weighs about 130lbs. He wrestled in High School and works on his family's dairy farm. He's single but tells us he's "interviewing" several lasses that have Mrs. Louis "potential."

Rollins and Louis give each other fits when they're together. But they are best friends in a big brother-kid brother kind of way, though neither would admit it to each other. The rest of the guys in my platoon were assigned to me about 6 months ago.

My platoon can administer basic first aid to the wounded on the battlefield. We also have the technical skills to provide surgical assistance to doctors in our mobile hospitals which are stationed a short distance from the front lines. So, I guess we can save people one day and shoot people the next if we must. (A paradox for sure.)

My outfit is the 648th Medical Clearing Company. My platoon's primary responsibility is evacuation of the wounded from the battlefield and providing safe transport to the clearing company where surgery and other treatment can be performed (if needed).

It seems simple to explain, but it's complex, kind of like playing an accordion. My platoon must be flexible enough to quickly leapfrog forward to remain with our infantry division or retreat on a moment's notice, depending on the combat situation.

Here's how the evacuation process is supposed to work.

Step #1: Combat Zone: A medic is summoned to administer first aid to a wounded man on the battlefield. It's hazardous duty, with bullets and bombs flying all over. The goal is to provide basic aid (Sulfa, torniquets, morphine) and quickly get the wounded man to a "safer" location called an Aid Station.

Step #2: Aid Station: Aid Stations are located out of the line of fire. I don't like the word "station" because it's misleading. An aid station is simply a gathering place for many wounded in a protected area. That could mean behind a tank, in a building, or in a large foxhole. The wounded are taken to the aid station and wait to be evacuated away from the battlefield.

Step #3: Collecting Company: These are located further away from the front lines. Each collecting company has ambulances which can shuttle the wounded from the Aid Station to the collecting company site. A Collecting

Company is just like it sounds; it's a temporary holding area where larger numbers of wounded are gathered. The goal is to move the wounded quickly from the collecting company to a medical clearing company where more extensive medical treatment can be performed.

Step #4: Medical Clearing Company: This is a mobile miniature hospital. There are tents for triage, surgery, and recovery. When not in combat, a medical clearing company can operate as a dental clinic, laboratory, dispensary, mess section, or a morgue. Doctors, mostly surgeons, are stationed at the clearing company.

My Role: I'm the Staff Sergeant who leads the 1st Platoon in the 648th Medical Clearing Company. We're considered army infantry medics and are part of Patton's Third Army. I report to the commanding officer of the 648th (Leibold). The 648th is a sub-component of the larger 65th Medical Regiment.

My Platoon is comprised of 40 men, all medics. We provide more in-depth triage to injured soldiers, sorting, and tagging the wounded by type of injury (shock, head, abdominal, amputations, and burns, etc.). The doctors take over from that point and determine the next course of treatment.

We have two platoons inside the 648th. If we're winning the battle and pushing deeper into enemy territory, one platoon can detach and move forward with the infantry. We set up our supplies and tents and the surgeons come with us. The second platoon stays behind to finish the evacuation of wounded soldiers and rejoins later.

We prefer to do our work in abandoned buildings, but if none are available, we set up our tents and supplies and conduct our work out in the open. We have large red crosses on the roofs of each tent to identify us as medical units so that the enemy knows not to drop bombs on us when they fly overhead. That's the theory, anyway.

A less thrilling aspect of our work is the digging of slit trenches behind every single treatment and convalescent tent. Digging a slit trench isn't enjoyable work, but they're designed to save lives. If we find ourselves in the crosshairs of a combat battle, a wounded soldier can be placed in a slit trench, so he's protected from flying shrapnel or gunfire. Sometimes, it's necessary for us to jump in with the injured patient so we dig the trenches a little deeper than what's required.

Well, not bad for my first entry. As I reread, it seems like I wrote out some type of book report on the Army Evacuation process. I'm no Mark Twain! Now I'm headed to lose some nickels and dimes to the card sharks next to me.

CHAPTER 26:
CAMP KILMER, NEW JERSEY SEPTEMBER 1943

THE ENTIRE 65th Medical unit arrived at Camp Kilmer, New Jersey on September 26th, 1943, after spending the previous night in a transitional barracks near the port. During the next 10 days, Camp Kilmer swelled to over 20,000 troops. There was excitement and apprehension in the air, this was no dress rehearsal. It was the real deal.

Krow's unit was assigned to board the troop ship *Monterey* which would take them to a European port. The men would not be told of their destination until they were out to sea.

As a luxury cruise ship, the SS Monterey was built for the maximum comfort of its passengers. But during wartime, these boats made excellent troop transport carriers for several reasons. The vessels were fully equipped and capable of ferrying large groups of troops and equipment across the oceans in a single trip. Anti-aircraft defenses and additional artillery were installed on deck to help protect and defend the ship in case of attack while at sea.

On October 6, 1943, the men began the boarding process.

✦ ✦ ✦

"Why the hell do we always have to walk so far with these dang heavy packs? Couldn't the army drop us off a little closer to this washtub? And why do we always have to travel at night? I can't see shit in front of me," Louis complained as he struggled under the weight of his pack.

Rollins was in line behind Louis and kicked the back of his friend's ankle, tripping him. "Do me a favor, Louis, and put a lid on it. You're getting on my nerves."

One by one, each man stepped onto the gangway to enter the rocking ship. The footbridge was 18 inches in diameter with two aluminum handrails the men could hold onto to stabilize themselves as they stepped aboard the ship . Each man simply followed the person in front of them until they got to their designated sleep quarters.

Krow dropped his barracks bag and looked at a maze of steel pipes in front of him. Ropes were attached to a forest of metal conduits, a strip of canvass stretched tightly between them. The cots were layered five high, from floor to ceiling.

During the moment of silence, Krow flashed past Louis and slid into a bottom bunk. He fluffed his tiny head pillow and interlocked his fingers behind his head. "Home, sweet home, Louis!"

"Hey, I was going to take the bottom bunk!" Louis moaned.

"Wipe that look off your face," Krow said in mock seriousness. "I'll have to contend with your backside protruding above me."

"Oh, I get it, Sarge. You want to look at my ass all night long!" Louis twisted his head from side to side to see if others heard his funny comeback.

"On the contrary, if you don't stop complaining, I'll be kicking the indentation of your ass for the next two weeks." Ed lifted his boot and kicked the empty hammock above him.

Truth be told, Krow had many of the same complaints as Louis. Their assigned deck was three levels below the waterline, and there were no portholes. The air circulation seemed less than adequate for the number of men in these confined spaces. Personal hygiene was going to be difficult, to put it mildly. Bodies and barracks bags were sprawled everywhere, and the shower and bath facilities weren't built to handle so many people.

It took two full days for all the men and equipment to be loaded onto the ship. Before sunrise on the second night, a tremor caused their hammocks to sway. Louis woke and leaned his head over his cot. "Sarge, you awake?" He probed none too quietly.

Krow cleared his throat. "Yes. I'm awake."

"Did you feel something?"

"It felt like a decoupling. A tugboat must be pulling us out to sea."

"Where do you think we're going?" Louis whispered.

"I don't know, Robert. I guess we'll find out when we get there." Krow rolled over on his side and shut his eyes. But he couldn't fall back to sleep.

CHAPTER 27:
CROSSING THE ATLANTIC
OCTOBER 1943

9 October 1943

Happy 24th Birthday Sweetheart!

I'm gazing at your beautiful face on one of the pictures you sent with me. (I can smell your perfume on the picture. You were right, it does make me feel like we're together, sort of.) I miss that I can't hug and kiss you on your special day.

By now, you must be back home and moved in with your parents. I hope you and your folks are back on speaking terms. When the opportunity presents itself, please extend my greetings to them and let them know I'm safe and sound.

Our ship is in a convoy with other ships, and we're told the Air Force is patrolling the skies above and providing a safe escort for us. Nothing to worry about here. Other than a touch of seasickness every now and again, everything so far has been going swell. Let me tell you a little bit about our boat. It's a retrofitted cruise liner. Our sleeping quarters are below deck, and since the bunk areas are cramped, we try to get to the upper deck to enjoy the fresh air as much as possible.

The Navy ship we're on has an Athletic Officer. One of the ship's ensigns told us he played football for the University of Michigan and got his law degree at Yale. Smart cookie! He probably could have received a military deferment as he's a little older than the rest of us but when Pearl Harbor was bombed, he enlisted in the Navy. Someone told me his name was Gerry Ford.

Anyway, he and his men rigged a couple of small basketball courts and created an obstacle course of ropes, steps, pull up bars, and other makeshift obstacles. It takes about 4 minutes to complete the course. I have my stopwatch from boot camp, so I timed all my men on the obstacle course. Louis was the fastest: he did it in 3 min 52 seconds.

The letters I'm writing to you aboard the ship won't be mailed until we land at our seaport. When you do receive my letters, you'll be rewarded with a nice stack of them.

Love always,
Ed

JOURNAL ENTRY
10 OCTOBER 1943

Traveling on a troop ship is shaping up to be an unforgettable experience. Honestly, I try to take the good from these situations but traveling this way can be unbearable at times. Here is the best way I can describe it.

The Good: After we departed New Jersey, we were allowed to explore the ship and get out from under the stifling conditions below deck. We enjoyed going to the top deck to get some fresh air. The first few days, the weather was nice and sunny, and I was able to play some cards with the guys on the top deck.

I read a little and stood in line to run the ship's newly designed obstacle course. It's a lot of fun and a good way to stay in shape and pass the hours while in transit.

The Unusual: We receive two meals a day. You stand in a long line in the mess area for at least two hours before you reach the front of the line to receive your meal. The chow is plopped onto the mess tray, and you follow the person in front of you to a chest high table with no chairs. This table, which is more like a thin countertop, runs the entire length of the ship (the length of two football fields).

You place your tray on the countertop and you eat your meal standing up while pushing your tray down the line toward the wash basins. You're expected to finish eating your meal by the time you make it to the end of the line and are responsible for washing your own tray. Walking and eating at the same time, no tables, or chairs.

Another new experience is taking a saltwater shower. When the water dries from your body, you're left with a thin coating of ocean salt on your skin. The only person who seems to enjoy the salt showers is Louis. He keeps licking his arms and asking anyone who will listen to him, "Can you taste the salt on your skin? Now all we need is margaritas!" He breaks me up sometimes.

The Ugly: Due to a bad storm at sea, we've all been forced to stay in the lower decks for two straight days. The constant tossing and turning of the ship caused many of us to become seasick. It seems like the entire platoon is barfing their guts out.

With so many people crammed below deck, combined with the poor ventilation, the situation is rapidly becoming unbearable. I tried closing my eyes to ward off the nausea, but it didn't work. It was most welcome when we finally put the bad weather behind us, and we were able to get some fresh air again.

✦ ✦ ✦

After 13 days at sea, the SS Monterey docked at its new destination. It was close to midnight when the troops received the "all clear" signal to debark from the vessel. The men were ready to get off the ship and be on solid ground again.

The Monterey had orders to make a fast turnaround. The ship draped cargo nets off the sides of the top deck, and the men were required to climb over the ship's top railing and shimmy three stories below to the docking area. With barracks bags, rifles, and steel helmets clanging against each other, the men started their descent from the ship.

"I can't see shit. Where's the dock?" Louis asked Rollins as they made their way down the nets.

"I don't think there is a dock. But I can make out an outline of a small boat below us. I presume that's our ride to shore."

"Where are we?" Louis asked.

"England," Rollins responded.

CHAPTER 28:
LIVERPOOL, ENGLAND
MID-OCTOBER 1943

AS THE men debarked from the ship, they were directed to a marshaling area where they reunited with the rest of the 65th Medical Regiment. While the Americans waited, they were greeted by the UK division of the Red Cross who were handing out free donuts and coffee to the grateful troops.

Even though it was late at night, the soldiers could see (and smell!) the food truck pumping out donuts by the tray full. Red Cross volunteers strolled by with platters full of these sweet delights, and it was a miracle there wasn't a brawl as the men were instructed to take only one donut upon entering their designated meeting area.

Inside the marshaling area, other volunteers from the UK Red Cross passed out packages to the troops. Each package contained pouches of freeze-dried coffee, boxes of raisins and prunes, and tins of powdered milk, corned beef, and spam. Other delights included cigarettes, chocolate bars, and chewing gum. The men became familiar with the English phrase, "Hey chum, got any gum?"

"It's the middle of the night. Why are you being so good to us?" Louis asked, flirting with one of the young female volunteers.

She looked to be in her early twenties, auburn-haired and trim. "We're confident we'll win the war now that you Americans are here. It's been hard for us, but now we have hope. We are grateful." The girl spoke politely but business-like, ignoring Louis' poor attempt at winning her over.

"Did the Germans bomb this part of England?" Louis asked innocently enough. It was night, foggy, and a black-out ordinance was in effect, so Louis couldn't see the war-torn city.

"The Luftwaffe air assaults on our city were nonstop early in the war. In the beginning, the Germans just bombed the Naval installations at the port. Then they started dropping firebombs on civilian areas, destroying our homes, and killing innocent people. The Nazi's have no soul." The girl lowered her gaze.

Louis followed her eyes and saw she wasn't wearing shoes. Or at least not the type of shoes he was used to seeing. Two thin pieces of wood served as the sole, tied together by strips of cloth.

He lifted his head to find the girl staring him down. "We have to make do," she said.

Louis blushed and attempted to hand the food box back to her. "I don't need this." The girl refused with a firm shake of her head.

"Thank you for your service to our country." She resumed her duty of delivering care packages to the newly arrived American soldiers.

That evening, the men slept in a transitional barracks set up not far from the dock. As the sun rose the next morning, the medics got their first view of the war-ravaged city. Liverpool was the second most heavily bombed city in all of England, and the destruction served as a stark introduction to the war. The port ferried war materials and troops from North America to England and was a regular target of the German Luftwaffe.

Krow had an early breakfast meeting with Leibold. "Our orders are to be at the Liverpool train station by 1000 hours. Tell your men to be on guard for pickpockets and beggars. It's rough times here for a lot of people." Leibold checked his watch. "We leave in three hours."

The Liverpool train station was a central hub for both military and civilians. The medics were dropped off by U.S. military trucks and made their way into the station. Louis pointed to a black sign on one of the pillars.

"Gate 11B is down that way." He adjusted his backpack, picked up his duffle bag and started walking toward the gate.

While they walked, they were deluged by calls of, "Hey Yank." As Leibold warned, the locals were out in full force asking for everything

from money to cigarettes. Some desperate-looking women were solicit-
ing for prostitution.

English bobbies stood guard between the military and civilian
stations. They warned, "We try to keep the crooks away the best we
can, but this is a central area. Pay the rabble no mind. If you encourage
them, they'll come back harder on the next person."

One hoodlum targeted Krow. "Hey, Yank. Did you know Hitler is
in America right now? You heard me right! He snuck into the U.S. and
has a secret plan to sabotage your Navy! I'll tell you the story while I
shine your boots."

Krow turned his back to him, attempting to put some distance
between them. Undeterred, the hoodlum switched his tactics. "Don't
turn your back to me, arsehole! You Americans are so fucking arrogant,
you pig-headed bastard!" He sneered and gave Krow the middle finger.

Krow dropped his pack and strode in the man's direction. He was
halfway to the bloke when he felt a vice grip locking down on his arm.

"Let him be, mate." A nearby policeman had listened to the entire
exchange. "The codger is baiting you. If you engage with him, his
accomplices will loot you of all your valuables." Krow was steamed but
heeded the warning.

Louis stepped next to Krow. "What was that BS about Hitler being
in America? "

The policeman chuckled. "It's been rumored that *a* Hitler *is* trying
to enlist in the American military, the United States Navy, in fact."
The bobbie talked as if it were common knowledge. "Adolf Hitler has
a nephew, William, who was raised in Liverpool. As an adult, William
Hitler moved to Germany where his uncle Adolf gave him a job in
government. Later, William became disenchanted with his uncle and
moved to America in the late 1930s. When this bloody war broke out
its been highly speculated that William Hitler is trying to enlist in the
U.S. Navy."

Louis was dumbfounded. "The United States of America would never
accept a person with the last name HITLER into our country, let alone
our military!"

"I'm afraid it's true. Adolf considered William a traitor at the highest level. When the Luftwaffe began shelling Liverpool, they targeted

Upper Stanhope Street and the boyhood home of William Hitler. The bombs obliterated the house and the surrounding neighborhood, many innocent Liverpudlians were killed in those raids." The bobby was interrupted by an announcement over a loudspeaker.

"*65th Medical Regiment report to train at Station 11B. Boarding will begin in ten minutes.*"

Louis reached for his duffle bag. "That's us," he said.

"Then you mates best be on your way." The bobby turned on his heel and resumed his post.

The men strode toward station 11B. "Sarge, do you believe that cockamamie Hitler story?" Louis asked.

"Seems farfetched to me. But I know what we need to do now." Krow said.

Louis cinched the front straps of his pack tighter to shift its weight to his shoulders. "Do what?"

Krow repeated the lines he'd seen on a propaganda poster at Camp Kilmer. "Loose lips sink ships."

"You plan to report that bullshit?" Louis barked.

"We have an obligation to report all intelligence gathered about the enemy. Hitler is enemy #1."

"Our officers are going to think you lost your effing mind when they read that doozy of a report!"

Krow grinned. "That's why I'll sign *your* name at the bottom of the document!" He laughed and stepped onto the train.

As the soldiers settled into their berths, the story of the two Hitlers faded to the background as the main topic of conversation became *where are we headed now?*

21 OCTOBER 1943

Hello sweetheart—

I wanted to let you know that we landed safe and sound at our final debarkation point and we're in a location that's far away from all the fighting. We are staying in a makeshift army barracks outside of town. Many of my guys are asking me where we are headed next. Honestly, I don't have an answer for them.

Captain Leibold has not told me where or when we'll depart so I guess we will all find out together.

Here is something swell to share. There is an American private here who started a little side business. He's an artist, and for a pack of cigarettes, he'll draw your picture. Coop and I had some free time, so we checked it out. We thought it might be a scam or something ridiculous, but it wasn't. This guy was a legit artist. If you sit with him for 15 minutes, he can draw a pretty good portrait of your face.

I asked him if he took drawing lessons or went to art school and he just said, "Nah, it comes easy to me. I can visualize it in my head and sketch it out."

Coop made him laugh (and me too) when he told the artist to charge me a second pack of cigarettes because "you're going to need more time to make a stiff like him (meaning me!) good looking." What a smart aleck!

I took a chance and paid him my one pack of cigarettes and he sketched a portrait of me. I'm including the portrait with this letter. I hope it doesn't get lost in the mail because it looks like a very handsome drawing of me, even if I do say so myself! You can be the judge.

Anyway, it's late and I better get some shut eye. The sun comes up early around here. I miss you dearly and hope the war can be over soon so we can be together again.

Love forever and always,
Ed

PS: I wrote my parents to let them know you would be stopping over to pick up my paperwork, birth certificate, military insurance etc. We'll have to update next of kin and beneficiary on some of the papers. Importantly, please give them my love. I think of them often.

CHAPTER 29:
CLEVELAND, OHIO
NOVEMBER 1943

WHEN ED was deployed overseas, Mary returned to her home in Cleveland. She reconciled her relationship with her father and mother and moved in with them for the duration of the war.

Many employers were hiring women for factory work and Mary found a job at Jack & Heinz, or "Jahco" for short. The company's manufacturing plant was in Maple Heights, a suburb of Cleveland. Jahco had won a large contract from the U.S. military to produce warplane parts.

The company had to bring on additional workers to fill the new orders, and Mary was hired as a parts inspector. Her contract stipulated she was expected to work twelve-hour shifts, seven days a week. She received one day off a month.

Those rules sounded unbearable, but Jahco was unlike any company. The employees were treated like gold and employment with Jahco was highly sought after by the locals. Besides, Mary felt it was her patriotic duty to contribute to the war effort. Who was she to complain when her husband and the other servicemen were sacrificing much more?

Mary's family kept tabs on the progress of the war effort by listening to the radio and reading the newspapers. But it was the letters from Ed which were the most eagerly anticipated.

The family developed a ritual for when a letter arrived from Ed. The unopened letter would be placed on the kitchen table so Mary could see it when she came home from work. After a private reading, Mary would share the news with everyone at the kitchen table. Next, she would place a phone call to Ed's parents to share the latest information from their son.

Mary saved every single one of Ed's letters and put them in a special keepsake box. She reread them often. She knew he was purposely leaving the bad stuff out of his letters to protect her from worrying about him. She worried anyway. But the latest letter included a special surprise.

"Look, it's a hand drawn portrait of Eddie! Mary showed it to her parents. "It looks just like him!"

Mary was excited to call Ed's parents and read the letter to them. And like every other time she called, Big Hand was the one who answered the phone. After exchanging niceties Mary read the letter to him.

"I look forward to seeing the drawing!" Big Hand exclaimed. They settled on a date for Mary to share the portrait and to retrieve the paperwork Ed requested.

On her next day off from work, Mary took the bus to the corner of Harvard Avenue and E 78th street, which was a short walk to her in-law's home. A few months earlier, the local newspaper had featured an article about this neighborhood's high concentration of men drafted into the armed services, and Ed's picture had been featured. Mary had gotten to know many of his neighborhood friends, and there had always been something fun going on. But now, she was struck by how quiet and empty it felt. Her eyes were drawn to homes with a gold star affixed to their front window, a signal that a loved one who served in the military had died: each time she spied a star, it sent a shiver up her spine.

When she arrived at Ed's house, she took a second to compose herself. This would be her first visit to Big Hand and Stella's since Ed's deployment, and she was frankly a bit nervous. She tugged her skirt, smoothed out her coat, and took a deep breath before knocking on the door.

Mary heard footsteps and saw Stella staring at her from behind one the window tiles on the door. Stella opened the door abruptly, startling Mary and causing her to flinch. Stella had clearly aged, and there were dark circles under her eyes.

She spoke in Polish, which Mary understood. "I know why you come here. It's for this!" Stella waved papers in her face. "He's not gone three months, and you are already here to steal it from me. Take it and go!" Stella threw the papers on the porch and slammed the door.

Mary was stunned and unsure of what just transpired. She picked the papers off the ground and scanned them. It was Ed's $5,000 military life insurance policy. *Stella thinks I married Ed for the money?*

She put her hand over her mouth and started to cry. She dropped the papers and darted off the porch, wanting to get away from the house as quickly as she could.

When Mary got to the sidewalk, she could hear the door open behind her. She could tell by the heavy footsteps that it was Big Hand, so she stopped and faced him.

"Mary! Don't go. Please, let me explain." He boomed as he bounded down the front porch steps, taking them two at a time.

Mary sighed heavily. "Do you think I came for that?" She pointed her finger in the direction of the insurance paperwork now scattered on the ground. "I was so excited to come see you, and this is how I'm greeted, like some gold digger? All I want is for Eddie to come home to me in one piece! It's been so hard, I'm trying to be strong."

"I'm sorry," Big Hand said, grimacing. "Stella has been unwell since Eddie left. Stays in her room day and night. Doesn't go anywhere. Doesn't eat much. Spends most nights crying. She doesn't want to see me or anyone else. Doctor says she's grieving, and her mind is full of dark thoughts. It might take a long time before she gets better, and I fear she never will. I'm so sorry she took it out on you."

Big Hand retrieved the insurance policy and gave it to Mary, who accepted it grimly. When he insisted on walking her back to the bus stop, she didn't object. On the way, Mary shared the sketch of Ed.

As Big Hand stared at it, he grabbed a hanky from his pocket and blew his nose. "It's a beautiful picture of him. Thank you for showing this to me."

Mary could see Big Hand was hurting as well. The two shared a heartfelt hug goodbye before Mary boarded the bus.

Later that evening Mary sat at her desk and penned a letter to Ed. She wrote about her job at Jahco and about their friends who were still stateside. She wrote about saving her paychecks so they could buy a beautiful house in the country. She treaded lightly on her meeting with his parents, not wanting to burden him about his mother's troubling behavior. As Mary concluded her letter, she included a poem which spoke to her. She hoped Ed would feel the same way.

Love Prevails

In distant lands where battles roar,
Brave souls fight on foreign shores,
I hold on to a steadfast belief,
That love will conquer the darkest grief.

Though war may test our souls so true,
Love shall prevail, and guide us through,
For every hardship, we'll find a way,
To strengthen bonds, come what may.

Someday soon we'll find our peace,
Embraced in love that will never cease,
Together, we'll paint a brighter day,
With love that guides us in every way.

CHAPTER 30:
DONHAGADEE, IRELAND OCTOBER 1943– MARCH 1944

THE 65TH Medical Regiment, inclusive of the 648th and Krow's platoon, were transferred to Donhagadee and remained on high alert for over 7 months. During their stay in Ireland, great stress was placed on physical conditioning by means of regularly scheduled 10-to-15-mile hikes. Medical platoons, including Ed's, underwent intense training with simulated casualties and worked on the best approaches for the various practice missions they were given. All medical, surgical, and dental technicians were employed in the practice missions, thereby augmenting their training with actual simulated battlefield experiences.

JOURNAL ENTRY
15 OCTOBER 1943

Map reading training today. Coordinates etc. I found a map of Europe and was able to place a piece of tracing paper over it so I could sketch a crude outline of UK, France, Germany, and Switzerland etc. I plan to keep this map with me and update it periodically with the dates and locations of our major combat campaigns. I used a color code of black, blue, and red which will help me illustrate the diagram.

JOURNAL ENTRY
30 OCTOBER 1943

Spending a lot of time training and reviewing our ward setups with simulated casualties. The goal is to triage, treat, recuperate, and evacuate. But there will always be special cases, and we need the flexibility to quickly adapt our wards to fit the type of injuries.

Burn victims require special handling and gas attack patients require an isolation ward. We're still learning if these deadly chemicals can be passed to other humans (mainly us) through contact. Ditto for communicable diseases (typhus & tuberculosis).

Treating enemy casualties requires different protocols. (Groups of people trying to kill each other would NOT make good bedfellows.) Enemy wounded are in a separate ward, isolated from our allied casualties. Guard duty and safety protocols go into effect.

JOURNAL ENTRY
27 NOVEMBER 1943

Rain, rain, and more rain. Back home, we get a chance to experience a change of seasons. Here in Northern Ireland, we have one shitty season. The guys invented a funny blend of words to describe our consistently lousy weather in Ireland. They merged gray, rain, and winter to call it "grainter."

All of us are sick and tired of wet feet, drenched tents, marches in the mud, and relentless drills. It's hard to keep all our medical supplies clean and dry. I only complain in my journal.

JOURNAL ENTRY
11 DECEMBER 1943

Today is my 26th birthday, and I'm celebrating it in "grainter" with a bunch of crazy men. During dinner, the guys sang "Happy Birthday" to me. Louis made a big deal out of saying he baked me a special cake. It was a chocolate cake, or so I thought. Instead of candles, he used "birthday" bullets.

Before I took a bite, Louis said it was a mud pie, and sure enough, it was a REAL mud pie! Apparently, he dug some sludge from outside and molded it into the pan. Ha-ha! The cooks took mercy on me and brought out a shortbread cookie. It's a local favorite. I broke it in half so I could save some for later. I'm eating the other half now as I write.

We have a blackout ordinance in effect, so I piled my jacket and blankets over my shoulders and head to block my flashlight. I'm lying on my stomach with my elbows propped up so I can scribble today's notes in my journal.

On my last birthday, Mary and I were living in Rossville and enjoying a mostly normal life. It's been three months since I've seen her. It gets lonely here sometimes.

JOURNAL ENTRY
7 JANUARY 1944

The Army brought in a bunch of English aviators to teach a training course on airplane recognition (friend and foe) and bombs (friend and foe). These guys were battle tested and have been fighting in the war for a few years now. I am sure that they're happy to be out of the line of fire for a while with this temporary non-combat assignment.

" Use your ears to identify the type of aircraft and the sort of bomb. It's easier to hear the differences versus trying to see the planes," they instructed us.

We learned to tell the difference between two types of Luftwaffe aerial bombs. High explosive bombs are designed to knock out buildings, and incendiary bombs are designed to set areas on fire. In combat, knowing which is which can help us bulk up on the right medical supplies for each situation (splints and sulfa vs gauze and ointments). Fast treatment saves lives.

JOURNAL ENTRY
22 MARCH 1944

We must be getting close to deployment. Lots of new training to make us feel prepared for when we become the uninvited guests of the German military. It's speculated the Nazis will deploy a sinister weapon to thwart our arrival on their soil. We learned it could be a lethal odorless, colorless, and tasteless gas compound.

It's a nerve agent which inhibits the muscles from doing their jobs. Our instructor told us it's a hundred times more deadly than cyanide! Death can occur when the muscles which control breathing stop functioning. The chemical can be put in a bomb or be used to contaminate our clean drinking water. It's a terrifying weapon.

As a result, the Army recently added gas masks to our field bags, and we practice field exercises using them.

Our training consists of a drill umpire placing canisters of low-grade tear gas in wooded areas and in open land. When the canisters disperse the tear gas, we have only six seconds to pull our masks over our heads and sprint like hell through the wafting gas to reach the wounded on the other side of the field.

Problems emerged right away. There is no such thing as low-grade tear gas, it was the real deal and a lot of guys got sick. Second, we could see the smoke erupting from the canisters. The deadly gas the Germans use is an invisible vapor, so we won't be able to see it in the air.

I asked the field umpire how we'll know to put our gas masks on if we can't see or smell the real thing. He replied less than cordially.

"If you see someone twitching like they're possessed by the devil, you know you only have six seconds before you experience the same thing." Very reassuring, A-hole.

Another issue is that the goggles fog up with any type of physical exertion, but you can't take them off to wipe away the condensation. It's hard to see where you're going when the lenses are blurry. We were required to treat the wounded wearing our foggy gas masks, and it was brutally hard to make out the type of injury and proper treatment.

Louis took it upon himself to ask the umpire what we all were thinking. "How the f&*k are we supposed to take care of the wounded when we have to wear these fogged up pieces of shit?" Here was the umpire's answer:

"If you see someone twitching like they are possessed by the devil you know you only have six seconds before you experience the same thing." A-hole, 2X!

JOURNAL ENTRY
20 APRIL 1944

Captain Leibold called me into his office today. My report on Hitler's nephew checked out positive! My jaw almost hit the floor. How the f&#k can the U.S. military accept a blood relative of Adolf Hitler into the U.S. military? Captain told me Hitler is in the U.S. Navy. I wonder how he makes out with THAT last name!

JOURNAL ENTRY
27 APRIL 1944

Long staff meeting today. Leibold explained we'll be leaving Donhagadee and relocating to a staging area in another country. Departure will be within the next ten days. He also requisitioned a photographer to take our formal platoon pictures.

For the first time in my life, I feel unsure of myself. Am I prepared for this? My burden is worrying about all my men making it through the end of the war alive. Will I live through it?

Cap "suggested" I give a speech to my men to prepare them for their role in this conflict.

Tomorrow, I better show up as their leader.

CHAPTER 31:
DONHAGADEE, IRELAND
APRIL 1944

MEMBERS OF Krow's platoon were congregating around the mess tent at 0900 hours. Krow met them there and gathered his men in a semicircle away from the front entrance. After a few minutes of pleasantries, he began his talk.

"Before any of us enlisted or were drafted, we all came from various parts of the country with different backgrounds. In our platoon, we have draftsmen, carpenters, mechanics, farmers, roofers, steel workers, a print setter, and one banker. I was a screw machine operator working in a factory when I was drafted into the Army." Some of the men chuckled.

"My point is that we would have been considered "regular Joes" before we were drafted. But we are NOT regular anymore. We have been given a great gift; we have learned how to save lives. Did any of you ever dream you would be assisting doctors during surgical procedures? Or be capable of delivering lifesaving plasma via a femoral artery?"

Krow felt surer of himself with every word. "How about having the balls to plunge a needle of morphine into *somebody else's body* to keep them from going into shock? American soldiers will live or die because of the decisions we make collectively or individually. It's a big responsibility we'll all need to shoulder. But there are no bigger shoulders than on the men of the 1st platoon who dutifully represent the 648th Medical Clearing Company. We accept all challenges." The men pumped their arms and Krow mirrored them.

"You're the best of the best, and our injured fighters will be lucky to have their lives in your hands. The time is getting close to when we'll be asked to muster out of here and go do our jobs. Are you ready to join me?" A cheer went up and soothed Krow's soul.

"The photographs we are about to take will memorialize us together for all time. I'd like you to think about how you want to be remembered in these snapshots. Take it seriously, men." He paused to make sure he still had their attention. "Please indulge me for one more minute. I would like each of you to close your eyes and visualize your future." Krow closed his eyes as well. "Visualize someone, known or unknown to you, who will be staring at your photograph in the future. It might be your child, grandchild, or great grandchild who might be curious about the ancestor who fought for the freedom of the entire world. They might even write a book report about you, some the bravest men on earth."

Krow opened his eyes and to his great surprise, many of the men still had their eyes closed, absorbed in their own thoughts of the future.

The photographer popped his head into the tent and gave Krow the thumbs up. "You men look good all dressed up. Let's head out and get our pictures taken."

A they filed out of the tent, Krow had high hopes that every one of his men would make it back home alive by the end of the war.

Unfortunately, not everyone did.

JOURNAL ENTRY
28 APRIL 1944

We're confined to the base and got word to organize all cargo for shipment. We can pack and unpack our gear in our sleep. I'm sick of training and so are my men. We're ready to get on with it.

JOURNAL ENTRY
4 MAY 1944

Captain Leibold called an afternoon staff meeting. We got our orders to move out for imminent transfer. This is it. Morale is good, anxiety high. My patience is being tested by my men constantly asking me where we're going.

Captain reminds us that our direct reports look to us for leadership. When the time comes, I hope I can perform as I am trained. I need to take my own advice and stop worrying about the unknowns or it will drive me batty.

JOURNAL ENTRY
6 MAY 1944

At 0700, we departed our current location and boarded troop trains to take us to our next embarkation port. We arrived at the port (Belfast) and immediately were ushered to an A.T.S. (Army Transport Ship). We pulled anchor and departed port.

Our Medical Units were told to stay below deck. We're traveling in a war zone and are being escorted by a small naval convoy. We were told to wear our life vests, presumably in case of mines or torpedoes which could scuttle our ship. Very reassuring (ha-ha). Once we set sail, we'll be notified of our debarkation point.

It's late and we finally reached our new "home." In the moonlight, we could see we passed a large mansion. The owner is allowing us to camp on his grounds.

It's obvious we're moving closer to engaging the enemy. Where and when is on everyone's mind. For now, it's shut-eye time, and I'm bushed.

CHAPTER 32:
DITCHLEY PARK, ENGLAND
MAY 1944

KROW'S PLATOON and the balance of the 648th Medical Clearing Company arrived at New Park Ditchley on May 9th, 1944. The following morning, Krow and the other Americans learned they were camping on the grounds of Ditchley Park, located in the rolling foothills of the Cotswolds. The owner was Ronald Tree, grandson of Marshall Field of Chicago department store fame. Tree's early life had been split between the U.S. and England, and after a successful business career in America, he had entered the world of British politics and been elected as a member of Parliament in 1933.

Tree became friends with Winston Churchill (who would become Prime Minister in 1940) and Anthony Eden (who Churchill would name Secretary of State for War). The three men became united in their belief Germany would soon become a threat to Britain.

As D-Day approached, Tree granted permission for the U.S. Army to use Ditchley Park as a staging area for American troop build-up. Its woodland setting provided the necessary camouflage to hide the buildup of U.S. troops in England.

JOURNAL ENTRY
12 MAY 1944

Today was a big day. I was invited along with our officers to a large family mansion in a beautiful country setting where we met our "landlord" (Ronald Tree). He told us he is part American and part British. We learned he has a high-ranking position in Britain's government.

The landlord gave us a history lesson regarding the use of this estate over the past four years. Apparently, the Prime Minister of England (Churchill) visited here several times in the early years of the war. While visiting, Churchill enjoyed helping himself to the landlord's personal cache of aged Scotch whiskey, and his love of a good cigar violated all the blackout rules on the grounds.

It's good our landlord peppered in these humorous stories during our visit. He's otherwise a very serious man. After he was done speaking, he let us know there would be a special guest joining us. The special guest turned out to be Sir Anthony Eden, England's Secretary of War. Eden thanked us for being here and said he wanted us to enjoy, to the best of our ability, the sights and hospitality of our new location.

Mr. Eden told us many young English men were conscripted into the Tommy army and it left many young ladies here looking for companionship. Families in these parts have one or two members in the war.

He lightheartedly told us we have the reputation of being cowboys and renegades. He mentioned the Brits may have watched too many American Western movies, which may have stereotyped us in this way. He suggested that the locals might be a little standoffish until they get to know us. But he impressed upon us that the people of England were grateful we're here.

At 1400 we joined in a local custom. They called it "teatime," where everyone spends a few minutes enjoying a cup of tea. It's a way of maintaining tradition and civility despite the dreariness of wartime. The servers showed us the proper way to hold a teacup. You hold the handle of the cup with your thumb and forefinger, and let the pinky hang away from the glass. Mr. Eden joined us for tea. "You are all proper Englishmen now," he joked.

After our tea, Mr. Eden stayed for a few photographs. He told us he would rather remain here and continue to socialize with us, but he had a cabinet meeting back in "the big city." Major Lang gave him a parting gift of American cigarettes and waterproof matches. It seems Mr. Eden fancies American tobacco.

Eden said something that blew past me at first, but I keep coming back to it. When Major Lang gave him the box of Camels and waterproof matches, Eden said, "Thank you kindly for the cigarettes, but you lads keep the waterproof matches. You are going to need them more than I will."

CHAPTER 33:
DITCHLEY PARK, ENGLAND
MAY 1944

15 May 1944

Hello sweetheart—

This afternoon I took in a variety show put on by the USO. The show was called "Yankee Doodlers." It's a troupe of American song and dance players and they're traveling to the various locations where American troops are stationed.

The opening act was called "Win this War." An actor came out on stage dressed as a professor wearing a cap and gown accompanied by two majorettes. I can't remember all the words, but it was a progressive sing-along routine.

There was a huge white board as a backdrop and on the white board were pictures and lyrics. When the professor wanted us to sing along, he had a pointer in his hand, and he would point to the words and/or pictures.

He would point to a caricature of Hitler with his little mustache and sing, "Isn't that old Hitler's pan?" And we'd all sing, "Yeah Man, Hitler's pan".

He sang, "Aren't we going to beat that man?" He would point at Hitler's little mustache again, and we'd all sing together, "Yeah Man, Beat that Man, Hitler's pan!"

Then he would point at a picture of Mussolini's big face and sing, "Isn't that Benito's jaw?" We'd scream, "Yeah Man, Benito's jaw. Haw, haw, haw, Benito's jaw. Win this War, we did before."

We got a chance to meet the actors afterward. Many were Vaudeville performers who, in a sense, risked their lives by traveling to a war zone to put on a show for us. They told us entertaining the troops was their way of contributing to the war effort. Oh boy, what a performance, we gave them a standing ovation!

It may sound from my letter that I am having a grand time overseas but I'm not. I've been here eight months. I'll never get back that lost time.

While I'm grateful we haven't had direct contact with the enemy, I know those days are coming. I wish we could get this war over with so I can come back home to you and the rest of the family. Please let my parents know that I'm safe and sound. I'm going to sign off now.

I love you always and forever,
Ed

CHAPTER 34:
DITCHLEY PARK, ENGLAND MAY 1944

EACH DAY more troops, supplies and heavy equipment were being amassed at Ditchley. Krow and Coop were in the quartermaster's tent repacking medical supplies when Corporal Dombrowski, the unit's clerk and radio man, found them. "Captain Leibold wants to meet with you two at his office at 1800 hours."

Coop was bent over, inspecting a box of sulfa powder. He put a canister back in its slot and turned his head toward the clerk. "What's this one about?"

Dombrowski grimaced. "Cap told me it was urgent and don't be late. Besides, if I told you, Leib would cut my balls off, leaving me as an unattractive mating partner to the women folk."

Coop gave Krow a sideway glance, "Dombo, you're already an unattractive fuck to the ladies. Cutting those marbles off isn't going to make a difference. Are you going to tell us what Cap wants us for or not?"

"Not." Dombo gave a half-hearted salute, turned on his heel, and made a beeline back to his jeep.

At precisely 1800 hours, Krow and Coop met Captain Leibold in his make-shift office at Ditchley. They took two seats on the opposite side of Leibold's desk.

"Leibold was all business and skipped any small talk. "We received our orders. We're getting ready to enter the theatre."

"Coop, you and the 1st section will be leaving for the Waterproofing School in Sudbury. We'll be making an amphibious landing and need to keep our jeeps and medical supplies dry." Leibold shifted in his chair.

"Krow, your unit will leave tomorrow morning to go to the Navy's amphibious warfare training center in Fowley, Cornwall. The Navy is conducting specialized training for Army medics on how to perform medical care on Navy ships."

Krow scrunched his forehead, his eyebrows meeting in the middle. "What's going on? We're Army infantry, what's this about a Navy ship?"

"Yesterday, the brass confirmed the worst kept secret in camp. We are preparing for an invasion on the French coast. It will be *of epic proportions*, their words, not mine, exact date still TBD."

Krow and Coop sat on the edge of their chairs, holding their breath.

Leibold leaned forward, his face grim. "The 648th is temporarily assigned to the Navy and will perform our duties as an amphibious medical team."

"Why?" Krow asked, completely shocked.

Leibold leaned back again and fidgeted with his pen. "I was presented two options and had to choose the lesser of two evils. Option #1 was to land on the French coast with the infantry divisions in the early waves. If the Krauts are ready for us, it could be a bloodbath until we gain a foothold on the beaches."

Krow rubbed the knuckle on his ring finger. "So, you went with Option #2?"

"Yes. I volunteered us for the Navy assignment." Leibold lifted a picture of his family from his desk. "Look, we aren't career military. Some of the guys in our unit are married with young children. We're civilian soldiers, and we all have lives to go back to after this thing is over." He put the picture down. "I believe this Naval assignment will improve our chances of making it out of there alive. My job is to serve the wounded, and God willing, keep all of us six feet above ground for the duration. Here is the way I see it." Leibold unfurled a map of the French coastline and placed it on top of his desk.

"Our Air Force will be dropping bombs on enemy artillery positions to weaken their fire power. Next, our paratroopers will land and attack the Krauts from the rear." Leibold ran his finger along a stretch of beaches. "The infantry will land on the coastline and fight it out with what's left of the German military until the beaches are secured. This is a coordinated plan and by mid-day, we should gain control of the coastline." Leibold stood and laid both palms on his desk, signs the captain was struggling to keep his calm.

"So, we land on the beaches to extract the wounded, right?" Coop asked, looking rather pale.

Leibold pointed at the coastline on the map. "Yes, we will land somewhere along here. The infantry medics in the first few waves are responsible for establishing the collecting stations for the wounded. Our job is to locate the collecting stations, land on the beach, transfer the casualties to our Navy ship, and get the hell out of there."

"What kind of ship will we be using?" Krow asked.

Leibold shuffled some papers around his desk until he found what he was looking for. He held up a black and white photograph. "It's called a land ship tank, or LST, and its primary purpose is to land on the beach and unload tanks. After it unloads, we'll quickly convert it to a triage center and cram as many casualties on board as we can. Then we'll transport the wounded back to England, re-load our medical supplies, and head back to the French coastline to extract more injured Americans."

Coop scratched the back of his head. "We'll still be in the crossfire big time."

"Correct," Leibold said, "but it's better than being targeted directly."

"We're hearing rumors of Rommel setting booby traps across the entire coast of France. And we'll be operating in E-Boat Alley.[3] How is this any safer?" Krow asked, clenching, and unclenching his fists.

Leibold sighed heavily. "The plan is the mine sweepers go in first and disable the underwater booby traps. By the time we arrive at the beachheads, many of these explosives should be neutralized. As for the E-boats and subs, we'll have to take our chances. We'll be flying our Geneva Convention Red Cross flags on the top deck, which should make it obvious we're a medical ship evacuating both American *and* *German* wounded."

Leibold lifted a piece of paper off his desk and read from his handwritten notes. "Our embarkation point is Port Falmouth in southwest England. Krow, your platoon will be assigned to a Naval LST stationed at the Port. Your boat will be transporting ambulances, medical supplies, litters, and life rafts. It will be our job to drive the ambulances onto the beach, load them with wounded, and take them back to the waiting LST.

---

3   E-Boat Alley is slang for Enemy Boat Alley.

"I'll need some of the men to stay on the boat with me to convert it to an emergency room. If necessary, we will be able to perform surgery on the ship." Leibold set the papers back on the desktop and paused for a reaction.

Coop leaned back and rocked in his chair. "I'll be sure to stock up on plenty of bottles of suntan oil for our trips to the beach." As usual, his snarky comment lifted the tension and Leibold finished describing other details of the plan.

"Any more questions?" Both men shook their heads. "Then you're dismissed," Leibold said.

At first blush, Leibold's decision to take the Naval assignment seemed to be a good one. If everything went according to plan it was the less dangerous option. As is well known now, the French beaches became the most dangerous place on earth.

And in war, nothing ever goes according to plan.

CHAPTER 35:
PORT FALMOUTH, ENGLAND
D-DAY, JUNE 6, 1944

THE LST left port and idled its way into the channel, taking a spot in the convoy. Nervous chatter spewed across the deck, and the ship's latrine entertained a constant flow of visitors. The ship resembled a metal shoebox without a lid, a twenty-foot wall of heavy steel on all sides. Sealed inside, members of the 1st platoon watched the night sky turn to early morning light with increasing trepidation.

It had only been a few hours since the first early morning troop-ships set sail for Normandy, but already full boatloads of American casualties were returning to the English ports. Krow heard some of his medics shouting "who's winning?" to the ships as they passed by. Blunt responses painted a bleak picture, and a larger line began to form at the ship's latrine.

+ + +

Bad weather leading up to D-Day had prevented the allied air force from fully taking out the German artillery armaments. Many of the aerial bombs missed their targets, leaving the enemy with their forti-fied cement blockhouses and their weapons largely intact and at full strength.

American paratroopers had been dropped scattershot behind the German lines, and hundreds of troopers landed miles away from their landing zone targets. Consequently, these units took longer than planned to coordinate an attack against the rear of the German army.

The Germans were able to focus their entire firepower on repelling the allied forces who were coming ashore on the Normandy beaches. In the early morning waves, the Americans were taking on the full brunt of the German response.

The LST filled with medics from the 648th neared the French coastline shortly before noon. As the ship got closer to the beaches, the men could hear the chest-thumping sounds of war.

Their ship lurched sideways as U.S. mine sweepers cleared a path forward. German 88s pummeled the beaches. Enemy machine gun fire caused a hailstorm of pinging noises that pounded against the ship's steel walls. The rapid fire *burp-burp-burp* sounds came in waves like how a hard rain pelts against the windshield of a car. Frequent detonations erupting from the water pitched the ship back and forth.

Whether it was the recent chemical warfare training, or an abundance of caution, Leibold gave the signal for his men to put on their gas masks. Then he braced himself at the front gate, poised to wave the green flag when it was safe to debark.

The ambulance drivers sat inside the vehicles waiting for the "go" signal. They would be the first to roll off the ship, with the medics following behind and using the vehicles as cover. A handful of men lifted their masks and retched as the boat lurched its way through the turbulent chop.

The ship's captain, who was struggling mightily to keep the boat steady, made the call to drop the front gate. When the gate lowered, Krow and the other medics expected the boat ramp to be flush with the beach. The cockswain gave the signal, and the winch screeched as it unwound the ramp.

It was chaos. The sea in front of them was filled with floating backpacks, helmets, and dead bodies. Allied soldiers with heavy packs ran haphazardly on the beach, desperately seeking cover from the shelling coming from above them. Machine gun fire seemed to come in all directions. The noise was overpowering, impossible to describe.

The ambulance drivers were so anxious to get off the ship, they almost flattened Leibold as he blocked their path. They expected him to be waving a green "go" flag. Instead, he waved a *red* flag like his life depended on it. Rather than dropping the ramp flush with the beach according to plan, the ship's captain had dropped the gate 200 yards offshore.

Leibold was furious and raced to the captain's nest. Krow could see the skipper pointing at something in the water and shaking his head *no,* while Leibold made circles with his hands.

Krow lifted his gas mask above his mouth and barked a quick set of orders to Coop. Coop nodded and jetted off toward Leibold. Enemy mortars were landing in the water all around them. They were a sitting duck, Krow turned to the men and gave his orders. "Drivers, stay with the ship, the rest of you, into the water with me!" Krow didn't wait for confirmation before he leaped into the turbulent sea.

One after another, each medic jumped and waded weaponless in the chest-high water, forming a single line. Their heavy backpacks made moving through the rising tide difficult, and almost immediately, their goggles fogged up and seawater seeped into their gas masks.

Krow heaved as he took a gulp of oily water instead of air. He tried holding his breath, but the exertion of slogging against the current made the urge to breathe unbearable. A bloated body floated into him, and he noted the soldier wasn't wearing a gas mask. His blurry goggles made it impossible for him to discern if the man was shot dead or gassed.

Krow had to decide fast. *Drown or die twitching.* He flung off his gas mask. Louis was behind him and followed his lead. When Louis looked back up, Krow was gone.

CHAPTER 36:
NORMANDY, FRANCE
D-DAY, JUNE 6, 1944

KROW'S HEAD was only a foot underwater, but the weight of his pack held him down, and he hadn't been able to catch a breath before he went under. He had slipped into a shallow indentation in the sandy seabed floor, caused when a mine sweeper triggered an underwater booby trap. The rising tide covered the gaping hole in the sand.

He struggled to shed his pack to no avail. Panic set in when he sensed something heavy land on top of him. Two knees clamped down on his shoulders, pinning his arms to his sides. Krow felt two quick tugs and his 100-pound pack dropped away. A split lifesaving second later, he was hauled up by his collar and gasped for breath. When he realized his savior was Louis, he thanked God for bringing his friend into his life.

As Krow's bearings returned, he looked for anything on the beach that could provide cover for his unit against the artillery fire. Spying smoldering and disabled vehicles, he shouted instructions to the men behind him, and his message was quickly passed down the line. When the unit hit the shore, the men sprinted for cover in teams of five. Miraculously, all made it and discovered their shelter was two husks of twisted metal resembling American tanks.

"What now?" Louis barked over the din.

"Dig!" Krow shouted back. "10-person foxholes." As the men scrambled to obey, he turned back to look for the ship but saw no sign of it.

Tamping down his unrest, he scanned the beach for flags indicating the location of collecting stations for casualties. He couldn't find any, but cries of "medic!" came from every direction.

Krow had to improvise and made his first command decision while in live combat. He decided to establish his own collecting station, using the tanks as cover. He instructed Louis to plant red cross flags on the roofs of the disabled tanks and delivered his orders to the men.

"Get to the wounded and bring them here for treatment." He also ordered two medics to stay behind to keep digging out a deeper and wider trench behind the dead tank.

Each time Krow lifted his head, he saw Louis shimmying through the sand like a water snake to reach another wounded soldier. If the soldier was too injured to move, Louis would put him on a litter and drag him through the sand to the relative safety of the foxholes. He displayed incredible bravery in the heat of battle, and Krow was truly awed. The number of wounded Louis pulled out of harm's way that day was more than any other medic with the platoon.

Krow was using his belt to apply a tourniquet to a soldier whose forearm was dangling from his elbow when Rollins piled in next to him. Rollins' face was covered in red sand, and his jacket had turned from brown to a dark cherry.

"Rolly, are you hit?" Krow blurted.

Rollins opened his arms and scanned his body quickly. "Not hit. But I can't fit many more of the wounded safely in my area. How do we get these guys off the beach?"

"We wait for our boat to return," Krow said.

"What if it doesn't?"

Krow clung to hope. "We flag down one of the ships coming in the next wave."

Rollins shook his head. "How do we do that?"

Krow twisted the tourniquet tight around the wounded soldier's arm, and the man groaned in pain. He jabbed a syrette of morphine into the man's thigh. "You'll feel better soon." He turned and looked at Rollins.

"Do you have your red smoke cannister? I'll use it to illuminate our position."

Rollins fished around his utility belt and pulled out the cannister. "The Germans on the cliffs will see the smoke. Won't they target us?"

"We'll have to work fast; I don't have any better ideas, do you?"

✦ ✦ ✦

After four hours of nonstop work, there was still no sign of the boat. There were so many injured soldiers in shallow wet foxholes, it was difficult to keep them all safe from the shelling around them.

Krow was scanning the water for an empty ship when he heard the creaking of tanks nearby and heavy machine gunfire coming from down the beach. Both sounds were deafening, and getting closer.

He used Louis's binoculars and spotted jeeps with white stars on their doors firing .50 caliber machine guns at German positions on the cliffs. American tanks flanked them, discharging their big guns in the same direction. A smile broke over his exhausted face when he saw that the tanks were also providing protection for a small convoy of ambulances. Krow could make out Coop in the driver's seat of one of the ambulances.

He struck a match and lit the wick on his smoke canister.

CHAPTER 37:
NORMANDY, FRANCE
D-DAY, JUNE 6, 1944

COOP SAW the thin line of red smoke trailing into the air. Krow watched impatiently as the tanks rerouted and headed toward the red smoke. But suddenly, the lead tank which provided cover for the ambulances stopped. Dismayed, Krow saw the tank swivel and reverse course, leaving the ambulance convoy unprotected. He fixed his sights on Cooper, who was giving hand signals to the other ambulance drivers.

Krow realized what was happening and swore to himself. He and his medics were in the middle of a vehicle graveyard. *A minefield.* The tank he was huddled behind was not disabled by a mortar shell. Rather, it had wheeled over a German anti-tank mine and was blown apart. With this revelation, Krow looked around him and saw many more vehicles disabled by the minefield.

In the meantime, American litter bearers jumped from their ambulances. Coop was on foot and in the lead. Krow could see him zigzagging like a pinball as he maneuvered his way across the minefield. The litter bearers behind him carefully followed in his footsteps. Krow cringed as he watched them jerk and dart their way toward his position.

Two harrowing minutes later, Coop slammed himself into Krow's foxhole. "You could have picked a safer place to set up shop!" He blurted after catching his breath.

"Where's the ship?" Krow asked.

"About a mile down the beach. It couldn't get any closer because of underwater booby traps in this section."

"Then we're stuck here. We can't chance taking the wounded through the minefield," Krow said.

"The American tank commander told me the underground explosives were designed to detonate only when they sensed heavy equipment rolling over the top of them. Men on foot shouldn't trigger the explosives. I say we trace my footsteps out of here and use these smoldering ruins as cover. Plus, the Germans seem to be focusing their firepower on another section of the beach right now. If we hurry, we should make it to the ambulances without being targeted." Coop took a deep breath.

Krow nodded and gave the order. Though Coop and team had to dodge periodic artillery fire, they succeeded in making several runs to claim all the wounded. Krow, Rollins, and Louis waited until all the casualties were evacuated and jumped in the last ambulance. When their jeep drove safely onto the ship, the skipper gave the order to lift the ramp and pull away from shore.

The boat's coxswain helped the captain navigate through the maze of sunken ships and other large obstacles in the water. The skipper successfully maneuvered the boat out of the most hazardous section and was almost to open water where he could open the throttles and cruise away from danger.

The coxswain's head swiveled as he used his binoculars to scan the area for enemy boats. He was about ready to give the "all clear" signal to the captain when he spotted a sizzling movement in the water about two thousand yards away. The object resembled a gray porpoise slicing through the waves at a high rate of speed, it was closing in on their position. He sounded the ship's alarm.

German E-boats had a top speed of 50 miles per hour and were the fastest of all boats on the water at the time. The enemy ships were launched from the port of Cherbourg, in lower Normandy, and they patrolled the corridor from the English Channel to the Normandy coasts.

The objective of the E-boats was to disrupt the flow of troops and equipment to the French shoreline. The E-boats would stealthily lay in wait for a target to appear, and when sighted, they fired their torpedoes and bolted from the area before they could be targeted themselves. E-boats were a constant worry for the allies. It wasn't until Cherbourg was captured on July 1st that the E-boat activity in the English Channel lessened.

The cockswain kept his wits and shouted instructions to the LST captain who, in turn, made a well-orchestrated defensive maneuver. The torpedo narrowly missed the bow of the boat as it zipped past. However, a Higgins boat filled with American troops heading to the French coastline took a direct hit.

Krow and the boat full of wounded soldiers returned safely to England without further incident. British aidmen removed the wounded and took them to hospitals in the area. Krow watched, nauseous and exhausted from the harrowing trip.

As he stepped off the boat, his eyes were drawn to hundreds of quarter-sized dings across the exterior wall of the ship. He barely made it to the other side of the ramp before he vomited out his guts.

After wiping his mouth with a blood-stained handkerchief, he unsteadily walked to dry land. As he approached a small building in the parking lot, he could see Leibold speaking with a Navy commander. Krow watched as Leibold nodded a few times and snapped a salute to the officer.

Leibold turned and dragged himself down the gravel road heading back toward the boat. Krow met him halfway. Leibold's voice was raspy, but his orders were clear.

"Restock the ship. We're going back."

CHAPTER 38:
ENGLAND AND FRANCE
JUNE-JULY 1944

JOURNAL ENTRY
28 JUNE 1944, ENGLAND

Our Naval LST assignment is over, and I'm ready to drop. None of us could have been prepared for the initial invasion on D-Day. Our role was to fill up the LSTs with causalities and get the hell out of there alive. I can't put into words the intensity of that experience. Remarkably, we all made it out of there uninjured. Yet, all of us are scarred for life.

JOURNAL ENTRY
1 JULY 1944, ENGLAND

I woke up this morning and on my pillow was a slimy puddle of green pus which had discharged out of my ears. My whole-body aches and the pain in my jaw is killing me. I took aspirin but it's not helping. The vertigo was so bad, Coop helped me to the hospital. It turns out my ear drums were blown out during one of our trips to the beaches.

Doc says the tissue in my ear drums didn't heal and since I was in the water during several runs, both ears became severely infected. At present, I can't hear well. When people talk to me their voices sound muffled, like

I'm wearing earplugs. Doc told me I might have an ongoing problem with this, as not much tissue is left in my ear drums.

The vertigo is making me nauseous. I'm on strong sulfa drugs, and they tell me I should be out of here in a few days. I feel foolish taking a hospital bed for this condition, as some of the boys here have catastrophic injuries and are in a bad way. I should be treating them verses the other way around.

JOURNAL ENTRY
6 JULY 1944, ENGLAND

Jesus H Christ. Some sons of a bitch here gave me dysentery. Now I have bloody shit coming out of my ears and my asshole.

JOURNAL ENTRY
12 JULY 1944, ENGLAND

I was discharged today from the hospital and when I got back to the outfit, I learned we've been alerted to get ready for our next assignment. My platoon will be landing on Utah Beach and will be temporarily assigned to provide aid to U.S. infantry units sustaining heavy casualties in the French low country. No more sailing back and forth, we will be on the continent full time assisting our infantry as we push to liberate Paris.

JOURNAL ENTRY
14 JULY 1944, UTAH BEACH, NORMANDY FRANCE

My platoon returned to Utah Beach this morning. Unlike our first visit here, our ride and landing were uneventful. We spent the day de-waterproofing our equipment and tested all our vehicles. We gave our ambulances touch-up paint jobs to make sure the Red Cross symbol can be clearly recognized on the roof and sides of every jeep.

We unfurled our large medical tents and left them open to dry. We used the leftover paint to touch them up as well. Can't be too careful!

We spent the nights sleeping in a transitional area consisting of rows and rows of foxholes that were dug out by troops who landed before we did. We were warned the Luftwaffe still strafed and bombed the beaches each night, trying to cut off the inflow of replacement troops to the front lines. Luckily, we haven't encountered any fire on our section of the beach.

My trench neighbors are Rolly and Coop. We talked about whether our experience here will be better or worse than it was during those early days in the invasion. We agreed it couldn't be worse than the insanity we experienced on D-Day.

Supplemental Entry:

Any time the wind blows into my ears, it feels like two screwdrivers are poking the soft tissue in my ear cavity. Like when you accidentally put a cotton swab too deep in your ear and it jabs the sensitive part of the eardrum. Yellow fluid (not pus) is leaking out of my ears again. Not as bad as before, but I've been using lots of cotton balls.

On a positive note, my asshole is back to its old jovial self.

CHAPTER 39:
SAINT-LÔ AND AVRANCHES, FRANCE JULY 1944

U.S. Archives

THE 1ST PLATOON was detached from the 648th and was placed on temporary assignment to assist in the care of wounded soldiers in Saint-Lô, France. The inland city was located approximately 25 miles southeast from the platoon's current position at Utah beach.

Capturing Saint-Lô was strategically important due its transportation roadways. If the allies could take Saint-Lô, it would prevent the Germans from transporting reinforcements and artillery to the frontlines. Importantly, securing Saint-Lô could provide the Americans a vital passageway to advance further east and enable them to liberate Paris, the French capital.

Unfortunately, American reconnaissance failed to understand how the Germans would use the many miles of natural French hedgerows to their advantage. Nazi machine gunners operated within an intricate system of entrenchments behind the hedgerows to conceal their location. Tunnels were built beneath the hedgerows to connect trench encampments. These underpasses allowed the enemy to stockpile and access additional ammunition, as well as to use them as escape routes should their positions become overrun.

As a result, the U.S. infantry battalions in Saint-Lô experienced high counts of injured and dead at the hand of Nazis who were defending their position in the city. Many of these soldiers were trapped and low on ammunition. The infantry battalions fighting in this area radioed for medical reinforcements: Krow's platoon arrived in the Saint-Lô area on July 17, 1944.

JOURNAL ENTRY
24 JULY 1944, ST. LÔ FRANCE

We've been here six days. Treating the large numbers of wounded has been intense and exhausting. It's been a difficult time.

Our medics didn't have to perform many amputations, as the Germans did it for us. The Nazi machine gunners hiding in the tall bushes cut these boys in half. Almost all the injuries we've treated so far have been due to missing extremities.

Early on, we ran out of torniquets and had to cut off the clothes from dead U.S. soldiers to make more. I ordered our litter teams to roll their dead bodies off to the side of the road so the American reinforcements coming behind us did not have to see them.

Our infantry troops captured the city of Saint-Lô (if you can call it a city). We got the "all clear" to enter the city limits and erect a first aid tent. When we entered, we passed a high pile of rubble with the American-flag draped body of a dead officer placed on top of the rock pile. Every American who passed into town saw this tribute.

We learned the officer led a daring rescue mission in the middle of the night. An infantry unit reported they were trapped and couldn't hold out much longer. He and a few others used only their bayonets as weapons as they crossed over enemy lines. They reached the trapped Americans and evacuated every single one of them. The brave officer was later killed by mortar fire.

The fighting at Saint-Lô was some of the fiercest of the conflict to date. It took a full month for the Americans to finally make their way through the Normandy hedgerows.

In addition to the battle at Saint-Lô, the medics of the 1st Platoon would provide medical aid during the battles to liberate the cities of Rennes, Laval, and Le Mans.

CHAPTER 40:
AVRANCHES, FRANCE
JULY 1944

U.S. Archives

AFTER LIBERATING Saint-Lô, the Americans pivoted 20 miles southwest to attempt to liberate the mountaintop city of Avranches, France. The city was the main gateway to access the French ports at Brittany and Brest. The Germans controlled Avranches and used those ports to ferry in large numbers of troops and ammunition.

If the Allies could wrest control of Avranches, they would be able to turn the tables on the Germans. The Americans would no longer have to be bogged down fighting in the hedgerows and swamps of Normandy. The battlefield could shift to more open ground, where U.S. artillery power and troop mobility would gain the advantage.

Hitler understood the stakes of controlling Avranches at all costs. To help his army defend the city, he doubled down on its defenses. He diverted additional troops and ammunition to the area, which made it difficult for the Americans to enter the city. Despite intense fighting and heavy casualties, the Americans made slow but steady progress toward Avranches.

A small unit of U.S. tanks had recently won control of a bridge over the See River just northwest of Avranches. The allies could use the bridge to infiltrate the city and fight the Germans who controlled the town. The American tank unit had orders to remain in place and hold the bridge.

Krow had established an aid station in the woods near the bridge, in a location concealed by timber and heavy brush. His men dug slit trenches, established guard duty, and used their binoculars to scan the main road for enemy activity.

Coop was on watch in a slit trench when he used his shortwave radio to alert Krow of a convoy of enemy vehicles on the outskirts of the city moving slowly toward the bridge. "You better come and see this," he said.

Two minutes later, Krow crawled next to him. Coop passed him the binoculars and pointed at the approaching motorcade. "It's three German ambulances heading toward the bridge."

Krow spotted the enemy medical convoy about a quarter mile away. He used his index fingers to adjust the lenses of his binoculars so he could get a closer look. As the first enemy ambulance slowly passed by, he could see that the German driver was sweating profusely. Krow then focused the binoculars on the drivers of the second and third ambulances. *Something's odd.*

"What's going on?" Cooper whispered.

"So far, our guys are holding their fire and allowing the German ambulances to pass. It seems the Krauts are using the bridge to evacuate their wounded into the city." Krow surmised.

Coop squinted in the direction of the bridge. "That's a nice gesture on our part. I hope the Krauts return the favor someday," he cracked.

Krow's eyes were glued on the enemy ambulances. Then it hit him like a ton of bricks.

No red crosses on helmets or armbands! Fuck!

✛   ✛   ✛

Krow quickly rolled on his side and unholstered his shortrange radio. He fumbled to find the universal channel to warn the tank crew. *It's taking too long!*

Cooper was startled. "What are you doing!"

"It's a trap!" Krow screamed into his radio. One of the men in the American tanks picked up the emergency call, but it was too late. The back doors of the enemy ambulances swung open and German artillerymen with anti-tank Panzerfausts fired at the U.S. tanks, scoring direct hits as more enemy soldiers poured out of the vehicles. It was the classic "Trojan horse" strategy. Leave it to the Nazis to violate the Geneva Convention.

Krow's eyes bulged as he watched the initial stages of the ambush. Instead of filling the ambulances with wounded, the Germans had loaded them with weapons and troops.

The American tank unit guarding the bridge was caught off-guard. Only one of the tank's machine gunners was able to return fire. But there were too many enemy soldiers coming at him and his tank would soon be overrun.

Suddenly all the shooting stopped. Plumes of black smoke obscured their view of the ambush site, but it seemed the fight was over. "What's going on? Why did shooting stop?" Coop blurted.

Krow focused his binoculars on the area surrounding the bridge. "There's too much smoke! I can't make anything out! "There's lots of movement, but I can't tell who's who." Krow kept the binoculars locked into the area. As the smoke cleared, what came into focus startled him.

"What the hell?" he murmured.

CHAPTER 41:
AVRANCHES, FRANCE
JULY 1944

REMARKABLY, THE American tank unit had won the skirmish. A U.S. sergeant was waving his rifle at a line of German prisoners who had their fingers interlaced behind their heads.

"Be on high alert; let's move toward them slowly," Krow told Cooper. They used the woods as cover and approached the bridge. As they got closer, they identified themselves as American medics. The tank commander, a sergeant named Armbruster, waved them over. He was clearly agitated.

"We barely had enough time to react. The Germans were spilling out of their trucks like ants, firing all kinds of weapons at us, at least at first," Armbruster explained.

"We tried to warn you," Coop said.

"Your warning came a second before the Krauts opened up on us. How did you know it was a trap?" Armbruster asked.

Krow pointed at his helmet and arm bands. "None of the German ambulance drivers were wearing Red Cross insignias on their helmets or shirt sleeves. Real medics would overtly display them on their helmets and uniforms to assure their safety."

Armbruster clutched his Gerard rifle and pointed to two smoldering husks of mangled steel. "Two of my tanks took direct hits. Six dead. Our machine gunner in tank #3 mowed down the initial waves of attackers and then sprayed flak at everyone else." His voice drifted off.

Coop looked at the smoldering American tanks, his face turning a bit green. "Any survivors?"

"Some of the Krauts coming out of the ambulances were weaponless and waved white flags. When I realized they were giving themselves up, I ordered a ceasefire, but it was too late. We chopped down a lot of them."

Armbruster dropped his head and rapped his knuckles against his helmet, like a little boy would when he realized he did something wrong and regretted it. He waved his rifle at the disfigured bodies of the dead German soldiers on the ground. "None of these fuckheads speak English, so I couldn't tell who was trying to surrender and who we should shoot!" Armbruster stomped his foot on the ground. "For fuck sakes! We showed these assholes common decency by allowing them to safely pass with their wounded. And they repay us by murdering my guys?" He was losing it.

Krow offered him a cigarette to calm him down. "Your order to cease fire saved some of the Krauts. Maybe we can get information from them."

Armbruster struck a match and took a deep pull off the cigarette. "I saved the wrong fucking people!" he choked out.

Krow pointed down the road toward the woods. "I established an aid station not far from here. I'll call more medics to tend to the wounded."

Krow was treating one of the enemy soldiers when he detected a familiar accent. He recalled Big Hand's advice to ask German fighters about their home countries. "Nationality?" Krow asked.

"Czech." The enemy soldier replied.

Krow asked the soldier several questions, and the picture become clearer. Most of the enemy soldiers were Czechoslovakians. When the Germans took control of their country, they were forced to fight for the "Fatherland." If they refused, their families were sent to the labor camps or murdered. "Many of us would rather lose our lives than continue fighting for Germany," the Czech said.

He told Krow of a hastily crafted mutiny plan concocted by his comrades to stop the ambush. "When the ambulances crossed the bridge, we disabled the drivers and swarmed the German guards inside the vehicles. We knew the plan was risky and we would take casualties, but this was our chance to help the American liberators."

"Why help us?" Krow asked.

"Because the Nazis are ruthless demons. They took our land and forced us to do things against our will including…" The Czech took a moment to wipe his eyes with his blood-soaked sleeve.

Krow reached into his back pocket to retrieve a clean handkerchief. "Here, use this." The Czech nodded and cleaned the streaks from his cheeks. Then he resumed speaking.

"They steal our children and use our sisters as if they are pieces of *property*. I wish we could have killed them all before they fired on your comrades." His hands were trembling as he looked at the bloody carnage around him. He pointed at a few bodies

"The dead men here are my friends. They sacrificed their lives to stop this from happening. I know most of their families." He broke down and sobbed.

Krow took it all in, and after a few more interviews, the mutiny story was confirmed. Three German drivers died from knife wounds. Other German guards in the ambulances had been shot or stabbed to death. Two conscripted Czech soldiers were found fatally wounded from fighting with German soldiers inside the ambulances.

The Czechoslovakians had indeed tried to stop the ambush. Many of them died trying.

CHAPTER 42:
AVRANCHES, FRANCE
JULY 1944

COMBAT CONDITIONS inside the city of Avranches were difficult. The Germans controlled the city and its labyrinth of narrow streets and passageways. Much of the fighting was house-to-house with the Americans moving cautiously, taking one building at a time. After four days of fierce fighting, Avranches was now largely under Allied control. But the city was by no means fully safe or secure.

The Nazi leaders inside the city communicated their dire situation to Hitler and recommended a retreat. In response, Hitler gave a direct order to stay and fight to the last man. To inspire hope in the remaining defensive troops, he ordered a counterattack and promised reinforcements. The remaining Germans inside the town would have to hold out at all costs, buying time for the plan to be put into place.

Consequently, sniper fire continued to prove troublesome for the Americans who were trying to snuff out the remaining pockets of resistance. The German snipers were familiar with the alleyways and were able to elude American return fire by stealthily moving from one place to another.

Rollins and Krow provided medical support to a small unit of ten American infantrymen who were clearing out the Germans building by building. They were making headway until the American unit was taken by surprise by Nazi machine gunners who hid behind a huge pile of rubble. U.S. casualties included two dead and six wounded, all shot in the street. To complicate matters, Nazi snipers provided cover from the second floor of a nearby building.

Krow and Rollins and two American infantry men (Washburn and D'Angelo) huddled inside the first floor of a dilapidated print store. While the infantry men returned fire, the medics tried to figure out how to rescue the injured American soldiers bleeding in the street. The alley in which they were situated was narrow and offered no cover.

Then something strange happened. The two Nazi machine gunners who were concealed in their firing nest began waving white flags, signaling for a cease fire. They were yelling in broken English in the direction of the print shop.

Rollins translated the message. "They're giving us five minutes to retrieve our wounded from the street, and they will do the same."

D'Angelo was crouched behind window, shards of sharp glass crunching under his boot as kept his eyes and rifle focused on the Germans. A bead of sweat dripped off the tip of his nose. "What if it's a trick? Back up will be here in a few minutes."

"Look!" Washburn blurted. The two Nazi machine gunners stood, exposing themselves to Americans. They were waving white cease fire flags. German medics bearing Red Cross armbands slowly walked out of one of the dilapidated buildings on the other side of the street. They were unarmed and held both hands high overhead, eyes downcast. They reached their wounded and began dragging them from the street.

Washburn was wild-eyed. "I'm zeroed in, and I can take out those fucking Nazi machine gunners right now!"

"Have you lost your mind?" Krow yelled. "We have a chance to get our guys before they bleed to death. You can't fire on them now."

"We watched those two goons shoot our guys to pieces. It's our turn to give it back to them."

Without responding, Krow and Rollins bolted out of the building, unarmed, and headed toward the wounded. One by one, they dragged the injured U.S. soldiers back to the safety of the print shop. Though Washburn still had his rifle zeroed in on the Nazi machine gunners, Krow was grateful he resisted firing on the Germans while they were retrieving the wounded.

The German machine gunners became more animated, vigorously waving their white flags. "*Schnell, schnell!*" The Americans heard the mechanical sounds of tank treads clacking on concrete.

"*Schnell, schnell!*" The enemy machine gunners were overly zealous trying to get their point across. "*Panzers. Panzers!*"

Rollins and Krow were dragging two more soldiers. "We won't have time to get the rest of our wounded before the German tanks arrive. What do we do?"

Krow shouted orders to American soldiers inside the print shop. "Help us get these wounded off the streets or they'll get trampled by the Panzers. Hurry!" The ground shook as the tank drew ever closer.

Precious seconds ticked away as the American soldiers remained under cover. Rollins was furious at the indecision. "Get your asses out here. Now!"

"Quickly!!" Krow screamed at the two young American soldiers in the building.

Washburn looked at D'Angelo, who had the higher rank. "What should we do?"

"Drop your weapon, Washburn. Let's go get our wounded."

CHAPTER 43:
AVRANCHES, FRANCE
JULY 1944

WASHBURN AND D'Angelo left their Browning automatic rifles inside the shop and flew out of the building. The minute their boots hit the pavement, the German sniper, who was still hidden in a building across the street, opened fire. The sniper's first shot blew the top off Washburn's head, killing him instantly. D'Angelo was struck in the left side of his chest, the bullet exiting through his back.

Rollins and Krow dove for cover. Both Americans were unarmed, laying on the ground without protection. Krow feared the worst. *We're going to die on this street. I hope Mary knows how much I loved her.*

The German machine gunner barked a quick set of orders, and Krow sensed movement around him. It was the two enemy medics; unbelievably, they were lugging the rest of the American wounded off the road.

"Up! *Schnell*! Up!" A German medic yelled frantically as he dragged a wounded American soldier to the curb.

Rollins and Krow sprang to their feet and quickly removed the rest of the U.S. wounded. Rollins retrieved D'Angelo's bloody body. Private Washburn had no chance.

The two American medics made it back to safety just as the German Panzer entered the alley. The enemy machine gunners were no longer visible. They had ducked back into their rubble-protected machine gun nest.

"What now?" Rollins looked at Krow.

"Grab the rifles! Prepare to defend ourselves if necessary."

Without warning, the German machine gunners opened fire down the alley, providing cover for the Panzer. But Krow and Rollins were heartened to see American troops with their anti-tank weapons bearing down on the Panzers from the opposite direction. They eagerly watched an American soldier climb four flights of stairs in an abandoned bell tower; they whooped and cheered as he fired an armor-piercing bazooka shell which took out the Panzer.

Sporadic machine gun fire continued until the Nazi machine guns ran out of ammunition. As a last-ditch effort, the Germans uncorked two short range missiles at American positions. The stubborn Germans then fired their rifles and discharged their side pistols until they were emptied.

The Nazi sniper had fled the area, stranding the German infantry-men without cover for a possible escape. Defeated at last, they raised their white flags of surrender, they slowly rose to a standing position, exposing themselves. The Americans held their fire as the Germans left their concealed perch in the rubble and fell to their knees.

D'Angelo was bleeding out badly, and Krow was doing his best to save him. He packed the hole in D'Angelo's chest with gauze and gave him a shot of morphine and rushed him into an arriving ambulance.

The American captain in charge of the infantry unit arrived a few minutes later. He gave the order to sweep the area for any remaining German resistance. The American wounded who were pulled out of harm's way were able to inform their leader what happened.

There was only one thing left to do, interrogate the Nazi machine gunners. The captain ordered them to their feet and with their hands held high, they made their way toward the American side of the road. The captain asked the questions while Rollins served as the interpreter.

"Ask the Krauts why their sniper shot our soldiers when they were clearly defenseless." Rollins relayed the captain's message to the enemy soldiers.

The German with the higher rank pointed at Rollins' Red Cross armband. "No shoot." And he pointed at all the American wounded and dead. "Soldat (soldier). Shoot."

Rollins provided further details. "He says their orders are to refrain from shooting medical personnel, provided those men are unarmed and wearing Geneva Convention Red Cross armbands and clearly attending to their wounded. They would expect the same reciprocity should the situation be reversed."

The American captain balled his fists. "Ask them why my two men were shot. They were unarmed and clearly gave themselves up to retrieve our wounded." Rollins relayed the message to the German.

The enemy machine gunner waved and pointed in the direction of where Washburn and D'Angelo sprung out of the building. He spoke rapidly and became agitated. Rollins was able to make the connection.

"He claims your men weren't wearing medical armbands and had weapons with them. They were considered armed and dangerous, and the Germans are under orders to shoot armed soldiers." Rollins looked at the captain.

"Bullshit. My men were murdered. They put their rifles down and went out to retrieve the wounded. They were defenseless!"

"*Nein! Nein* (no, no)!" The German gunner patted his hips and belt.

Rollins turned away and jabbed his finger at the side of his belt. "He says the sniper shot the two American soldiers because they came out of their hiding places with their side arms in place. The snipers have orders to kill enemy soldiers who are armed."

With a grim expression on his grizzled face, the captain kneeled over Washburn's lifeless body and lifted the bloody olive drab blanket that covered him. As the German had attested, Washburn's Colt M1911 semiautomatic pistol was resting in its holster.

The captain ordered the Germans to be sent to a POW enclosure outside the city. Krow called in jeeps to evacuate the wounded and take them to a medical clearing station operating two miles from the front. Later that evening, he received word that D'Angelo died from his chest wounds. He couldn't help but feel responsible for his and Washburn's deaths, especially as the two of them had ultimately pitched in to clear the American wounded upon his request.

In the end, Hitler's counterattack was not well coordinated and was thwarted by the American forces. The city of Avranches was taken on July 31st, 1944. Bulldozers cleared the roads, and the Allies were able to push large numbers of fresh troops and supplies through the city.

The Americans now controlled the French fighting terrain and no longer had to do battle in the swamps and hedgerows of Normandy. The

Germans were on the run and the Americans began liberating French towns at a rapid rate as they advanced toward Paris.

Shortly after Avranches was secured, Krow received word that their field assignment on the front lines had ended. His new orders were to rejoin the balance of the 648th in Fougères, France, located 30 miles south of their current position.

CHAPTER 44:
FOUGÈRES, FRANCE
AUGUST 1944

JOURNAL ENTRY
AUGUST 1944, FOUGÈRES, FRANCE

My platoon received its orders to rejoin the 648th at Fougères, France. We arrived four days ago after our three-week field assignment concluded. Here, we will be operating as a clearing company attached to the 34th Evacuation Hospital.

When we arrived in Fougères, the balance of the outfit met us outside the mess tent and gave us a standing ovation. It sure was good to see all the guys again. It was a boost to our morale after witnessing the devasting effects of war.

The men and I celebrated our arrival by taking a hot shower in one of the hospital tents. I could barely stand to smell myself. No hot shower since our arrival on this continent. By my math, it's been about 22 days.

My uniform is now more or less a blood-filled sponge. When it rained, our uniforms leaked like a red ink pen. On rare occasion, I was able to take off my uniform and give my body the once over with a bar of soap.

I tried to keep my hygiene up the best I could but there were several days where I didn't get a chance to brush my teeth. I estimate I'm down about 10 pounds. Honestly, I barely remember eating anything. I know I must have as my C-Rats (C-Rations) are depleted, but we certainly never had a nice sit-down dinner while on the front lines.

Our mess cooks were told in advance we were coming. They prepared chicken and some vegetables for us. We devoured it. I'm not sure where they secured the cherry tarts, but it was the best tasting dessert I've ever had!

Leibold gave us a three-day reprieve from our duties so we could catch up on badly needed rest. The 2nd platoon will be handling the day-to-day duties. Cap wrote a nice note to our C.O. and in it said the company left with 20 men and came back with 20 men. The big man upstairs had us in the palm of his hand considering the cards we were dealt.

Nothing could have prepared us for what we experienced. The manner of injuries. The utter devastation of cities. The noise level from bombing, shelling, tanks, and all manner of weaponry defies description. It was heartwrenching to look into the faces of the local people who endured the destruction of their homes and villages.

On the other hand, it was invigorating when we saw thousands of U.S. bombers overhead coming to our aid in Saint-Lô. We flattened the city; there is nothing left of it. Our bulldozers cleared the rubble so we could move our equipment through the town. We must have achieved aerial superiority, as we didn't see many Luftwaffe aircraft, thank God.

It seems to me after being in direct engagements with the enemy that the lines are blurred between what's right and what's wrong. The universal rule is to use any means necessary to survive.

The Germans have muddied the waters by despicably using Red Crosses as deception for military engagements. I saw this firsthand with the enemy tank battle in Avranches. We are now suspicious of everything.

I used to think I could make a career out of being in the military. Basic training was a breeze. I liked learning new things, including map reading, aerial recognition, and basic medical treatments. I scored well on all exams and was promoted several times. Bragging to others with each new stripe on my sleeve.

It's easy to lead when the war games are for practice. Maneuvers do not prepare you for actual warfare. Out here, nothing is by the book.

Now I better understand the burden of leadership. I'm no longer brash or cocky, or at least, less inclined to be so. Decision making in combat is life or death. Knowing a split-second decision might lead to death of our comrades is hard to bear.

I remain positive and assured on the outside so that I can keep up my platoon's morale. I pray I have the strength and foresight to make the right decisions.

CHAPTER 45:
FOUGÈRES, FRANCE AUGUST 1944

IN FOUGÈRES, Allied leaders made the decision to use enemy POWs for labor in the American field hospitals rather than sending them to an allied prison camp. The prisoners would be assigned the grunt work of digging out latrines, trash disposal, and the tilling of slit trenches and foxholes in and around camp. Using enemy POWs for menial labor allowed the American medics to concentrate on treating the sick and injured.

A stringent vetting process was put in place for the selection of POWs to work in the American camps. Only after a series of interviews and rigorous interrogations could enemy personnel be assigned to work at one of the American medical clearing stations. The POWs were housed in separate tents and always placed under guard.

Leibold insisted his team be part of the POW vetting process. After all, the American platoon leaders would have to guard, feed, and house the prisoners. Krow and Coop led the initial screening of candidates. They interviewed the POWs in the mess tent, and the MPs brought the prisoners in one at a time.

"I know this guy." Krow whispered to Coop.

"What's his story?"

"He was one of the mutineers in Avranches; he risked his life to help stop the German ambush. I did triage on him and interrogated him after the incident. His story checked out." Krow tapped Coop in the ribs with his elbow. "And he's *not* a German."

"So, what is he?"

"He's Czechoslovakian. When his village was taken over by the Krauts, he was forced into the Wehrmacht Army. The Krauts threatened to kill his family if he didn't pledge his loyalty to the Fatherland and fight for the Reich."

Coop inadvertently snapped the pencil he was holding in half. He took another from the cup holder and finished writing his notes. "I'll lead the questioning for this one. You can translate."

Coop led off with a doozy. "Have you killed any Americans?"

"What's your name, rank and military background?" Krow translated to Czech.

"Andrew Radminsky. Private. Quartermaster Clerk."

Coop shot Krow a puzzled look and Krow obliged him. "*Czy zabiłeś żadnych Amerykanów*?" *(Have you killed any Americans?)*

Private Radminsky's back stiffened. He emphatically denied killing anyone.

Coop refused to waver from his line of questioning. "Ask him why he was a willing participant in an ambush that did, in fact, kill two U.S. soldiers and wounded other Americans."

Radminsky explained he served as a field supply clerk, and that he had never been placed in combat before he and the other Czechs were recruited for the ambulance operation. They knew it would be a suicide mission since the Americans had cut the supply lines.

Radminsky emphatically reminded Krow that several Czechs carrying white flags were gunned down by American fire during the ordeal. Some of his friends sacrificed their lives for the sake of their fellow countrymen. Unfortunately, they were unable to subdue all the Germans and the Nazi gunners got off several shots before they were eliminated.

Cooper tapped his pencil on the table. "Can we trust him?"

Krow thought back to his father's advice. "Yes, I believe we can. Would you agree to stamp him for a second round of vetting?"

Cooper nodded and passed Radminsky along for further interrogation. After successfully completing several more background checks, Private Andrew Radminsky was handed a shovel and began his new career as a POW latrine digger.

Radminsky would not stay a POW for long. They would meet again, under circumstances Krow could never have predicted.

CHAPTER 46:
FOUGÈRES, FRANCE AUGUST 1944

13 August 1944

Hello my Dearest Mary,

Please accept my deepest regrets for being unable to write to you during the past few weeks. I was on a special assignment, and my men and I have been busy taking care of patients. The most I can divulge is I am somewhere in France chasing the bad guys around the countryside. All is good here, and I am safe and sound.

When I returned to camp, the postmaster gave me a nice stack of your letters! What a great pick-me-up. I loved reading them, and some I read twice! I miss our fun days of living in our little apartment off base and playing ping pong or cards with our friends. We all hope this thing will be over quickly and we can get back home to enjoy our lives and be with our loved ones.

Congratulations on your new job at Jack & Heinz. You will be the best airline parts inspector in the company! After reading your letter, I must say your schedule looks more intimidating than mine. Working 7 days a week for 12 hours a day leaves you no time for having fun. I especially like your dream for us to save our money and buy our own little grocery market and raise our family there. Thinking about you and having a family together makes me happy! I hope we can have a boy and a girl. One of each!

I have some military news I can share. A few days ago, I led a unit that helped evacuate about 600 of our American wounded boys back across the pond to jolly old England. Many of the GIs had the "million-dollar" wounds which got them free tickets back to the states. I wanted to jump on one of those planes and have them fly me back home too! But I guess it's better to come back in one piece versus being all mucked up like some of those poor fellows. I'm starting to go down a rat hole so let's go to more positive news.

At present, we're in farm country and the people here are very friendly. I used my $4 invasion money to purchase a few things from the locals. The townspeople trade goods and services in exchange for cigarettes and chocolates. Since I don't smoke, I've been using my cigarette ration to purchase things. Some of the guys have exchanged their goods for French wine and champagne. As you know, I don't indulge much but I did have a glass of the highly acclaimed French champagne and enjoyed it. What I really have a hankering for is a Coca Cola and Dan Dee chips! They don't have either here in France.

Lastly, I want you to know there will be periods of time when I'm unable to write to you but please do not mistake that as a lapse of my love or thoughts for you. I have the same dreams to be together as you do. I cannot wait to hold you in my arms, smell your perfume, and give you the best loving kiss a husband could give to his wife. Until then, I will hold your photographs close to me and your loving letters closer to my heart.

Fondly and with all my love,
Ed

CHAPTER 47:
DIGNY AND VERDUN, FRANCE FALL 1944

AFTER FOUGÈRES, Krow's platoon advanced with the infantry units who were liberating French cities at a fast clip. The platoon worked around the clock to treat hundreds of wounded in Digny and Estampes. When they arrived in the city of Verdun, they were assigned to the 109th Evacuation Hospital and provided overflow capacity.

The medics were able to stay in Verdun a few extra days for some well-earned rest. Since its liberation, Verdun was a popular spot for troops on leave.

Wherever large numbers of U.S. troops congregated, there also tended to be an ample supply of brothels and prostitutes eager to shed Americans of their dollars. While there were prophylactic kits easily available to them, soldiers still indulged in unprotected sex with the local population. Many of the young men were naïve or ignored the risk of contracting sexually transmitted diseases.

After many years of fighting, there seemed to be a shortage of eligible young French men. The fresh supply of twenty-year-old American males happily volunteered to fill the gender gap. Due to his medic role, Krow understood that this could lead to some undesirable consequences.

One day, Krow was taking inventory in the pharmacy tent with Corporal Dombrowski, who was single. Krow noticed lower than usual inventories on some items and couldn't help himself from razzing the corporal.

"Dombo, why the hell does it always seem like we are running low on penicillin? Are there supply issues on this antibiotic?" Krow stifled his grin when Dombrowski's cheeks turned red.

"Sarge, from time to time, the men find themselves at the mercy of some of the local women who want to show their appreciation for liberating their city."

"How does this relate to draining our inventories?" Krow gave him a hard look.

Sweat dotted Dombrowski's upper lip and forehead. "Well, um occasionally some of the men, not me of course, accept the women's gratitude in the form of fleshly activity."

Krow answered with a zinger. "You mean they choose to copulate not capitulate?"

"Huh?" Dombrowski didn't get the play on words.

Krow broke it down for him. "Our soldiers are getting the clap due to having unprotected sex. Hence, they are exhausting our precious supply of penicillin. Am I right?"

"Yes, I guess that's accurate." Dombrowski flushed.

"How do they get the penicillin?"

"They get it from our dispensary. And take the shot from our pharmacists or one of the medics."

"What type of tests are administered to confirm the GI has some form of VD?" Krow asked, his voice turning more serious.

"Probably a visual check," Dombrowski responded. "It's kind of obvious when a man comes down with the clap."

Krow sighed. "Dombo, do you recall our combat experience in Saint-Lô and Avranches?"

Dombrowski looked down at his shoes. "Yes, I remember. It was bad."

"Right! And do you recall how we ran critically low on supplies and were forced to call in airdrops of penicillin and other materials? Some of those drops landed behind enemy lines, and we risked our lives to retrieve them. We don't want to have to do it again, especially on account of running low on penicillin due to men being irresponsible when having sex.

"The next time you or your friends indulge in acts of "fleshly activity," use a prophylactic or I'll have to write a letter to your mommies and tell them you've been very bad boys."

Dombrowski stared at the floor. "Yes, sir," was all he could muster.

CHAPTER 48:
METZ, FRANCE
NOVEMBER 1944

U.S. Archives

EVEN THOUGH American troops liberated the city of Metz the day before Thanksgiving 1944, there was still heavy fighting in the area. The Germans were determined to remain in control of the strong forts on the outskirts of Metz. Allied infantry units were called in to root out the remaining German ground forces in these fortresses.

The men of the 648th had just finished their Thanksgiving meals when they received the order to relocate to Metz. A small team, including Krow and his three friends, was dispatched in advance to find a suitable building which could act as a hospital. Everyone preferred working in buildings instead of treating casualties in tents and spending cold, damp nights sleeping in slit trenches.

When the medical team arrived in Metz, they found a building which met their requirements. However, the infantry commander in the area explained he could not spare any soldiers to protect their location or guard their escape route. "It's mostly safe inside the city, and the Krauts are confined to the fortresses outside of town. I need all my men to clear them out so I can fully secure the town and the supply route. You guys will have to provide your own security for the next few days."

Krow understood the drill. They would set up their medical equipment in the building and establish a rotation of guard duty. While on security detail, the men switched from their Red Cross dress to infantry gear. They carried their rifles and had a full accompaniment of grenades.

Plummeting temperatures and a brisk wind made guard duty an unpleasant experience, it hovered near zero degrees with frequent snow squalls. Some of the men required treatment for frostbite. As such, sentry watches were shortened from four-hour to two-hour shifts. It was currently 2200 hours and time to rotate out guard duty.

Louis was the tip of the spear, meaning his guard duty was on the furthermost edge of camp. Bundled up, he settled into a slit trench on the side of the road for his shift.

Across the road, 100 yards behind him, was Rollins, and a few more guards were positioned behind him. They needed to defend both sides of the road in case a quick retreat was needed.

It was getting close to midnight and Louis's two-hour shift was coming to an end. He cupped his hands and was blowing hot air into them when Coop slid in next to him.

"It's your lucky night, Louis. I'm your replacement on this fine evening."

"It's about damn time, I can barely feel my toes!" Louis griped as he pointed eastward toward a small town named Jean. "There's been sporadic firing and shelling over there."

"Not your worry anymore, it's my turn to watch the fireworks," Coop responded in his trademark fashion. "And out of the goodness of my heart, I brought you a present." He handed Louis a thermos.

"Coffee!" Louis said. "Despite what everyone says about you, you really *are* a swell guy."

Coop grinned. "Be nice or I'll keep it for myself. And it's not coffee, it's something special."

Louis twisted the lid and relished the steam. He took a sniff and his face lit up. "Hot chocolate! Where did you get it!"

"The cooks surprised us and served it with our Thanksgiving rations. I saved some for you. It's still hot, so don't let the Krauts get a whiff. Now get out of here so I can take a nap."

Coop wasn't in the trench more than ten minutes when his SCR-536 handheld transceiver cackled to life. It was Rollins.

"Coop, do you see movement between us? I see something coming out of the woods."

Coop swiveled around to look behind him. It was dark and the snow was blowing fiercely, pelting him in the face. "It's probably Louis. He should be passing your area right about now," Cooper radioed.

"It's not him. There are too many shapes coming out of the woods," Rollins whispered through his radio.

The squall lessened and Coop got a glimpse. "I confirm movement of a large group of individuals moving toward the road. The snow is blowing in my face, and I can't make out the uniforms. Can you tell who they are?"

"I can't see clearly, but they're gathering in the middle of the road about 60 yards away from me. Maybe 50 shapes, which is about the size of an enemy platoon."

"Do we have our wires (booby traps) strung this far out?" Coop asked.

"No, the wires are behind us. Set yours out over the road. They probably won't see you if you stay low. We'll pen them in."

"Copy." Cooper crawled out of his trench and got to work.

"Sarge, are you getting this?" Rollins asked over his short wave.

Krow was on radio duty and had listened in on the entire exchange. He had already given the order to deploy reinforcements and put the unit on alert to prepare for a retreat.

"Roger. Flying monkey's out of the cages."

"How the hell did an enemy platoon this size get through our defenses?" Leibold huffed when he was appraised of the situation. "The last of the Krauts were supposed to be holed up in those fortresses outside of town."

"Maybe the Krauts dropped paratroopers to provide reinforcements?" Krow suggested.

"In this weather?" Leibold took charge. "Rollins, we're about 100 yards behind you. Do you still have eyes on the butterflies?"

"Roger, Captain. About 50 total. Snow squall making it difficult to identify who these guys are. Not Americans for sure."

"How can you tell?" Leibold barked.

"Not wearing helmets. They're probably not German for the same reason."

Louis was sipping on his hot chocolate on his way back to camp when he practically ran headfirst into the squad of unknown hostiles. He was 25 yards from the main group before he realized he needed to take cover. Louis crouched low and looked around him. He could see footprints in the snow behind and in front of him. He was caught in no man's land and would be in serious trouble if more enemy troops came up behind him.

He spotted a snow-covered log off to the side of the road about 10 yards from the edge of the woods. Louis shimmied his way toward the log, taking a silent inventory of his weapons. He was carrying his M1 rifle, a holstered Browning Colt .45 semi-automatic pistol, and four hand grenades. He reasoned if he could get to the log, he could set up his M1 behind it, using the stump as a barrier to protect himself from enemy return fire.

Louis's head was on a swivel until he made it safely to his destination. He leaned his carbine on the log, quickly checked his grenades, and unclipped his radio.

"Rolly and Coop, do you guys see this? Hostiles on the road. I repeat, hostiles on the road."

Suddenly, Louis was caught by surprise when an arm thrust out of the log. A thin bony hand grabbed at his utility belt where he kept his grenades.

Louis looked down and two sunken eyes stared back at him. The hump that resembled a snow-covered log was actually a half-frozen body. "Cnaba Gory" were the last words spoken by the hostile. Louis used the stock of his Browning automatic rifle to deliver two smashing blows to the man's skull, killing him instantly.

Between his shriek of surprise and the cracking of bone, the skirmish with the "log-man" gave away Louis's position. Americans converged from every direction, thrusting flashlight beams onto the hostiles. All rifles and weaponry were trained on the intruders.

The Americans quickly discerned the enemy was unarmed. Leibold demanded the hostiles identify themselves. What happened next will be forever seared in the memory of each American who witnessed the event.

Many of the prisoners dropped to their knees and clasped their hands in prayer. Some went into a fetal position. Others crawled on the ground toward the Americans. Most were weeping.

Louis identified himself as he bolted out of the woods. He was upset and out of sorts. Flashlights trained on him as he came forward to join the group. The flashlights cast an eerie glow on many more "snow covered logs" off in the distance.

The medics discovered these men were not hostiles, but allies. They were Russian POWs who had been held in a Nazi labor camp located near the city of Boulay-Moselle.

Earlier that day, the U.S. Army fought their way into the camp and liberated it. Due to the heavy fighting, they couldn't relocate the POWs to a safer location. Many of the prisoners used the distraction to escape on foot. Some were too weak and emaciated to make it to safety and died from exposure or exhaustion.

Leibold gave the command for the American medical ambulances to come forward. "Isolate them from the rest of our wounded until we know what diseases they might carry."

Cnaba Gory are Russian words. The English translation is "Thank God."

CHAPTER 49:
METZ, FRANCE
DECEMBER 1944

JOURNAL ENTRY
4 DECEMBER 1944

We experienced for the first time the savage brutality of the Nazi regime. We are treating over 60 Russian POWs. I would describe these poor ill-fed men as human husks or ghouls. They don't resemble human beings. I'm at a loss of words to adequately describe their ghastly appearance.

What happened to these Russians goes way beyond any rational rule of war. What kind of people could do this to another living, breathing, person?

These men were not wounded in the conventional sense of armed combat. Instead, they have been tortured, mutilated, and dehumanized. Their injuries are psychological as well as physical.

They are suffering from many diseases such as dysentery, dehydration, advanced emaciation, large ulcers on feet and hands, leg edemas, and pneumonia. We suspect some have typhus and probably tuberculosis. Despite the cold weather, these men are infested with lice and other vermin. We put their fecal-stained, wretched-smelling clothing in large piles and burned them.

I served as an interpreter and explained we were going to use our gas-powered DDT sprayers to delouse them. Initially, they became agitated, apparently the DDT dispensing container resembled other gas containers being used for various disciplinary purposes in the Nazi POW camp. We alleviated their fears by spraying the DDT on ourselves to show them it wasn't harmful to us. After we did this, they posed no further protest.

We had them strip naked. I explained it would be necessary to shave their body hair from their personal areas. All complied without complaint. We liberally sprayed these people with the DDT, killing any remaining lice or other parasites on their bodies.

Over half of these men were diagnosed with tuberculosis and were separated and placed in quarantine. The cacophony of coughing fits within this group of men was strident and could be heard throughout the camp. It was disturbing to say the least.

Because they are so badly malnourished, we resorted to feeding them soups and other lighter fare until their digestive workings recover. Initially, we provided them ample amounts of our army rations, but this caused them much intestinal distress. We had to forcibly stop them from gorging on these rations as their fragile digestive systems couldn't handle the sudden influx of solid foods.

In total, we found over 40 dead in the woods. Mostly from exhaustion or hypothermia, we suspect. Many tried to stay alive by placing the dead body of one of their comrades on top of themselves for warmth. This was the case with the man that Louis killed. The Russian soldier underneath was still clinging to life. We found several of the dead who perished in this manner.

Robert (Louis) has been beside himself with grief. Others and I have talked to him several times. He was defending himself in a combat zone. He made a split-second decision and given the circumstance, I suspect I might have done the same thing.

It's haunting him. He said he looked into the man's eyes before he bore down on him. Louis thinks he panicked under pressure. No action will be taken against him as this was considered an accident and was documented as such.

He wants to write the Russian man's family in condolence. I wouldn't know the right words to use under the situation. Maybe the chaplain could help; I'll suggest it to Robert.

JOURNAL ENTRY
11 DECEMBER 1944

The entire platoon was called to a meeting today. We were told English speaking Germans were apprehended at one of our checkpoints. They had stolen American uniforms and vehicles and were posing as American soldiers.

They were seeking intelligence on our activities. We've been alerted to be aware and if we have any suspicions, we should ask a series of questions only Americans could answer. Things like state capitals, sports questions, etc.

We were also briefed on American soldiers who were murdered at Malmedy in Belgium. Leibold told us the Germans murdered almost 100 defenseless American POWs. Many were killed by close range shots to the head.

This has really riled us up and galvanized our resolve to take revenge. I'm a medic and trained to save lives, but I'm not sure I can medically treat another Kraut soldier ever again. We're fighting with a high level of purpose now. There will be less mercy shown to captured or wounded Kraut soldiers.

JOURNAL ENTRY-SUPPLEMENTAL
11 DECEMBER 1944

Almost forgot. Today is my 27th birthday. Happy Birthday to me.

CHAPTER 50:
FROM METZ TO MONTMÉDY, FRANCE DECEMBER 1944

ON DECEMBER 22nd, the 648th Clearing Company was still in Metz, but eight days earlier the Germans had launched their largest offensive of the war in the nearby Ardennes. This conflict would become known as the "Battle of the Bulge," one of the fiercest and bloodiest battles in American history.

Leibold called Krow to his tent to deliver a new set of orders. "As far as we can tell, the German offensive has done considerable damage to our ability to hold the front lines near the Ardennes. This is turning out to be the largest conflict since Normandy. In the event we cannot hold off the German advance and the Krauts continue to push the front lines backward, we will need to find a safe place further to the rear to treat the casualties."

The captain unfurled a map and placed it over a makeshift table. He pointed his finger at a city on the French and Belgian border. "I need you to take a scouting party to Montmédy. If the Germans break us at Bastogne, they will race to the Meuse River. Our infantry will take a stand there to prevent them from crossing. We need a "safe" place for the clearing company to operate. Find a location to keep us out of the line of fire, but close enough to the river and roads so we have evacuation options."

"When do we leave?" Krow asked.

"Tomorrow morning," Leibold said. "There's one more thing. Your route will take you south of a German Panzer division which is striking near the Meuse. Our intelligence says the Krauts should stay north of you, but with the bad weather and poor visibility, you should stay vigilant in case you, or they, get lost."

JOURNAL ENTRY
22 DECEMBER 1944

We leave for Montmédy tomorrow morning. This has changed so fast. At Thanksgiving time, we all thought we would be home by Christmas.

Now our friends near Bastogne have said they are fighting the entire German army. This morning, we started to receive truckloads of badly wounded men from that sector. The injuries were ghastly and reminded me of the types of injuries we dealt with back in the Normandy days.

I also must tell four of my men goodbye. We have a rough seniority system in place where we keep a record of each medic and their days spent directly on the front lines. I try not to select any surgical techs to go to the front lines as their skills in surgery are needed. So, the selection comes down to the recent replacement medics who have joined our platoon. All of them are young and inexperienced but have put in at least three months of aid training with us.

The captain said this is a permanent reassignment, meaning these men won't be coming back to our unit. We send away four trained men and in return, we will be getting another set of green replacements, and the cycle continues.

Unfortunately, McCaulley, Pfeister, Fress, and Jefferry have the least front-line combat experience. Two of them are only 18 years old, cocky and itching for a fight. I was the same way until the bullets started to fly. Combat reveals the true make-up of a person's fortitude and integrity. They will learn on the battlefield that it's sometimes hard to do the right thing or to know what that is.

At 0700 the next morning, Krow and the other nine men crammed inside their vehicles and departed Metz. Day break clouds gave way to a clear blue sky and the men witnessed the awesome power of hundreds of U.S. war planes flying overhead.

After a week of bad weather, the U.S. Air Force was back in business. C-47 cargo planes dropped supplies to the beleaguered troops who were holding down the city of Bastogne. American bombers pounded the German forces ringing the city.

Krow's scouting party was 30 miles from Montmédy when one of its jeeps hit a patch of black ice on a curved section of the road and slid into an ice-covered gully. No one was injured but pushing the vehicle out of the ditch proved troublesome. They were deploying the winch from the other truck when they heard the high-pitched sound of mechanical treads coming up behind them. From their vantage point, the men couldn't see *who* it was, but they knew *what* it was.

"Tanks coming from the rear! Get the winch hooked up and let's get the hell out of here!" Krow barked. "Coop, look behind us and tell me what you see. Everybody else, get behind the jeep and push like hell!"

Coop spied motion and figures approaching the bend in the road. He pointed his finger in their direction. "Germans! I see horses pulling mobile petroleum tanks, and two Krauts guiding the horses, flanked by Panzers."

Krow reacted fast and barked out a set of orders. "Get your weapons and jump into the ditch. Go for the fuel tanks first, and then fire at the Panzers!"

The men scrambled to remove their gear from the trucks. While the medics concentrated their efforts based on what was coming up behind them, they failed to see two German soldiers slowly creeping out of the woods directly *across* from them. The Germans had their weapons drawn and caught the unsuspecting medics by surprise.

"Hands up and drop to your knees." one of the enemy soldiers commanded.

Krow was shocked. "What the…" He quickly considered his options but came up blank. *We're fucked.* He nodded reluctantly and slowly dropped to his knees.

"Do everything I say, and you will live." Krow noted the enemy soldier had an odd accent for someone wearing a German uniform. He narrowed his eyes and gave the man a puzzled look.

"*Oui*, I am French. I will explain soon. Keep your hands up in the air," he demanded.

Krow's eyes nearly came out of their sockets when he recognized the second "enemy" soldier. It was Andrew Radminsky. The last time he had seen Radminsky, he was a POW digging latrines for the U.S. Army. Radminsky nodded at him, as if everything was under control.

"Stay still," the French soldier whispered to the medics while he kept his eyes locked on the approaching Panzers. He waved and signaled for the Germans to continue moving toward them.

Krow desperately tried to assess the situation. *What the hell is happening?*

When the Panzers came within 70 yards of their position, tremendous flashes of light burst from the woods on both sides of the road. All became suddenly clear, the German tanks had been lured into a crossfire ambush.

Concealed in the woods on both sides of the road, French artillery launched anti-tank missiles, scoring direct hits on the German Panzers, killing them instantly. French sharpshooters took out the horse carriage drivers. The surprise attack was a success and took less than two minutes. The horses began to spook but were calmed down and taken by Frenchmen.

"You may stand up and relax, *messieurs*. We are friends," said the Frenchman in the German uniform. He explained they were part of the

French Resistance. Their militia acted as a guerrilla group harassing the Germans, blowing up weapons depots, stealing supplies, etc.

The Frenchman further explained that he was wounded during one of these fights and was treated in Fougères. It was there where he met Radminsky, who offered his services to the French leader. After a stout round of vetting, the Frenchman secured Radminsky's release from camp.

As a former German Quartermaster now working for the resistance, Radminsky had proven himself a clever and resourceful ally for the French. The Czech was more than happy to take vengeance on the Germans for sending him on the suicide mission in Avranches.

"Why are you wearing the German uniforms?" Krow asked.

A wry smile came across the Frenchman's face. "Let's say one good turn deserves another. The Nazi bastards kill Americans and steal their uniforms and vehicles. English-speaking Germans wear the U.S. army uniforms and cross over the lines and act as spies for the Krauts. It only seems fitting that we 'borrow' German uniforms and return the favor."

The Frenchman reached in his breast pocket for a packet of cigarettes and continued explaining. "Radminsky speaks excellent German. He lures the supply units to our hidden position in the woods and we strike them down. We keep their horses and fuel supplies. It's a good game, no?"

He pointed at the American jeep still stuck in the ditch. "Let us help you get your vehicle out of the gully and get you on your way." He lit the cigarette and waved for additional manpower to push the jeep back onto the road.

Twenty minutes later, the medics were back en route to Montmédy.

Coop was the first to speak. "Krow, can you pull the jeep over for a minute?"

Krow gave him a sideways glance. "What for?"

"I need to rummage through my pack for something,"

"It's a bad time to stop. What do you need?" Krow asked him.

"I need some clean underwear because I shit my pants back there."

CHAPTER 51:
MONTMÉDY, FRANCE
DECEMBER 1944

WHEN THE American medics arrived in Montmédy, they went to work on selecting an appropriate location where they could safely store their vehicles and equipment. Despite the Germans destroying many buildings and structures during their retreat from Montmédy, they seemed to have missed several miles of fortified blockhouses which ringed the city. Krow's team found an abandoned blockhouse outside the city limits that seemed to suit their purpose well.

The first day was spent canvassing the entire area for signs of German soldiers. Having found none, the team of medics returned to the blockhouse and stayed there for the evening. The men woke on Christmas Eve to bitter temperatures. It was safer, though certainly not warmer, to do reconnaissance on foot instead of driving a vehicle on icy and snow packed streets. The medics found several adjoining blockhouses that could serve as wards for their clearing company, and later located a hospital that was vacated by the Germans upon their retreat. After checking it out, Krow and his unit determined that it remained undamaged and could support the entire 109th Evacuation Hospital. They called in their findings and returned to their blockhouse to hunker down for the evening.

Upon their return, the medics covered the small windows and firing holes with towels and other objects to establish blackout conditions inside the cement hut. They drew straws for guard duty shifts, rotating every two hours until sunrise. Some of the medics ignited their shoe polish-shaped cans of Sterno to warm their hands and cook their C-rations. The small blue flame sizzling from the Sterno cans produced the only light inside the hut. It was like being in a dark cave with eight flickering fireflies.

"Would anybody like to join me for some Christmas Spam?" Rollins popped the top and shoveled a teaspoon of the lukewarm mystery meat into his mouth.

There was a general sullenness in the room with most of the men pecking at their bland rations. It was the night before Christmas, and the medics were spending their holiday in a colorless cement hut built for the sole purpose of killing anyone who came near it.

Coop offered a more creative idea. "How about we go through our sacks and see what we can find and do one of those white elephant gift exchanges? It might liven this place up a bit."

Louis was pouring hot water into a tin cup and was suddenly energized. "That's a swell idea! I miss being home tonight just like you sad sacks do. But it doesn't do us any good to mope about it." He pointed his finger at each man, egging them on to get into the spirit of the game.

The last person he came to was Krow. "Sarge, you in?"

Krow didn't hesitate. "I'm in, and I hope I don't get bamboozled by any gift-stealing sharks!"

That sealed it. The men rummaged through their duffle bags for suitable gifts. No wrapping was necessary. Coop ripped a piece of paper into ten pieces and wrote numbers from one to ten. Then he flipped his steel helmet over like a bucket and dumped the numbers into it. "Everyone bring your Sternos and put them in front of you so we can see what we're doing."

Louis put a blanket on the floor and the men gathered around and piled their "gifts" in the center. When Louis proclaimed himself the master of ceremonies, Coop didn't object.

"Okay, boys and girls, welcome to Christmas in Montmédy. For tonight's game, we offer the following gifts for your perusal: one deck of used playing cards, one set of dice, two colored pencils, one French postcard, one box of dried apricots, one chocolate bar, and three cigarettes. Quite a nice selection, if I do say so myself!"

When guard duty rotated, a postcard from Verdun, four sticks of chewing gum, and a pinup poster of Veronica Farmer from Yank magazine were added the pile. The poster was contributed by 18-year-old Steven McCaulley.

His friend Pfiester let a zinger fly. "McCaulley, how are you going to *yank* yourself without that poster?" After a good laugh, the game got underway.

The first person selected a gift, and one by one, each player could pick a gift or steal one from another person. The game was indeed a fun distraction from the melancholy of not being home for the holidays. At the end, Krow's "present" was the French postcard.

"Could you men sign your names to this card? I don't believe any of us will ever forget where we were on Christmas Eve 1944." After everyone signed the card, he gently folded it and put it in his wallet for safe keeping.

Afterward, Krow moved away from the group and leaned his stiff back against a wall. He wrapped his army issued blanket over his shoulders and with the adrenaline from the game wearing off, exhaustion set in. In the dim light, he could see the other guys settling in for the evening. Some used their rucksacks as pillows, while others pulled their blankets over their heads to stay warm.

Krow closed his eyes. *I'll never forget this night.*

JOURNAL ENTRY
25 DECEMBER 1944

It's Christmas Day and I said goodbye to four of the men this morning. McCaulley, Pfeister, Fress, and Jefferry are heading to the front lines to replace infantry aidmen who were killed or wounded. Six of us remain to finish our recon work.

Once the villagers learned we were Americans, we became local celebrities. The townspeople seemed weary but buoyant. Their city had been in German control since 1940 and liberated by Americans only a few months ago. The locals are rebuilding their village, and don't want to hear that the liberators have lost any ground. They tell *us they already burned their swastika flags, so it needs to stay that way.*

The mayor of the town spoke some English and invited us to celebrate Christmas church services with them. The village priest didn't speak English, but we followed along well enough. It's interesting that we all sing the same Christmas carols: Silent Night, Noel, and Hark the Herald Angels, only the language is different. After church, the Belgians invited us to the rectory where they served black bread and pea soup for lunch.

The guys and I searched our packs and gave out chocolate bars and boxes of raisins and dried apricots to the children. The kids got excited and jumped up and down when we presented our impromptu gifts to them.

Spending time with these young ones reminded me of home. I should be spending Christmas with Mary and celebrating with my family. Instead, I'm stuck in this godforsaken place, with no end in sight. A few weeks ago, the Krauts were on the run, but now, they may have taken the upper hand in this never-ending war. I sure as hell don't want to spend a third Christmas here, as nice as everyone is being to us.

It neared 2000 hours and Krow was getting ready for his night guard duty shift. He wore a long sleeve wool shirt under his jacket and used a spare undershirt as a scarf to cover his neck and mouth. He made a headband out of three lightly used socks to protect his sensitive ears from the icy wind. But despite banging on the top of his metal helmet, he couldn't make it fit over the headband. Letting the helmet sit askew on his head was the best he could do.

The early guard detail chipped out slit trenches two-feet deep, two-feet wide, and six-feet long. The trenches resembled burial coffins and were dug on alternate sides of the main road.

Louis had finished his shift a few hours earlier and except for taking off his helmet, was still bundled up. He flipped over a steel bucket, used it as a chair, and became preoccupied digging through his belongings. He took out what he was looking for and sat on it like a hen keeping her eggs warm. A moment later, a large shadow cast over him. He glanced up and chuckled when Krow walked past him toward the door.

"Sarge, you look like a vagrant." Louis rubbed his hands together.

"Are the trenches deep enough?" Krow asked as he bent over to grab his M1 Garrard rifle.

"Merry Christmas to you too, Sarge," Louis wisecracked.

Krow shot him an exasperated look. He was in no mood for humor.

Louis softened his voice. "The coffins are plenty deep, Sarge." Louis waited until Krow was ready to pull the door open and timed his delivery perfectly. "Hey Sarge!"

Krow wheeled toward him. "What now?"

Louis reached under his butt and tossed something to Krow. "I kept these warm for you."

Krow caught a pair of hand-made wool mittens. "Huh? Where did you get these?"

"I traded my stash of cigarettes to a local bootlegger. Stay warm out there," Louis smiled.

Krow pulled on the mittens, and indeed they were warm. Louis's thoughtfulness got the better of him, and he kept his eyes riveted on the floor as his sight became blurry. He pressed his lips together and clapped the mittens a few times as a distraction. Krow didn't want to have a full meltdown in front of his men.

"Merry Christmas, Sarge." Louis winked.

Krow couldn't speak, so he simply nodded his thanks. He grabbed his rifle and reached for the door handle. A rush of cold air smacked into his face as he trudged into the darkness. A recent flurry blanketed the ground with powdery snowflakes, and it left an insulated quietness across the countryside. Coop was already in his trench, and Krow was replacing Rollins a hundred yards ahead.

Krow stayed low as he maneuvered from the hut to his slit trench. At 50 yards, he clicked his chirper to signal to Coop he was passing by. When he neared Rollins, he clicked again and Rollins returned a two click response, indicating he understood a "friendly" was approaching.

At 10 yards away, Krow dropped completely to his stomach and shimmied the rest of the way toward Rollins. When he got to the trench, Rollins was bundled up in a wool blanket. He had icicles hanging from his nose and was shivering badly.

"Rolly, you okay?" Krow asked.

"My ball sack is up to my neck, and I can't feel my toes," he said through trembling lips.

"Sorry to hear about your marbles. Anything to report?"

"No, Sarge, all quiet."

"You're relieved. Stay as low as possible on your way back to camp. The high moon produces a shadow and betrays any movement."

Rollins nodded and rolled out of the trench. He did the required clicks as he passed Coop on his return, and everything became dead quiet once again. But not for long.

Coop was laying on his stomach in his trench when he thought he heard a noise. Like a turtle, he slowly inched his head above the trench. He listened for a few minutes and thought he recognized the sounds. He didn't want to use his radio due to the stillness of the night. The crackle from turning it on might give away his position.

He decided to leave his post and snake his way to Krow. When he was within 10 yards, he clicked twice. No response. Cooper slowly crawled on his elbows another 5 yards, he chirped again and waited. He heard Krow's return click and a second later, he was beside the trench peering down at him.

Krow was on high alert and had his rifle in the firing position. "What the hell is going on?"

Coop chuckled quietly when he saw Krow in his makeshift garb. "Louis was right," he said.

"About what?"

"About you looking like a vagrant."

"You came all this way just to blow me crap?"

"Take off your helmet and your headband," Coop insisted. Krow did as instructed and plucked the cotton balls out of his ears. He grimaced as the frigid air seeped inside.

"Can you hear those sounds?" Coop asked him.

"I can't hear shit! Wait a minute … yes, yes, I can hear it now. I'll be damned!"

Somewhere in the distance, they heard a single flute-like tonette, but as they listened intently, more tonettes joined in. The instruments were played off-key and without rhythm; it was clearly a bunch of musical amateurs. But to the two medics on guard duty, it was a lovely rendition of *Silent Night*. Despite being so far away from home, Krow and Coop drew comfort knowing they weren't alone. Other American units were nearby, spending Christmas 1944 in their foxholes.

CHAPTER 52:
BELGIUM DECEMBER 1944– FEBRUARY 1945

KROW AND his men rejoined the balance of the 1st Platoon in Metz on December 27th. Upon arrival, they were given orders to relocate their clearing company near the city of Bastogne, Belgium. Fighting in sub-zero temperatures was brutal, and the brave soldiers defending the city of Bastogne suffered greatly. Many developed severe frostbite requiring amputations of fingers and toes. Krow's platoon stayed south of Bastogne through most of February treating the injured.

JOURNAL ENTRY
NEAR BASTOGNE, BELGIUM
29 DECEMBER 1944

The American tank took a direct hit from German 88s. The men trapped inside were burned to a crisp, except for one unlucky soul. How he slithered out of the inferno no one knows. But he wouldn't make it either. He knew it, and I knew it.

His face was badly disfigured, and he couldn't speak. When we made eye contact, I knew what he wanted me to do. Still, I asked him the question to be sure. Blink once for yes, or twice for no. He blinked once.

Two syrettes of morphine were all it took. Out here it's called mercy, back home it's called something else.

I closed his eyes, took his tags, and left his body there. Smoldering.

JOURNAL ENTRY
SOUTH OF BASTOGNE, BELGIUM
28 JANUARY 1945

I received word today that medic, Steven McCaulley, was killed in action. Six months ago, he was a kid in high school with his whole life in front of him. I picked him to go to the front. It's been hard not to think about it.

After a continuous 12 weeks of working in a combat zone, the men of the 1st Platoon were ready to be relieved. In early March, the unit was reassigned to the 34th Medical Hospital in Asch, Luxembourg devoted to the care of accidental and self-inflicted wounds. They spent two weeks in Luxemburg and their work was light.

The men were able to improve their hygiene, as well as spend time sightseeing and eating at the local diners which catered to American soldiers. The combat-weary medics enjoyed their down time immensely.

JOURNAL ENTRY
LUXEMBOURG, BELGIUM
23 MARCH 1945

Captain Leibold called me into his office today. He told me the Third Army is in a heated battle to capture Frankfurt. We'll be leaving in two days to set up our clearing company in the combat area. Looks like our relaxing time in Luxembourg is drawing to a close.

The last two weeks have been blissful. We had a chance to decompress and take real showers. I got my hair cut without the fear of stray bullets scalping me. After only being able to send Mary a letter once a week at most, I was able to write her every day. It strikes me that we've been apart longer than we've been married.

I'm having a hard time staying positive in my letters. In truth, I thought being a medic would be a noble thing. It's not. Each day is the same. We treat ghastly wounds and listen to the last breaths of dying soldiers. The infantry men can leave the blood and guts behind them after each skirmish and catch a break from it on some days, though I don't envy them either.

There are amputations every day. After doing this for so long, we feel numb when we dispose of limbs and body parts once belonging to someone. In the Ardennes, we didn't have time for proper disposal of extremities, so we had the German POWs dig large pits in the fields away from the hospital. We would have them take wheelbarrows full of arms, legs, and other body parts and dump them into pits and cover them with lime. Each night, the POWs would shovel the dirt back into the holes.

In combat, I can count more than 100 times when I left someone's body parts on the battlefield. I tried my best to retrieve as many as I could but it's not always possible. Back in the Ardennes, I treated a soldier whose leg was blown off by a German 88. I put a tourniquet on the wound to stop the bleeding and dumped sulfa powder on the exposed part, followed by a shot of morphine. Then I noticed his blown off leg a few feet away, the leg still had his boot on it. I grabbed it and used adhesive tape to tie the leg tightly to the man's chest. I told him to hold on to his leg as I buckled him securely onto a litter.

Chances are always low our surgeons can reattach the limb, but it seemed like a clean break, so I took the chance. The next day, I checked on the man, and the attending surgeon told me the leg I strapped to the wounded man's chest was someone else's leg. And it was the wrong side. The Doc told me if he attached the limb, the boy would have ended up with two right legs. What the fuck was I thinking?

Easy mistake to make, right? Heat of the battle, body parts laying everywhere, bombs going off, I've been thinking about the boy every day since. It's bothering me that I gave him hope his leg might be reattached. I looked into his eyes and told him to hold onto to his leg tightly. I can't imagine how he felt when he learned he had been clutching someone else's blown off leg the entire time he was evacuated. I feel like a fucking dumbass and probably gave the kid nightmares for life.

Being around death, whether it be humans or animals, sometimes seems easier than being with the living wounded. The most difficult decisions are how to prioritize which soldiers need immediate aid. In combat, there are always more wounded soldiers than medics to treat them. There are many times where I had to decide in a split second who gets immediate aid and who doesn't. It's crass, but on the battlefield, my way of screening wounded for treatment is a "pink man" gets priority over a "gray man."

In the Ardennes, I had to leave several soldiers on the battlefield, telling them I would return. I always did return, but often, it was too late. They were already gone. Watching someone perish is something I will never forget. The reduction in breaths, the death rattle, and it's over.

More than once, I've witnessed grown men asking for their mothers before dying. No matter how hard I try to push these scenes to the back of my brain, I know I'll never forget their cries.

A few months ago, I came upon a boy who was incinerated inside a burning tank. He had no skin, no facial features, and his body was cooked like a purple beet. He had no chance at surviving and was suffering greatly. Yet, he was still conscious.

He begged me for mercy. What was I to do? Should I have left him there to die in unfathomable agony? If I gave him two shots of morpho, there'd be two fewer syrettes to use with someone who has a fighting chance at survival. He used his eyes to blink his wishes to me. I gave him the shots. What's the right thing?

I wonder sometimes if I'm suffering from shell shock. After rereading my journal notes I can feel the anxiety building in my chest, I realize that I show some signs. When I'm busy during the day, I'm generally not affected by it. The devil visits me at night.

I need to get the platoon ready to leave for Germany in two days. There will be more killing before we win this thing, and now we're going to play on the Krauts' home court. My writing today is more negative than positive.

The source of my negativity is that each time we make a major push forward, we find these Germans to be clever in their dastardly methods of defense. We think we've seen every tactic by now, so we know what to expect. But we're hearing rumors of a secret weapon Hitler is developing, and no one has seen it.

I'll counterbalance with some optimism. In the larger picture, we're winning the war. We have momentum. All of us can sense it. After all, the Krauts are on the run, and we're about to enter their country.

CHAPTER 53:
GERMANY
MARCH 1945

U.S. Archives

JOURNAL ENTRY
BELGIUM-GERMAN BORDER
25 March 1945,

The 1st Platoon, as it seems is our lot, was the first to break camp and relocate to our next location. We left Luxemburg about a week ago and entered Germany. As we crossed the Luxembourg-German border, we were greeted by large signs.

ENTERING GERMANY. AN ENEMY COUNTRY.

DO NOT FRATERNIZE.

For the past three and a half years, we read and heard so much about this country. And now here I am, an American soldier standing on German soil. This will be a day all of us will never forget.

✦ ✦ ✦

After the German infantry moved their soldiers across the Rhine into Germany, they destroyed the bridges to slow the crossing of Allied troops. The Germans were hoping to buy time to regroup and determine their next plan of action.

The Allies planned to press forward to prevent the Germans from having a chance to reorganize. The heroes of the Rhine River crossing were the Army Corps of Engineers. These ingenious soldiers assembled a series of pontoon bridges over the Rhine in record time.

To camouflage this work, the engineers utilized huge canisters filled with a chemical mixture that produced enormous smoke screens when ignited. This would provide cover for American troops and equipment entering Germany.

Though they couldn't see the pontoon bridges, the Nazis still dispatched small guerrilla artillery groups and positioned them on the banks of the Rhine to harass the Americans who were trying to cross the river. The Germans lobbed their rockets into the smokescreen to buy more time for their retreating army. Most of the bombs landed harmlessly in the river.

Except for one.

✦ ✦ ✦

"Why do we always have to do important shit in the dark? I can't see two feet in front of me inside this smokescreen. How am I supposed to drive like this?" Louis griped to Rollins, who was in the passenger seat of their medical ambulance loaded with supplies. They were in a line of vehicles assembled at Pontoon Bridge "G", waiting for their turn to cross the Rhine and move deeper into Germany territory, God willing.

Rollins rolled his eyes. "Stop your yapping and pay attention. The flagger signaled for us to proceed." Louis pulled even with the flagger and received his instructions.

"No more than 10 miles an hour," the flagger said. "Give the truck in front of you plenty of room, as we don't want any wrecks on these bridges. Don't stop moving and stay inside your vehicle at all times."

Louis made a sour face. The guard laughed and waved them ahead. Louis pressed the gas pedal and his vehicle slowly lurched forward onto the wobbly pontoon platform. "Holy shit!" he screeched. Trying to steady the vehicle while staying between the cables on either side of him was incredibly challenging, especially with the thick smoke that made visibility almost nil.

"Rolly, can you see the vehicle ahead of us?"

"Nope," Rollins said." I can't see a blessed thing. Keep going nice and slow, and we should remain separated by 20 yards. Do you feel like your tires are still inside the grooves?"

"Yeah," Louis replied, hands gripping the wheel." I can feel the rims banging the sides of the rails. We're good."

Their eyes were glued on the windshield, trying to make sure they didn't get too close to the jeep in front of them. As a result, neither man noticed the dislodged latch on the back door of the ambulance. Each time the jeep drove over a buckle connecting the bridge links, boxes of cargo spilled out the back door.

They were one third of the way into their journey when Rollins asked. "Louis, is somebody honking their horn at us?"

"Huh, what?" Louis was too busy focusing to hear anything.

"Someone honked, from somewhere behind us," Rollins repeated.

"What do you want me to do? I'm not supposed to stop!" Louis barked back.

Rollins put his head out the passenger window to get a look behind him. At first, he couldn't see anything but a movement behind the truck caught his eye. "Shit, the back doors are swinging open! We're losing our cargo! Slow down and I'll jump out and secure the back doors."

"You might get run over!" Louis barked. "The security guard told us to keep moving and stay inside."

Rollins squinted into the smoke. "The guys behind us are the ones honking at us. They must be running into the boxes of cargo. Slow down and I'll hop out. I'll be fast."

Louis was unbending. "You are not exiting this vehicle."

Rollins huffed. "I personally loaded and packed this ambulance. The penicillin was the last third of the cargo I loaded. If it was anything else I'd forget about it, but we really need the penicillin."

Louis understood penicillin was a miracle drug. He also understood that Germany and its vicious army loomed at the end of the pontoon bridge. He knew the Nazis would fight like cornered animals to defend their country, resulting in lots of casualties.

"Fuck! Ok! Don't spend any time trying to retrieve cargo which dropped behind us. Just secure the latch and get your lame ass back here." Louis slowed the truck and Rollins leaped out the passenger door.

When his feet hit the ground, Rollins felt the unsteadiness of the pontoon bridge. It was undulating heavily under the weight of all the vehicles. He gripped the side of the ambulance and shimmied his way to the back of the truck. He was about to latch the rear door when he noticed a box of penicillin at his feet. Rollins thought about picking it up and tossing it into the back of the truck.

He waited one second too long…

CHAPTER 54:
CROSSING THE RHINE, GERMANY MARCH 1945

"CAN'T THOSE guys hear our horn!" Krow barked. "Speed up and I'll try yelling at them."

For the last few minutes, the ambulance driven by Coop was running over boxes dropped out of the back door of the ambulance ahead of them. The boxes were starting to get stuck underneath the carriage of their vehicle, which made Krow concerned it would grind them to a halt.

Rollins was bent over lifting the box of penicillin when he saw the trailing ambulance bearing down on him. His eyes went wide.

"Coop!!! Hit the brakes!! Stop!!" Krow screeched as Rollins materialized a mere three feet in front of him.

Coop tried, but he didn't have enough warning. Rollins was about to get crushed when a "screaming Mimi" detonated in the water next to them. The concussive effect of the bomb vaulted Rollins off the bridge and spun him like a top into the water below.

Krow and Coop face-planted into their dashboard as they crashed into the jeep in front of them. Luckily, they were able to brace themselves just before impact. They were shaken but not injured.

"Where's Rollins? Did I hit him?" Cooper screamed.

Krow leaped from the passenger door and gripped the side mirror to steady himself. As quickly as possible, he moved to the spot where he thought Rollins landed in the river.

Louis appeared out of the mist two seconds later. "Do you see Rolly? I shouldn't have stopped. Oh God, where is he?" he screamed.

Both men scanned the brown water below, screaming Rollins name at the top of their lungs. But there was no sign of him in the dark, murky water.

Though they couldn't see him, Rollins was alive when he plunged into the river. During maneuvers, the men had trained for being submerged in water with their gear. There was a three-step process. Coat off. Use holsters as paddles. Swim to the light. Rollins was able to get two out of the three maneuvers completed. He had a leg wound, and "swim to the light" was a problem. Between the smokescreen and the murky river water, he was disorientated and saw only blackness.

Krow ordered Louis back into his ambulance and told him to get his vehicle moving. He did the same with Coop. Krow knew the mission was paramount, though it pained him deeply to leave Rollins behind. As they moved deeper into enemy territory, he couldn't risk causing more collisions, or halting progress all together to search for a man overboard. Heart aching, Krow jumped in the jeep with Coop but yelled out the window to Rollins as loudly as he could.

Rollins did his best not to panic. He kept blowing bubbles and followed their ascent toward the surface. When his head popped out of water, he gulped the air. He still couldn't see anything due to the lingering smokescreen, but he did, however, hear the convoy's heavy wheels creaking as they rolled over the joints of the pontoon bridge.

The river's current was taking him away from the bridge. As he assessed the situation, his only chance to live was to use the current to his advantage. Meanwhile, Krow was still hanging his head out the window and yelling nonstop.

Despite his cranky ears, Krow thought he heard something. "Coop, did you hear that? It's coming from your side."

"Rolly, can you hear me?" Coop screamed loud enough to wake the dead.

"Yes!" Rollins screamed back for all he was worth. "I'm behind you but the current is taking me away from the bridge." Rollins didn't realize he was leaving a small red trail as he drifted away.

Krow made a split-second call. "I'm going after him. Hand me the life vests under the seat. Send a message to Leibold telling him two men are overboard and that we'll do our best to rendezvous somewhere downriver on the German side."

Coop frowned and pointed to Krow's ears. "You'll get disorientated, and you're a terrible swimmer. We don't want two dead bodies. I'll go." Krow was reluctant but agreed with Coop's logic.

Coop stopped the vehicle, grabbed the life vests, and dove into the water. Krow slid into the driver's seat, thrust the gear shift into drive, and resumed moving. Immediately, he regretted his decision to allow Coop to go after Rollins. *Now two men under my command are in the water.*

Rollins and Coop used their voices to locate each other. Once they came into contact, Coop helped Rollins secure his life vest and helped him to paddle with the current. Unfortunately, they drifted out of the protective shield of the smokescreen and became visible in open water. Behind them, they could see the massive smokescreens concealing the movement of Allied troops across the Rhine. The crack of a German Karabiner 98 rifle broke the silence.

"We're being fired upon!" Coop yelled. "Dive!"

They tried to wrestle their way out of their life vests. Rollins struggled, his lips turning purple, and his injured leg hindering his progress. Seeing his friend's distress, Coop grabbed the back of Rollins' shirt and yanked him under. Bullets sliced through the water all around them but miraculously, they evaded them.

The men surfaced and gulped some air and continued to take periodic sniper fire from the hillside.

Rollins was laboring and it became a struggle for Coop to keep him alert. The exertion and his injury weakened him considerably. His face was becoming ashen, and his lips turned deep purple.

"C'mon Rolly, stay with me!" Coop barked, trying to keep his friend alert. He was starting to fear the worst when he heard a motorized vessel pounding its way in their direction. It was a nimble U.S. Higgins boat and the soldiers on board were firing twin .30 caliber machine guns toward the German gunners on the other side of the Rhine. Coop had his left arm around Rollins' neck and paddled with his right arm toward the Higgins.

The lead boat curled around them as a second Higgins sprayed the hillside with machine gun fire to provide cover for the rescue boat.

A muscular arm hauled in Rollins. Another arm heaved Coop into the boat.

Bullets continued to zip past as the pilot hit full throttle to get them out of the area. The second Higgins hung behind to provide cover fire while the rescue boat sped away to safer water.

Coop was on his back, heaving from the exertion. "Rolly, we made it!" No answer.

"Rolly, thank God, we made it!" Cooper repeated. Still, no answer.

Rollins was barely conscious; he lost a lot of blood and his pulse had slowed substantially. Cooper grabbed him by the collar and repeatedly yelled his name.

Rollins blinked and locked eyes with his friend. He tried to open his mouth to whisper a thank you, but he was too weak.

A heartbeat later, he was gone.

CHAPTER 55:
FRANKFURT, GERMANY
MARCH 1945

LATER, IT was revealed that a sniper's bullet was the official cause of death. The slug entered through Rollins' back and nicked his aorta, which caused him to bleed out. Whether the bullet struck him when he was lifted into the Higgins or before, no one knew for sure.

Only Coop knew of Rollins' death. Krow and the rest of his platoon were unaware of the loss of their dear friend. They had to focus on the here and now as they were moving through enemy territory. Germans were everywhere. Both soldiers and civilians.

The platoon passed through small German villages on their way to Frankfort. However, unlike the jubilant scenes witnessed in allied territories, where enthusiastic crowds would line the streets to cheer the American "liberators," a stark contrast awaited them. Suspicious townspeople cautiously peered through cracked doors, their expressions filled with dismay. It was evident that these conquered people struggled to comprehend the magnitude of the circumstances that had just befallen them.

JOURNAL ENTRY
26 MARCH 1945, FRANKFURT, GERMANY

We arrived in Frankfurt with no incident. It was here I learned the devastating news of Rollins' death. This morning he was alive, and this evening he is dead. I feel it's because of me that Rolly is gone. What did I think would happen when I asked Coop to blare his horn? Of course, Louis or Rollins would exit their vehicle to see what the problem was.

No one stops and no one gets out of the vehicle. Those were our instructions. If I would have simply followed orders, Scott might still be alive.

What the fuck was I supposed to do? Cargo was falling out of their truck; it was getting stuck under our vehicle, and we were dragging it. If it continued, it could have stopped us in our tracks or worse, our tires would have elevated over the rails and who knows what would have happened. Either way, all the vehicles behind us would have ground to a dead stop or rammed right into us. Worse yet, we would have all been sitting ducks.

I keep replaying the scene in my mind. I saw the look of shock on Scott's face when he thought our truck would hit him. But then the explosion threw him off the bridge and into the river. Because of the smoke screen, it was as if the river had swallowed him up.

One second, one fucking split second. Scott was there, and then he was gone. My grief and despair have overtaken me. I put these men in this situation. I'm the leader. I make the decisions and they follow them. Today I made the most horrible mistake imaginable. I keep rethinking the situation over and over again. There are no words for this, none. I can hardly bear it.

Leibold interviewed everyone involved in the incident. Each description was the same. It was a freak accident. It was no one's fault, so the official record reads. The army would write the standard "sorry for your loss" letter to Rollin's widow, the mother of the yet unborn child who would never know his or her brave father. Krow knew Janice Rollins deserved more, and he set out to describe the circumstances of Scott's death.

> *Dear Janice,*
>
> *It is with profound sadness and utmost grief I write to you about the circumstances of Scott's death. I was with Scott moments before he was killed. The truck he was on was hauling precious supplies of medicine across a pontoon bridge into enemy territory. For reasons still unknown, the lock on the rear door of the cargo truck disengaged and cases of valuable medicine were inadvertently being discharged from the back of his supply truck. Under the dark cloak of a protective smokescreen, and with the looming threat of enemy fire, Scott jumped from his vehicle and bravely retrieved many boxes of badly needed medicine from being destroyed or damaged.*
>
> *A German bomb exploded a few yards from where Scott was standing, and its impact caused him to fall into the river below. He was alive and we made contact with him, but due to the heavy smoke being used to camouflage our convoy, visibility between us was nearly zero and we could not determine his location.*
>
> *Dean Cooper bravely dove into the river and successfully located Scott. He was alive and resilient, but by then, both men had drifted outside of the camouflage of the smokescreen and became exposed to enemy fire.*
>
> *An American rescue boat was dispatched to locate and pick them up. The rescue boat was taking German fire from the riverbank and returned counter fire in kind. A second boat provided the necessary cover so Scott and Dean could be hauled to safety.*
>
> *What I am about to tell you grieves me terribly. I am certain your profound loss and sadness will not be comforted in the least*

by learning Scott was killed by enemy sniper fire as he was being pulled from the water by the soldiers onboard the rescue boat. It happened quickly, and he would not have suffered.

There is little more I can say to alleviate your sorrow. But you may be consoled with the knowledge that Scott risked his life countless times and treated and rescued many American soldiers during combat who might have otherwise perished on the battlefield. He was a hero in the truest sense.

In closing, I write this letter to you with the deepest grief imaginable. Please accept my heartfelt sympathy to you and other members of your family.

—Krow

Krow reread his letter to Janice Rollins several times. He couldn't reconcile his part in her husband's death and worried he didn't explain the circumstances fully. Ultimately, he elected to rewrite portions of the letter later when he was thinking more clearly. Thus, he folded it and put it inside his journal for safe keeping.

Sadly, Scott Rollins' tragic death would not be the only memory that would plague these men. They were about to enter the most gruesome, inhumane place on earth.

CHAPTER 56:
GERMANY
APRIL 1945

JOURNAL ENTRY
APRIL 1945, TRAVELING TO SUHL, GERMANY

We stayed in Frankfurt for 10 days. On our way out, we saw scenes of destruction inflicted by our American Air Force on the larger German cities. We're traveling to Suhl, and much of this country has only recently been conquered. The smoking ruins of buildings and other equipment are still visible.

There are civilians hiding or living in these ruins, and I can literally feel the weight of all their eyes on our convoy as they stare through blown out windows and doorways. We observed a few sweeping up rubble from the street. For what purpose it was unclear. Maybe to have something to keep them busy. Maybe it was a sense of guilt.

Most of my men kept to themselves on this part of the journey. I didn't feel like talking either.

In mid-April 1945, the men of the 648th found themselves in Erfurt, Germany. The unit was treating many patients suffering from malnutrition. Their wounds were inconsistent with combat injuries. Most were Soviets or Poles who were captured and sent to labor camps in

Germany. Krow picked out a Polish resistance fighter and asked what happened to him.

Leibold stood by for the translation. "What did he say?"

"I'm not sure I understood him correctly," Krow replied. "He may be hallucinating or is mentally unstable. He says he's been a prisoner for about three years, and he talks of long lines of naked inmates waiting to enter a shower building. He says they go inside but never come out."

Leibold shook his head. "Ask him what he thinks happened to these inmates."

Krow translated the question into Polish and listened intently to the man's response. "He says it was a trick. The guards made it seem like everything was normal. They played loud music to drown out the screams but dying shrieks could be heard outside the building."

Leibold sighed heavily. "Ask him where they put all the dead bodies."

Krow translated and the soldier began to weep. Krow patted him on the knee and asked him to continue when he was ready. The man wiped his nose and spoke softly.

Krow felt chilled. What this man told him was too awful to be true. "He says the bodies were sent to the "bakery" and burned, and that he never got used to the smell."

"Are you sure you are translating this correctly?" Leibold asked, crossing his arms.

"Yes, pretty sure. I speak Americanized Polish but fundamentally, the words are the same."

Leibold excused himself and placed a call into Regiment HQ. He was told that a large, multi-campus POW camp, Buchenwald, had recently been liberated. The camp was located near the city of Weimar and was only 15 miles from their current location.

HQ asked Leibold if the 648th could spare any doctors and technicians, as they were needed at the camp. "What type of equipment should we bring to perform surgeries?"

This was the surprising response. "Bring your gas masks and tell your men to prepare themselves for the worst."

✦   ✦   ✦

Leibold selected Krow, Louis, Coop, and a few surgical techs to accompany him. As they drove through the front gates of the camp, the smell of decomposing flesh was overpowering. Krow covered his nose with his sleeve, but the stench still seeped through the fabric. The men witnessed hundreds of emaciated bodies shuffling about in filthy, fecal stained tattered uniforms. These poor souls were barely alive, eyes sunken and teeth rotted. How these skeletal prisoners had the strength to stand, Krow couldn't fathom.

Leibold and his medics were battle hardened and their jobs weren't for the faint of heart. But no level of experience prepared the tough medics for the atrocities they were about to witness.

They drove to the HQ tent where Captain W.R. Spaltman, the American medical liaison, was waiting for them. The men saluted, and Spaltman got right to it.

"Initially, our guys believed they liberated a POW camp. But the prisoners told them this was a death camp. The Krauts used the prisoners as slave laborers. When the POWs could no longer perform their work, they were executed. Bodies were buried in mass graves or burned in large crematoriums, many of them Jewish civilians." The men shook their heads, disbelieving. The Polish resistance fighter's story was true, and worse than they could ever have imagined.

"Bring your gas masks and follow me. I'll take you on an unvarnished tour of the grounds," Spaltman said.

Buchenwald would later come to be known for the bizarre medical experiments performed by Nazi doctors. Prisoners were taken against their will and subjected to the cruelest clinical experiments, more accurately described as medical torture.

Spaltman walked them to a building: a sign on the door was printed in German.

"What's the translation?" Leibold asked.

"It's the Center for Typhus and Virus Research of the Hygiene Institute of the Waffen SS. Victims were injected with various diseases and infections to test experimental vaccines. As a precaution, make sure your gas mask is secure as we walk through this facility."

As they walked inside, they came across two American MPs who were guarding a display table in the foyer.

"Are those from humans?" Louis pointed to rows and rows of form-aldehyde jars containing brains and other organs, his eyes practically popping from their sockets.

"Yes, though it's unclear what experiments were conducted on them. There's no need to go any further." Spaltman waved his hand at the door and the men shuffled out, stunned to silence.

Spaltman walked them up a steep grade, passing by a horse corral and stables. There was a well-maintained mansion on the top of the hill overlooking the camp. They stopped at the front door.

"This is the commandant's residence. Don't let the pristine setting fool you. Prisoners who worked here as maids helped the MPs discover some of the more disturbing pieces of evidence. You can remove your gas masks in here."

Spaltman led them into the living room, where an MP was guarding a bookshelf that held additional artifacts. Leibold walked to the shelf and examined the contents. "Are those what I think they are?"

"I am afraid so," Spaltman answered. "The prisoners told us they came from tortured Polish or Soviet soldiers."

Leibold was mesmerized by the tan leather faces of two shrunken heads. Krow stood a step behind, becoming increasingly horrified with every new revelation.

Louis was absorbed by the unusual patterns on several lampshades. "What's the story with this artwork?"

Spaltman winced. "The lampshades are made of human skin. What you think is "artwork" are tattoos cut from the bodies of the prisoners and sent to the camp tannery where they were fashioned into lamp-shades, wallets, and other goods. We're told the camp commandant gifted these products to visiting Nazi dignitaries."

Leibold swore. "I can't believe this! Please take us to the surgical tent so we can prep for surgery."

"You won't be needed for surgery," Spaltman answered softly but firmly.

"Then why are we here?" Leibold asked, blinking.

"So that you never forget this place and the atrocities that happened here."

19 April 1945

Dearest Mary—

By now you must be aware of the German concentration camps that our Army is liberating. We need to make the world aware of these awful places. We are supposed to document what we've seen to verify the existence of these hideous prisons. I visited such a camp a few days ago.

The contents of this letter will be gruesome for you to read. I'm not sure that my descriptions could ever adequately describe what I have witnessed. Nor do I believe that I will ever be able to erase these awful scenes from my memory.

I closed my eyes more than once, my brain denying that all of this is real, and yet this place exists, which disturbs me greatly. I don't know how to soften the tone of my writing. It's impossible to tamp down the subject matter so I've decided to share exactly what I have witnessed and detail it to you as graphically as I have experienced it.

As you enter camp, you see thousands of emaciated bodies shuffling about, eyes sunken. They are barely alive, more like living skeletons.

There are piles of dead and naked bodies everywhere, hundreds of them, maybe thousands. They are the color of greenish grey from their bodies decomposing. Rigor mortis setting in, leaving arms and legs in all manner of awkward positions. Contorted purple heads, eyes bulging from their sockets, mouths permanently opened in screams. A hundred vacant stares looked back at me.

The Nazis were in a hurry to get out of here, and they left behind boxcars full of dead POWs. They loaded the bodies with the intention of shipping them to another camp, wishing to hide the evidence of their atrocities.

The MPs here told us the story of when they opened the railroad cars: many dead bodies fell to the ground due to overcrowded conditions in each box car. When the bodies fell to the ground, one could hear the squishing sounds when they landed on top of each other.

Before the camp was liberated, the SS guards shot more pathetic souls. They marched them by the hundreds to large pits dug outside the grounds of the camp. They lined them up and murdered them, each person falling to their death into the pit below. They bulldozed the dirt over these mass graves; it appears that some poor souls were buried alive.

The heartless Nazi's blew up the water towers on their way out of camp. It's truly heartbreaking that thousands of prisoners died of dehydration so close to being saved. Without water, the sanitation conditions throughout the camp are unbearable. Excrement is everywhere. Dysentery and other diseases are running rife.

This next part is difficult for me to write. I witnessed it with my own eyes. To facilitate elimination of the dead bodies, the Germans built large ovens and cremated the dead.

In the area I inspected, there still were charred human bones visible in these large ovens. I put a handkerchief over my mouth and nose and even then, the odor of burned flesh invaded my nostrils.

Even more despicable, the SS guards in charge of the ovens took the gold wedding rings off the fingers of the dead bodies before they cremated them. Wedding rings were discovered in large casks inside one of the buildings. Thousands of rings. They did the same with gold fillings. Popped them out of the mouths of these poor dead people.

Does no one in Germany possess a single shred of moral decency? It's pure evil in the strongest measure possible.

I'm afraid that I am turning into a person who only knows blood, death, hate, and revenge. How am I to live a happy and normal life after seeing this place?

I'm sure of one thing. This has given us purpose about why we're fighting this godless war. There will be no place to hide for any German wearing a uniform.

We will find them and administer justice. The men and I are resolute on this issue.

Your loving husband,
Ed

Krow put the letter in his journal and never mailed it.

CHAPTER 57:
BUCHENWALD CONCENTRATION CAMP APRIL 1945

IT WAS late afternoon by the time the tour of the Buchenwald Concentration camp concluded. Leibold stayed with the medical techs to provide non-surgical aid to the POWs. He instructed Krow to return to Erfurt and start the process to break camp. He said he would catch up with them in a few hours.

Krow, Coop, and Louis walked to their vehicle. It had been a long, disturbing day, and each man was absorbed by his own thoughts.

They slowly drove out of camp along a road with several abandoned German guard shacks lining each side. During the liberation of the camp, these watch posts were blasted to shreds. Rubble and smoldering debris was everywhere. It seemed the world had permanently turned a lifeless shade of gray, a depressing overcast sky and a putrid smokey haze emitted from the rubble.

As they idled past one of the partially pulverized guard shacks Coop thought he heard a noise. It sounded like crying, Louis heard it, too. Krow was driving and Coop jabbed him in the side and used hand signals to communicate with him.

Instinct took over, Krow signaled he was going to stop. The men jumped out of their vehicle and formed a defensive position using the jeep as cover.

The sounds could have been a child or animal, or it could have been a trick. The men had learned to take no chances, regardless of how situations appeared. Here, in this part of the world, anything could happen.

Krow signaled that he and Coop would move towards the shack to investigate. Louis would stay behind the jeep and provide cover.

As the two men started toward the building Krow heard another noise that made the hair on the back of his neck stand up. Even with two bad ears, the sound was unmistakable. *Growling.*

Krow used his hands to give the danger signal. The SS used trained canines for many different types of jobs, including attacks, bomb sniffing, guard duty, and prisoner tracking. Slowly, carefully, Krow inched toward the growling and sniffling sounds and stepped over bricks that cluttered the front door. Krow motioned for Coop to provide cover. The men closely inspected the area for booby traps, and seeing none, carefully picked their way into the building.

The growling morphed into protective barking. The element of surprise was gone; if it was an ambush, it would come soon enough.

Krow turned a corner, and what he saw surprised him. There was a kitchen table, and underneath was a child, a little girl, maybe two or three years old. She looked scared, lost, or both. A noble looking German Shepherd guarded her. The large canine sat on its hind legs and was perched directly in front of the young child, preventing Krow from getting any closer.

He bent down on one knee, so he was eye level with the German Shepherd and the girl. The dog stopped barking and uttered a low growl. The message was clear. *Stay back.* Krow turned his attention from the animal to the girl.

Still on one knee, he removed his helmet and placed it on the ground next to him. He smiled at the young girl. To his surprise and delight, the babe threw a tentative smile back at him. Krow noticed her face was dirty and tears had created dingy tracks down her cheeks. She had brownish hair, olive skin, and cobalt blue eyes, and her smile highlighted two adorable dimples on each chubby little cheek. Clearly, the German Shepherd wasn't going to attack, but it wasn't going to let him get any closer, either. Krow had an idea.

He slowly picked up his helmet and handed it to Coop. "Ask Louis if we have any canned Spam in our packs and fill my helmet full with however much you can find," Krow instructed.

When Coop left, Krow smiled and pointed his index finger at the little girl. She grinned impishly and pointed her tiny finger right back at him. Next, Krow touched his nose with his index finger, and the child did the same. Then he took his thumb and index finger, grabbed his earlobe, and pulled down on it twice. The girl repeated the gesture. *Monkey see. Monkey do.* Both Krow and the girl were giggling now, while the dog's head swiveled back and forth.

Coop returned with Krow's helmet filled with the stinky Spam. Krow put a little of the meat in the palm of his hand and extended it toward the dog. Still growling, the German Shepherd inched forward, sniffed his palm, and dared to give it a test lick. Afterward, he licked his chops and sniffed the air, clearly wanting more.

Krow placed the helmet on the ground, five feet away. The big canine buried his snout in the helmet and began eating. The distraction gave Krow the opportunity to move closer to the girl. He motioned for her to come out from beneath the table.

She was tentative, but with a little coaxing, she came out but kept her distance. Neither moved a muscle. It was a standoff, with neither sure of the other's intention.

Krow broke the awkwardness by opening his arms in an invitation for a hug. Apparently, that was all that was necessary as the cherubic little girl came forward and put her small arms around his neck, hugging him mightily. Unexpectedly, she planted a mushy kiss on Krow's cheek. The two formed an instant connection with each other.

Krow's eyes welled up as he realized he had not been hugged or kissed by another human being for almost two years. And here, outside the gates of the most heinous place on earth, he fell in love with this little angel.

He scooped her up and carried her in his arms out of the building and out into the street where the others were waiting. The dog stayed in the doorway, no longer barking or growling but tracking their movements.

Louis, who had been on high alert, relaxed and smiled as Coop, Krow, and the girl emerged from the shack. He began to rummage through his pack for chocolate bars, packaged raisins, and other things a small child might like.

Krow sat down on a tree stump and placed the child on his knee. Louis and Coop gathered around. "It's time we find out this little one's name and where she's from," Krow said.

He spoke in English and asked, "What's your name?" The girl just shook her head, not comprehending.

"Ok, let's try it in another language. *Wie heiben sie?*"

She smiled and nodded. "Dowee."

Krow tried to hide his disappointment. *She's German.*

Coop knelt next to Krow. "What's her story?"

"She's probably from the village and must have been separated from her parents when they came to tour the camp. Speaking German, Krow reaffirmed her name. "*Wie heiben, sie Dowee?*"

She smiled and pointed at herself. "*Ja. Dowee.*"

Dowee turned toward Krow and asked for his name. "Jak masz na imie."

Krow's eyes grew wide. *She spoke Polish!*

"*Nazywan sie Krow,*" he spoke in his native language. *My name is Krow.*

Krow could feel the light coming back into his heart. "We need to take this child to the Red Cross Displaced Person's (DP) camp. Hopefully someone might know her."

When they stood up, Krow felt something warm slipping into his palm. She wanted to hold his hand. As they walked to the jeep, Dowee told Krow her story, at times he had to stop and bend down to her level, his bad ears and her soft voice making it difficult for him to hear her words.

Her explanation had many holes, but Krow deduced she was recently placed in a home as a foster child. She was staying with her *new* mommy and daddy. Krow asked where her *new* mommy and daddy were now. She shrugged.

In response, the little girl let go of Krow's hand and stepped back to get a better look at him. Then she looked up with her sweet blue eyes and asked him a question he would remember for the rest of his life.

"*Jestes moim nowym tatusiem?*" *Are you my new daddy?*

CHAPTER 58:
NEAR WEIMAR, GERMANY APRIL 1945

KROW MELTED. He wanted to tell Dowee that *Yes, I am your new daddy, and I will never leave you.* But as much as he wanted that to be true, the priority wasn't on finding her parents, old or new. As they neared the DP camp, his heart filled with a profound sense of loss.

When they arrived, Krow found the administrative nurse whose job it was to reunite family members who were separated during their imprisonment at the camp. He explained what Dowee told him. The administrator took notes and began interviewing Dowee herself. Krow didn't leave the child's side. He informed his men to leave a jeep and he would meet them back at Erfurt.

"So, what's your take on her story?" Krow asked when the interview concluded.

"We're still trying to put all the puzzle pieces together, but most of these children were stolen from their home countries and transported to Germany. Sometimes they were seized in broad daylight and in plain view of their parents. These children were taken because they fit the racial profile Hitler outlined for his Lebensborn program."

Krow tried to take this all in, but it was hard for him to comprehend. "You mean these kids were kidnapped from other countries because they fit some type of German racial profile?"

"I'm afraid so," the nurse said. "We have information outlining the German policy for this program. It's likely your little friend might be part of a group of children who recently passed the Germanisation test. Their original birth records would have been destroyed before they were sent to live with SS foster parents. The idea is that these children would be "rehabilitated" and become working, brainwashed members of the Reich."

Krow might have thrown up if there was any food in his stomach. "What happened to the children who didn't pass the "Germanisation" test?"

The nurse gripped the corners of the table so tightly, her fingernails turned red. Her eyes narrowed and she spoke in a whisper. "The information is a little sketchy, but it seems the older male children were used as slave labor. If the boys become incapable of working, we believe they were exterminated." She paused and closed her eyes. "If the older girls were cursed with being attractive and well developed, they may have been sent to the camp brothels."

Krow slammed his fist on the table so hard, the MPs took a step in his direction. The nurse waved them off as Krow ran his fingers through his hair. "What will happen to Dowee?"

"We'll speak with the captured German officials to see if we can locate any records of where she came from and who her parents might have been. If we can't find any of her family members, she'll be sent to an orphanage for displaced children and be put up for adoption. But she will have a difficult time being adopted by any families living in Europe." The nurse sagged in her chair.

"Why?" Krow asked.

"If word gets out that she's associated with the *Lebensborn* program, she will likely be rejected by other countries. Even German families themselves aren't likely to take these children into their homes for foster care or adoption."

Krow couldn't follow the logic. The nurse leaned forward and talked softly yet honestly. "Look, we both know that Germany is losing the war. If you were a German family and your country was taken over by the allied powers, would you want to have a stolen baby in your home that was part of Hitler's scheme to breed a master race of Germans?"

Krow shrugged. This was beyond his capability to imagine.

The nurse pressed on. "Even if these children get adopted by a European family, they'll have a rough upbringing. These countries are in a state of ruins, and a shortage of food and shelter is going to put an economic strain on families. Another mouth to feed would be an undue burden for a family already experiencing hardship."

Krow ground his fist into the palm of his left hand. "My God, they're just kids!" He yelled, incredulous.

"We feel the same way; it's heartbreaking. We'll do our best to look after these children, but we're only a temporary organization for displaced persons. For now, your sweet princess will have to stay with us. She'll be well taken care of by our Red Cross volunteers, I promise you. I'll open a case file for her, and the search for her family will begin right away."

How can I leave this beautiful little girl? She placed her trust in me. I wish I could take her away from all this, but I can't. The war isn't over for me yet.

Dowee was finishing a snack and sitting with an aid worker when Krow walked up to her. He crouched down on one knee and patted his thigh. Dowee immediately sat on his leg and looked at him with her sparkling blue eyes. He dreaded what he had to say next.

"It's time for me to go, but I promise that I'll come back here and visit you every chance I get." Dowee's shook her head *no* and wrapped her arms around his neck. She had no intention of letting him go.

His voice cracked as he spoke to her in Polish. "I love you, sweetheart, and I promise I'll come back to see you again." The nurse intervened and gently peeled Dowee from Krow's neck and held her for one last wave goodbye. Dowee stayed brave but started to cry when she realized Krow was really leaving her.

The nurse smiled at Krow. "You're smitten by this little one, aren't you?"

"Truly, I am," he admitted. We bonded."

The nurse laughed. "Then you should know you've been calling her by the wrong name."

Krow was flabbergasted. "What do you mean? She told me several times her name was Dowee."

The nurse grinned. "She has a cute speech impediment that causes her to roll her R's so *Dory* sounds like *Dowee*."

"No kidding," Krow said.

The nurse nodded. "Her formal name is Dorthea."

✦ ✦ ✦

Krow was true to his word. Over the next few days, he visited Dory at the DP camp two more times. Every visit, he inquired if she was being well taken care of, which she was, and whether anyone had come forward with any information about her.

The last time Krow visited Dory, she was wearing a Buchenwald armband. The administrator told him that if no one came forward to claim her, she was scheduled to go to an orphanage in Switzerland, which had an organization devoted to international war orphan adoptions.

Four weeks later, Krow received a short letter from the DP administrator letting him know that Dory had left the camp for Switzerland. Much to his regret, he never saw her again.

CHAPTER 59:
GERMANY
APRIL–MAY 1945

JOURNAL ENTRY
28 APRIL 1945, BAMBURG, GERMANY

Momentum is in our favor. At present, I'm with the 1st Platoon in Bamburg, Germany. We're serving with our friends at the 34th Evacuation Hospital. On our move to Bamburg, we encountered what looked to be a downtrodden, beaten German Army. The Krauts are disorganized, retreating haphazardly at best, and surrendering by the thousands.

We're beginning to receive more German patients than Americans, though we aren't the ones treating them. All of this is a damn good sign we are winning this war.

We're camping outdoors along a pleasant trout stream. Most of the American casualties we treat consist of accidental injuries like vehicle accidents, methyl alcohol poisoning, and injuries incurred while examining enemy explosive devices.

JOURNAL ENTRY
5 MAY 1945, AUERBACH, GERMANY

Cap informed us of rumors the Soviets have taken Berlin and Hitler has been killed. I can physically feel my body relax after months of being on high alert.

When we heard about the supposed death of Hitler, our unit did not celebrate in the usual way. It was more of subdued relief that the fighting will end soon. There was no party; we simply reported for duty to care for a dwindling number of American patients.

JOURNAL ENTRY
8 MAY 1945, AUERBACH, GERMANY

We received word today from Captain Leibold that SHAEF announced the war ended. We officially proclaimed today as V-E Day.

If we were in France, our victory parade would know no bounds. In our present location there is no celebration. Germany's surrender has caused bewilderment among the townspeople. We are distrustful of them, and they of us.

We're in charge now and will not tolerate any missteps by the locals. Anyone caught stealing food or supplies will be dealt with harshly. Our mood is foul because we're still stuck here and unable to return home yet.

JOURNAL ENTRY
12 MAY 1945, AUERBACH, GERMANY

Our Chaplain conducted a small service today praising God for his mercy about ending the war. God didn't end this war. The American fighters did. God is not here.

14 May 1945

Dearest Mary—

Thank you for the latest batch of letters. I especially enjoyed smelling your perfume on a few of them. I'm not sure you intended to leave those wonderful smells on the envelopes, but I closed my eyes and pretended we were together. Hopefully soon.

Blackout conditions were lifted, so we opened our tents and let our lights brighten the camp. Several of us, including me, enjoyed building small bonfires between our pup tents. Sitting around the fire and watching the logs and embers burning was a welcome relief to all of us who lived under strict blackout conditions for two years.

A few of us decided to try to replicate a good old-fashioned American cookout. High on the list was to have a little contest on who could craft the most delicious hot dog. A few guys entered the competition and it was Louis who had the winning "frankfurter," as he called it. I honestly don't know how he comes up with this stuff.

Somehow, Louis worked out a deal with "Black Market Bill" and procured cow intestines. He worked with our mess cooks and combined Spam with the "meat" from our C-rats. He liberally sprinkled in garlic and some other seasonings and cut the intestines into links and tied off each end. We found some long twigs and put the hot dogs on the end of them and roasted our creations over the fire. We didn't have buns but one of the guys had a small supply of German black bread, and we used a piece of it to wrap each frankfurter. Honestly, those frankfurters were damn good! It sure did remind us of home and the things we took for granted before the war.

While we ate our hot dogs, Coop facetiously narrated the Cleveland Indians versus the Detroit Tigers baseball game. He faked the whole thing. It was really swell. We even sang "Take Me Out to the Ball Game" during the seventh inning stretch.

As you can tell, our general mood is one of relief. New discussions center around how many points are needed to go home. There are rumors that the Army will offer promotions if we stay on and fight the Japs. No way!

I'll close by saying to you how much I miss you. I can't help but wonder how much you and I have changed. Will we look the same to each other? All I know is the first time I hug you, everything will fall into the right place. I hope you feel the same way.

For now, I kindly ask you to pass along all assurances to my folks that I am safe and think of them frequently. In the meantime, my love for you keeps me going forward. Thank you for waiting for me to come home.

Love always and forever,
Ed

CHAPTER 60:
AUERBACH, GERMANY MAY 1945

IMMEDIATELY AFTER Germany's formal surrender, the Allies faced the dilemma of how best to treat the thousands of wounded enemy soldiers who were now Prisoners of War. These POWs were placed under the custody of the American military. High Command decided to use some of the Nazi concentration camps to house the thousands of German POWs, and to utilize the hospitals inside those camps for treatment.

The roles were now reversed. The Germans became POWs, sent to concentration camps. But the major difference was that they weren't being sent to be exterminated, but to be hospitalized, treated, and processed out. Despite the inhumanity of the Nazi regime, the Allied powers showed a remarkable degree of humanity to the defeated German soldiers.

The 648th was given administrative control of the hospitals inside several of the extermination camps. These hospitals tended almost exclusively to German patients. When Leibold received these orders, he called Krow into his office and explained the situation to him.

"When your platoon arrives at these camps, find the location of the enemy supply dumps. We aren't going to be able to provide enough American drugs and medical gear to do this job properly. It's important to get our hands on German supplies before they hit the black market. German medical personnel should be used exclusively to treat German wounded. All efforts should be made to treat DP personnel with medical personnel of their home country."

Leibold took a swig from his canteen. "Our secondary job will be to develop a transportation process for enemy wounded who are now healthy enough to be discharged from our care. Enemy POW patients will be processed by American interrogators before being released from their service. Displaced patients, when discharged, will return to the DP Camps for interviews and relocation. What questions do you have?"

Krow's hands tightened into fists and his face grew hot. He knew he shouldn't get upset but couldn't help himself. "Our orders are to treat these bastards for their war injuries? We should leave them to rot in hell like they did with our guys."

Leibold slapped his hand down hard against his desk, making it shake. "We have our orders. I'm not happy about this either, but most of the enemy wounded are rank and file Wehrmacht, not the Nazi scum that dictated the horrors we've witnessed. These men just want to go back to their families. We have administrative responsibility for military hospitals in these four concentration camps: Ingolstadt, Schrobenhausen, Paffenhausen, and Dachau.

Krow flinched upon hearing the words "concentration camps."

Grimacing, Leibold continued. "Each of these encampments will have American hospitals to treat the enemy wounded. Also, we're responsible for the DP hospitals in these locations."

The fight left Krow as he gradually realized that Leibold shared his distaste for the assignment and was only following orders. "Will any of my men be responsible for treating any Germans?" he asked. "If so, I need to prepare them."

Leibold leaned back. "Your team is responsible for establishing medical and logistical processes and to get the German doctors to tend to their own wounded. God willing, that will be all."

Krow crossed his arms. "I can't guarantee my men won't lose it when they see the German wounded. I'll do my best to keep them at a safe distance so they don't do anything disruptive."

Leibold's eyes hardened. "Tell your men to do their jobs. If nobody does anything stupid, we can all go home soon."

In the coming days it wouldn't be Krow's men who would be disruptive...it would be the Germans.

CHAPTER 61:
INGOLSTADT, GERMANY
MAY 1945

JOURNAL ENTRY
GERMAN HOSPITAL & ALLIED DP CAMP

We met with the German medical officers in charge of the hospital. After our meeting, they accompanied Captain Leibold and me into the tent with the German wounded.

"Achtung!" one of the Nazi officers yelled.

At his command, all the injured soldiers were expected to get off their cots and stand at attention as we walked past. Even the most severely injured soldiers were expected to get on their feet despite the risk of further injury. These pathetic souls were required to salute Captain Leibold as he walked by. Not by Leibold's instruction, but at the behest of their German commanding officers.

These Germans prisoners were savagely wounded. There were amputees, burn victims, head injuries, and post-operative patients, all with blood-soaked bandages and various types of full body wraps and plaster casts.

Many of these patients had head wounds requiring a complete wrapping in gauze and other bandages. But if they were breathing and conscious, their superiors expected these injured men to stand at attention as we strode past.

Painfully, these war-weary soldiers were made to get off of their cots and do their level best to stand rigidly as we passed them by. If any of them resisted or failed to move from their beds, they were verbally berated by the officers in charge of their unit.

The German officers put on a show with a lot of yelling and ordering their men to stand at attention. Some of these patients recently had their legs or arms amputated. It was positively barbaric.

In a few instances, I witnessed German officers roughly grab dazed and morphine-drugged wounded soldiers from their beds and brutally hoist them to their feet (if they had any). Some of these poor souls were barely conscious.

One patient had his lower jaw blown off at its hinge, and his upper teeth were missing; only his nose and eyes remained. He must have just come out of surgery and was still heavily sedated. As we approached, his superior officer berated him to stand up and salute. The Kraut leader bent over him, yelling in his face. The kid didn't move. I'll never forget what happened next.

The German officer grabbed him by the hair and tried to forcibly roust him to his feet. The boy wailed in agony. The officer ordered two other patients to grab the man's arms to get him to stand up.

Blood from his surgically altered face dripped on the floor. I've seen it all, but this was too much. I had to look away or I might have thrown up.

"Put him down," Leibold ordered in a louder, more commanding voice than I'd ever heard him use before." No more patients will stand and salute for us, is that clear?"

The look the German leader gave Leibold was like a snake who's just snared its dinner. I wanted to beat the tar out of that Kraut officer, and I know Leibold would have joined me. This was not done as a sign of respect. What it was, I simply can't comprehend. How could the German people have followed such a warped military hierarchy? I shudder to think what would have happened to us all if Hitler and the Nazi elite had won this bloody war.

I'm rambling and cannot fully articulate these exact circumstances. I hate this place with a passion.

JOURNAL ENTRY
24 MAY 1945, DP HOSPITAL

When we arrived at these concentration camps, we learned we needed to do more than "organize the process." We were overwhelmed with the enormity of DPs and wounded who were being housed and treated on these sites.

There are thousands of people in these camps. We immediately set up a delousing station and kept a liberal supply of DDT on hand in each institution. As new enemy wounded arrived, we used German interpreters to explain we would be covering them in DDT and to let them know they would be receiving shots for typhoid diseases. The Krauts are distrustful of these shots. The German medical officers made an announcement that these shots are safe and necessary for their protection.

We checked our own immunization register to make sure we were up to date on all our booster shots against these diseases. It was amusing when one of our men voluntarily came forward to "announce" it was time to receive his booster shot in the ass.

Even though we used humor to break up the gravity of the situation, the serious nature of these deadly diseases did not go unheeded by any of us.

JOURNAL ENTRY
28 MAY 1945, DP HOSPITAL, INGOLSTADT, GERMANY

Working at allied DP hospital in Ingolstadt. Many housed in the DP camps are ready to go back to their homelands. From time to time, we can evacuate whole trainloads of DPs directly to their home country.

At such times, the work necessary to assemble and equip an entire hospital train is shared by our company and the ETO at Munich. Meals must be served on the train, the cars must be cleaned and deloused, equipment— blankets, litters, and cots, medical supplies, bandages, and drugs—must be assembled and stocked on the train before the patients are loaded.

When ready, convoys of ambulances carry the litter patients to the train, and our men and officers supervise the loading.

JOURNAL ENTRY
29 MAY 1945, DP CAMP AND GERMAN POW HOSPITAL

It will be hard for anyone outside of the 40 of us to understand the joy we feel when we send these war-weary DPs home. In general, the allied personnel and "friendlies" are so appreciative of our work here. They tell us they will never forget our help. It makes our efforts in these hellholes more bearable.

On the other hand, there's a stark contrast when dealing with the German wounded. Despite their injuries, we're taking no chances. We don't fraternize with them. We perform our jobs and let the German medical teams do their work.

Despite no fraternization, I've noticed there are three types of enemy wounded. The first group want to heal and go home to their families. They're regular army types. The second group are in a daze that Germany has lost the war, upset that we (Americans) interfered in "their" European war.

The third group are the enemy soldiers who recognize their country has committed horrific sins. They, too, for the first time are seeing the emaciated allied soldiers and DPs who are housed in the various parts of these camps. These Germans are having trouble coping. But it's hard to tell what any of them are truly feeling. Many feign ignorance.

JOURNAL ENTRY
30 MAY 1945, DP CAMP

I've been thinking about the sweet little girl, Dory, I met back in Buchenwald. She was shipped to Switzerland on one of these trains, and it's been hard for me to think she was traveling all alone.

I can look at injuries and wounds and not let it bother me, but this young girl shot an arrow into my heart. Her little cherub face and the conversations we shared are going to stick with me for the rest of my life. I hope and pray everything works out for her.

CHAPTER 62:
GERMANY
AUGUST–SEPTEMBER 1945

AFTER THE 1st Platoon finished their work of establishing operations in each of the four former concentration camps, they were sent to Starnberg, Germany. Starnberg is a resort town located in German Bavaria, 30km southwest of Munich. It's known as the "land of five lakes."

Amid its natural beauty, Starnberg bore a sinister secret: a sub-camp of the Dachau extermination camp was built there. German officers lived in resort-like homes overlooking the picturesque lakes while prisoners lived in putrid, inhumane conditions. After the war, the Dachau sub-camp was converted into a DP camp in the U.S. zone in Bavaria.

It was here where the 648th set up operations.

JOURNAL ENTRY
STARNBERG, AUGUST 1945

We arrived in Starnberg last week. This region was unaffected by the war and could be one of the more beautiful places I've ever seen. Pristine lakes all over and lots of outdoor recreation activities are available to us.

Captain Leibold was able to secure several large houses overlooking one of the lakes for us to occupy. Our infantry kicked the Krauts out of these homes and seized control of them. We are the new tenants.

I'm staying in a room which has four beds and a balcony overlooking a lake. Each morning, we drink our Nescafe on the deck and watch the mist burn off the lake. We're getting good rest here. Other units are handling medical duties at the DP camp.

We were given light duty and are only treating American soldiers who were wounded in this region. We set up a small ten-bed dispensary treating patients up to five days. The severely injured are evacuated by ambulance to the 132 Evac Hospital in Munich.

This is the best part. No more C-Rats! Our mess is cooking fresh meat and vegetables, and sometimes we get fruit.

I'm reluctant to put this next part in writing. But when I reread it 100 years from now, I might remember how hard I laughed. When we were in the field, we dug pits and trenches for our latrines. We sat on wood planks with holes in them and dropped our loads in the pit. Your ass froze in the winter, and you pinched your nose in the summer.

Now we have real flushing toilets. To celebrate, some of the younger guys had the kooky idea to replace the word "hello" with the phrase "it's a joy to take a shit on a real toilet." As stupid as it sounds, it means things are gradually returning to normal. I tried to be serious and told the boys to act their age, but inside I laughed.

In September Major Lang paid the men a visit in Starnberg. He was there to present the unit with their military service stripes. The men of the 1st platoon stood at attention while Lang presented the final stripe to their platoon leader, S/Sgt Edmund D. Kruszynski. On his left arm, he bore four horizontal and one diagonal bar indicating his service time in live combat.

Lang also told the unit they would be receiving medals for each combat campaign in which they faced an armed enemy. He read them off as Normandy, Northern France, Ardennes, Central Europe, and Rhineland. Lastly, Major Lang presented the entire 648th Medical Clearing Company an award of distinction given exclusively to a select few units. Lang read off the merit award.

"The 648th is awarded the Meritorious Service insignia for the months of October 1944 through April 1945. The award is given for superior performance of duty and outstanding devotion to duty in the performance of exceptionally difficult tasks, achievements, and maintenance of a high standard of discipline while engaged in combat against an armed enemy."

Each medic in the platoon was given an insignia to be worn on the right sleeve of his uniform. Lang impressed on the men that the unit's Meritorious Service award was the equivalent of the Army's prestigious Legion of Merit award, which was given to individuals for their outstanding devotion to duty.

Before Lang left Starnberg, he called out the names of several men and asked if he could speak with them privately in the officer's mess. Krow, Cooper and Louis were part of the group.

Lang had a freshly lit cigar hanging from his mouth. He pulled a draw from the cigar and slowly exhaled a blue cloud of smoke into the air as Krow and his direct reports walked inside the tent.

"Men, I called your names because you have accumulated enough service points to go home. You will be leaving via train headed for Marseille. From there, a troop ship will take you back home. Get your affairs in order. You will be leaving within the next few days."

And suddenly, it was over. Krow and the other medics had dreamed of the day they could leave this place. But Krow knew Europe and this war would never ever leave him or his men.

"Any questions?" Lang asked.

One hand shot in the air. It was Louis, grinning like the Cheshire cat. "Major, you got any more of those stogies? The cigars would pair great with the champagne I plan on drinking tonight!"

The men roared. And Lang laughed with them. They were actually going home!

CHAPTER 63:
BOSTON, MASSACHUSETTS OCTOBER 1945

KROW, COOPER, and Louis said their goodbyes to their friends who remained behind in Starnberg before traveling to Marseille. Once there, they boarded a troop ship to take them stateside. The men were only two days into the journey when the captain made an announcement. The skipper informed his passengers he would be pushing the vessel at top speeds to try to beat a tropical storm which formed south of their position. "It's calm now, but the next few days will be rough sailing."

Indeed, the ship faced gale force winds for much of the voyage. Krow could only keep down chicken soup, so that's what he ate for the duration.

The weather finally broke in their favor, with the sun peeking through the clouds as the boat entered the Boston Harbor. Krow stood on the top deck, holding onto the railing, as the ship cruised through the channel. He returned to America with five bronze battle stars, one silver combat star, and four years of military service to his credit.

Cooper, Louis and Krow had their barracks bags strapped over their shoulders and were in a line that zigzagged through the ship's narrow corridors and headed toward the exits. As they left the ship, they shielded their eyes to block the blast of sunlight.

"What are you guys going to do now? We talked about staying overnight. Is that still the plan?" Louis squinted as he stepped onto the gangplank leading to shore.

The Army provided a transitional barracks area where returning soldiers could spend the night before boarding their respective trains home. Bathrooms, showers, and clean beds were provided. A same-day laundry service was offered to clean and press their uniforms. They were expected to leave the following morning so the next round of incoming troops could use the same facilities.

Krow shook his head in the affirmative. "I never thought I'd say this but it's the one time I'm glad we're in the Army and not the Navy. I'm wiped out from the rough ride back. I could use a hot shower, a shave, and a good night's sleep before boarding the train back to Ohio. What about you, Coop?"

"That's my plan too. I haven't eaten in a few days, and I want to take advantage of the laundry service. The aroma of sweat and bile on my shirtsleeves isn't very romantic. I want to smell as fresh as a daisy when I reunite with Mrs. Cooper." A broad smile creased his face.

Krow woke the next morning in time to view the sunrise through the barracks windows. He propped himself on one elbow and looked across the long row of beds filled with returning troops. Half of the men were still asleep, while the other half were packing their belongings and would soon be heading off to hometowns across the U.S.

Ed swung his legs over the side of his bed and stretched. He frowned when he noticed a softball-sized yellowy stain on his pillow. Sometimes, especially at night, the cotton balls he used failed to absorb all the fluid being discharged from his ears. He didn't worry about it in the field, but now that he would be sleeping with Mary he became hyper-aware of it.

Heading to the showers, he scrubbed the last of the salt water from his skin and double lathered his hair with shampoo. When he was as clean as possible, he wrapped a fresh towel around his waist and walked to the sink.

Ed used the thick corner of the comb to make a nice tight part in his hair. He put fresh cotton balls in his ears and slipped on a clean uniform. He stripped his bed, packed his barracks bag, and set off to meet Coop and Louis for their last breakfast together.

+ + +

There was a melancholic silence at the breakfast table when the three friends met, though Krow did his best to sound upbeat. "Hey this won't be the last time we see each other. Let's plan to get together after the holidays."

Coop hadn't touched his eggs and toast, a rarity for him. "We've been in the thick of it together for the last four years. I know you goons better than my brothers and sisters. I'll never forget you guys," he murmured.

Louis covered his eyes with his hand, his fingers shaking.

"Louis, are you okay?" Krow asked.

Louis kept his head down and focused on his breakfast plate as he spoke. "I can't stop thinking about Rolly. He was always so afraid he wouldn't come back. I shouldn't have let him get out of that truck. That will always haunt me, just like the poor, desperate Russian POW I killed." Louis pinched the bridge of his nose, but he couldn't hold back giant sobs. Still, he pressed on with what he needed to say. "Every day, I replay what happened to them in my head. I remember the look on their faces, and it haunts me terribly." He covered his eyes with a napkin.

Cooper slid over and put his arm around Louis's shoulders. "None of it was your fault, do you hear me? You were a hero at Normandy and every day since. You saved hundreds of soldiers, and all those men get to come back home to their families because of you."

Louis waved them off and tried to compose himself. "I don't know if I'll ever get over this feeling, I have a huge hole in my heart that will never heal."

Ed put his hand on Louis's forearm. "It's over, Robert. We need to put the war behind us and move on with our lives. The faster we can do that, the better off we'll be. Besides, if you ever want to talk we are only a phone call away. We'll always be friends…always."

"Ditto," Coop said.

Eventually, the three of them said their final goodbyes and slid away from the table. Sadly, Krow would be unable to take his own advice. He couldn't just put the war behind him, at least not right away. His personal struggles simmered below the surface, but as always, he put forth a brave front.

CHAPTER 64:
CLEVELAND, OHIO
OCTOBER 1945

IT WAS Saturday morning and Ed was on a passenger train from Boston to Cleveland. He took a window seat so he could look at the scenery on the way home. After four years of colorless devastation, he was mesmerized by the panorama of fall colors whistling past him. Pastures were filled with cattle and sheep, farmers were busy harvesting corn, and wagons were filled with pumpkins. He felt like a blind man who had just regained his sight, and was startled when the conductor announced, "Approaching Cleveland Union Terminal Depot." *We're here already? How is that possible?*

He wanted to call Mary the evening before, but the line for the phone was a mile long. He was also exhausted from the journey home and the heart-wrenching separation from his closest friends. *I'll have to surprise Mary and my parents.*

It was quite a sight when the train pulled into the terminal. A metal barricade separated the troops coming off the train from a throng of civilians on the other side. Family members behind the barricade erupted with cheers when they spotted "their" soldier exiting the box cars. Most were happy reunions, but some were heartbreaking. Ed watched an amputee exit the train, the boy's left leg was severed just below the hip bone. It made him recall a similarly gruesome injury he treated on the battlefield. *Hold on to your leg, soldier. The doctors might be able to reattach it.*

Ed stepped off the train, jumped over the gap, and looked for signs for taxis and buses. On his way out, he read a poster hanging from a circular pillar in the main terminal. *Boys and Girls, help your Uncle Sam. Save your quarters and buy War Stamps!*

He weaved his way through the crowd of people and breathed a sigh of relief when he finally exited the station. Dropping his barracks bag to the ground, he gazed skyward and embraced the warm October sun on his face. *I'm home. I'm really home.*

"Hey, soldier! How about a flower bouquet for your sweetheart? Guys in uniform get a 50 percent discount." A junior high-aged girl was working a flower stand just outside the terminal building. The cart looked like a rickshaw with a single wheel in front and two wheels in back.

Ed waved to acknowledge her call as he walked over. "I'll take two of the fall arrangements."

The girl wrapped tissue around the bouquets. "Are you just coming back from the war?"

"Yes, from Europe," Ed replied.

"My two older brothers served in Europe. The younger one Kirk is still there, and my oldest brother David died in France, shortly after D-Day." The girl finished preparing the bouquets, surprisingly stoic.

"I'm sorry for your loss," Ed said with feeling as he reached for his wallet.

The teen pointed to the stripes on his army jacket. "Did you ever have to shoot anyone?"

A rolodex of ugly images rattled through his brain and a prickly sensation surged through his body. Ed had to shake them off before answering. "I was a medic."

"Then you were one of the lucky ones!" The girl smiled and handed him his change. "If you're looking for a cab, they're parked in long lines two blocks south of here." She handed him his flowers, and Ed started to walk in the direction of the cabs.

"Hey Mister!" she called out. He turned and saw her pointing at something on the ground.

"You forgot to take your duffle bag!"

The cabs were exactly where the girl told him, and Ed had no trouble hailing one. The yellow taxi pulled forward, and a less than enthusiastic driver took his luggage and put it in the trunk. "Where to?"

Ed gave the driver directions and noted the inside of the cab smelled like onions and vinegar. He couldn't tell if it was the man's lunch, or his body odor. The cabbie turned the key and pulled away from the train station. "You on furlough or discharged?"

"Discharged, today is my first day back home." Ed smiled as the cab passed his high school and the bowling alley where he worked as a kid. The trip down memory lane was cut short by another question from the cabbie.

"What was it like over there?" the driver asked before stuffing a half-eaten sandwich in his mouth.

Ed kept it short but answered politely. "War isn't pretty."

The cabbie nodded, seemingly satisfied with Ed's cryptic answer. A few minutes later, they left downtown behind and passed through a residential community with saltbox homes. Ed noticed some children playing hopscotch on the sidewalk. The family's driveway was lined with red roses still in full bloom. *Beautiful.*

The driver eyeballed him through the rear-view mirror. "See any combat?"

Ed was done with being interrogated. "Some," he clipped.

The cab passed a young mother pushing a baby stroller. It brought to mind Rollins's pregnant wife, and the smell from the cabbie mixed with the scent from the flowers began to turn his stomach. He fiddled with the bouquets on his lap as the car slowed at a four-way stop.

In the front yard of one of the houses was a picnic table filled with baskets of homegrown corn, green beans, and tomatoes. Ed had heard Americans were planting Victory Gardens in their yards to help supplement the food supply at home and abroad.

The cabbie waved an annoyed hand at the gray-haired lady sitting behind the picnic table. "See the old broad across the street? She was forced to plant a garden to make ends meet. We've been on a lousy food rationing program the past five years. I guess they sent all the good shit to you guys while the rest of us made sacrifices."

Ed wanted to punch the guy. "It looks like you had no problem find-ing all the *good stuff.*" Luckily, the cabbie didn't respond.

The taxi took a left turn and pulled onto a street Ed recognized well. *I've walked to Mary's home a hundred times on this street.* Mary's parents' house was only about a mile away, and he absolutely couldn't wait to see her.

"I heard the Japs were meaner than the Krauts." The cabbie's eyebrows bobbed, making him look like Groucho Marx. "C'mon you were there, what was it like?"

Ed smashed the palm of his hand into the driver's head rest. "If you wanted to know what it was like to be in a fucking war, you should have enlisted. Pull over. I'm walking the rest of the way."

The startled cabbie rubbed the back of his neck and pulled the car over to the curb. "Suit yourself, buddy. I was just making conversation."

Ed got his bags and quickly paid the fare. But as he watched the cab pull away, he felt a little remorseful. *I overreacted. The guy was just curi-ous, I should have apologized.* Still, he was grateful to be on foot so he could calm down before seeing Mary.

His heart rate gradually receded as he strode down the street. A few neighbors who were in their yards shouted, "Welcome home, soldier!" Ed waved each time he heard the greeting.

He was a few blocks away from Mary's house when he detected a fast-moving object closing in from behind him. He whipped around and saw a young boy peddling like a madman in his direction. The boy hit the brakes and did a fish tail stop inches from Ed's feet. Then he removed a brown lunch sack from his basket and held it high in the air. Ed noticed buttery grease marks on the bottom of the sack.

"My grandmother saw you walking down the street," the boy said breathlessly. "She asked me to give you a bag of her homemade choco-late chip cookies!"

"You almost ran me over!" Ed said with a laugh as he accepted the gift from the boy. He pulled two cookies out of the bag and breathed in the chocolatey goodness. "One for you, and one for me, and tell your grandmother thank you." The youngster snatched his cookie and ate it in one messy bite before jumping back on his bike and peddling away.

The warm cookie melted in Ed's mouth and was devoured in a flash. He couldn't resist pulling out a second cookie. *Quality Control.*

A block later, licking the chocolate from his mouth, he saw Mary's house. As he walked toward the front steps his heart pounded in anticipation, just like it had on their very first date.

I hope Mary's home!

CHAPTER 65:
CLEVELAND, OHIO OCTOBER 1945

ED LOOKED at the familiar gray steps leading to the porch. He and Mary had sat together on the top step a hundred times, drinking coffee and stealing secret kisses. The stairs creaked as he tiptoed his way to the front door.

He set the duffle bag down and laid the flower bouquets on top of it. Before knocking, he took off his hat and ran his fingers through his hair. He was nervous and excited, like how he felt on their first date. He was about to rap his knuckles on the door when he spotted a familiar face through the other side of the screen. It was Mary's brother Ray, now ten years old, playing a solitary game of jacks.

Ray was only six years old when Ed was drafted and sent to Fort Oglethorpe. Ed remembered how he used to play jacks for hours with his friends when he was Ray's age. An idea popped into his head.

Ed knocked on the door ever so quietly and then hid. Ray sprang to his feet and ran full steam across the living room floor, executing a perfect baseball slide in front of the screen door. He looked out but didn't see a soul. Ray's eyes darted in all directions as he tried to spy which one of his friends had tried to spook him.

Ed jumped out from his hiding spot. "BOO!"

Ray fell backward, landing rump first on the floor. It took a few seconds for reality to sink in, and finally grasping who it was, Ray's eyes grew as big as saucers. "Is it really you?"

Ed grinned and pressed his index finger to his mouth, signaling for Ray to be quiet. When Ray complied, Ed whispered his plan through the screen door. Ray shook his head vigorously, his eyes alight with mischief.

Mary and her mother, Anna, were in the kitchen prepping for dinner. Wearing aprons, the ladies were making dough for noodles and dumplings when Ray burst through the kitchen door holding two flower arrangements.

"Look what I have! One for mom and one for Mary."

Mary brushed off her hands. "Who gave you those flowers?"

Ray summoned his best acting skills. "Some *guy* knocked on the door and dropped them off."

His mother raised one eyebrow. "What guy? Raymond, I've told you to never speak with strangers."

Ray turned and gestured behind him. "Who said he was a stranger?"

Ed stepped into the kitchen right on cue. "Hello, Mary." Her blank expression unsettled him. "Do you recognize me?"

Tear's sprung from Mary's eyes. "I almost didn't believe it. Oh my God, you're really here!" she screamed and ran into his arms. Ed smelled a mixture of light perfume and baking flour on Mary's face as he kissed her with all the passion in his heart.

A heavy object rammed into the left side of Ed's rib cage, breaking up their kiss. It was Mary's mother and her cutting board.

"We're so glad to see you! So glad!!" Anna's face flushed as she kept repeating those lines.

After a minute, Anna pulled away. Ed kept his arms around Mary's waist and gazed deeply into her eyes. "You have flour on your nose," he laughed.

Mary outlined his lips with her fingertips and began crying in earnest. "And you smell like cookies!"

Their tender moment was cut short when Ed felt someone tugging on his rear pants pocket. He looked down and grinned. Ray was staring up at him, beaming.

"We did good, didn't we?"

Ed detached one of his arms and mussed up Ray's hair. "We sure did! You can be my partner in crime any day."

CHAPTER 66:
CLEVELAND, OHIO
OCTOBER 1945

MARY KNEW that Ed was anxious to see his parents, and now regretted that she'd never written him about her troubling last encounter with Stella. As they neared his house, she felt compelled to prepare Ed for what he might encounter. "Your mother is convinced I only married you for your money. Don't be surprised if she isn't herself when you see her. Big Hand told me she'd been in a dark place ever since you left."

Ed stopped in his tracks. "I wish you would have told me sooner. You know my parents rarely wrote me letters."

Mary squeezed his hand and leaned into him. "I didn't want to worry you. You had enough on your plate."

"I suppose that's true," Ed admitted. "I hope when she sees me, she'll snap out of it."

They walked quietly, with Ed staring at every house and every bush. He noted the familiar bump at the end of his neighbor's driveway. He and his childhood pal, Woodrow Golunski, loved to zoom their bikes over the bump and go airborne.

Mary gave him a double elbow poke in his side. "Look ahead, sweetheart." She pointed up the road.

Two driveways away, a handsome hulk leapt from a porch chair with an open newspaper in his meaty hand. He bounded down the short flight of steps two at a time and charged toward them. Ed was relieved beyond measure to view the familiar toothy grin.

"Edmuuuund!" his father yelped. Big Hand thrust his arms around Ed and lifted him in the air. "I thought you were a mirage! I took off my glasses, rubbed them clean, and put them back on again. That's when I knew. My Eddie came home!" Big Hand lifted Ed again and they both laughed. "When did you arrive?" Big Hand asked when he set Ed back down.

"A couple of hours ago," Ed explained. "If it's okay with you, I'd like to go home and see how Mom's doing."

Big Hand shot Mary a knowing look. "I think she'll be happy to see you, but don't be troubled if she acts confused. Rest assured, I'm happy enough for both of us that you're back home safe and sound!"

Everything looked exactly the same as when Ed left. The blue globe and the bird feeder sat in their familiar spots in the front yard. The red brick walkway and the blue-gray paint on the porch pillars hadn't changed, and neither did the black door with metal knocker.

"She's in her bedroom," Big Hand said once they stepped inside. "Do you want me to come upstairs with you?"

"No," Ed said. "I'll greet her by myself." Even though the steps were carpeted, the wood creaked underneath his weight. There was a short hallway with two bedrooms on each side. The last door on the right was the master bedroom, and it was cracked open. Ed peered inside and found his mother Stella sitting in her rocker with the shades drawn, absorbed by her knitting.

"Hi Mom. I'm home."

Stella stopped rocking, lifted her head, and gasped. "Edmund? Is it really you?"

"It's really me, mom," he said, his heart lifting as her face brightened. "I'm so happy to see you again!"

"Come over here so I can hug you!" she gushed.

Ed bent over and Stella gave him a tight squeeze. "I prayed for you every day," she said, clutching him even tighter. He could feel her fingers pinching his mid-section. Stella pushed him away and scrutinized him from head to toe. "You're too skinny," she declared.

"Then I guess you'll have to cook *all* of my favorite foods to fatten me up!" Ed said with a chuckle.

Stella slapped her knees and erupted in unfiltered laughter. Her joyful outburst could be heard all the way down the steps. She clapped her hands and then abruptly stopped. "Is Mary with you?"

Ed braced himself. "Yes, she's downstairs with Pop. Why?"

Stella's face softened. "She's worked hard while waiting for you to come home. If I were in your shoes, I wouldn't waste any more time with me. Go be with your wife."

Ed felt a pressure valve release. It seemed his mother had dropped her unfair accusations against Mary. The last thing he ever wanted was for his two favorite women to be at war. He leaned over and kissed Stella on the cheek. "Are you going to be okay, Mom?"

"I am now." Stella took his hand and squeezed it. "Go downstairs before your father scares her away."

There was ironic foreshadowing in Stella's words to her son. It wouldn't be Big Hand who would scare Mary.

It would be Ed.

CHAPTER 67:
CLEVELAND, OHIO DECEMBER 1945

IN DECEMBER 1945, the holiday season was in full force. America had won the war, and the stifling blackout ordinances were finally lifted. Christmas lights were everywhere and cities across the country resumed their tree lighting ceremonies. The joy of being home for the holidays kept Ed's mind from dwelling on his intrusive combat memories, though he frequently found himself arguing with ghosts.

Stay in the truck, Rolly! D'Angelo, don't listen to me! McCaulley, you're staying with us!

As the hoopla from the holidays faded away, winter settled over northeast Ohio like a wet, suffocating blanket. The short January days combined with rain, snow, cold and gray clouds were hauntingly like Europe's "grainter" winter of 1944. As the weather darkened, so did Ed's mood.

Whether it was called shell shock or war neuroses, the effect was the same. But the word "neuroses" implied being weak minded. Ed, a former leader of a platoon who earned a Meritorious Achievement Award for valor during combat, didn't want the stigma of being viewed as weak minded.

Ed began to struggle more and more with memories of his time in combat. During the heat of the battle, he was continually forced to make life or death decisions on the fly. He didn't have time to think about his feelings or the long-term effects of his decisions. He wanted to bury these unpleasant memories, but there were too many reminders. When Mary suggested they go out with old friends, he couldn't tolerate constant questions of, "What was it like over there? How many people did you shoot?"

He had a short fuse when listening to the blowhards who didn't serve but acted as if they knew everything about the war. Ed almost leveled one of his old friends when the guy bragged about how rich he became by staying stateside and profiting from the government's fat supply of war contracts.

His broken promise to Dory kept playing in his mind like a never-ending soundtrack. The scent of a dead animal on the street took his mind to the concentration camps. *Bodies were stacked like firewood.* A backfire from a car's exhaust pipe would startle him into thinking they were being attacked. *Hit the deck!* When he passed by disfigured veterans, he couldn't help but feel responsible, like there was something he should have done to save their limbs.

As the weeks passed, decisions made in the heat of the battle cycled through Ed's brain. It was like a skipping record, repeating the same words over and again. *D'Angelo, Washburn, McCaulley, Rollins, Nazis, fear, hate, revenge...*

He privately re-read certain parts of his journal, searching for answers. But reliving those events only made things worse. There were so many injured and dead. And then there were the living skeletons from the NAZI death camps. He was plagued by dreams where he was told, *"We're going back in,"* while wounded men called out, *"Help me!"*

Ed understood he was shell shocked, but he was powerless to turn it off. The more he tried, the more frustrated he became. He was sleeping less and had trouble thinking clearly. Not being able to control the negative drumbeat of his thoughts made his symptoms worsen.

It all came to a head in one horrific night. Ed dreamed he was in hand-to-hand combat with an enemy soldier. He pinned his rival to the ground and wrapped his hands around his adversary's neck to choke the life out of him. A burst of light flashed, and he was tackled from behind and yanked off his foe. Ed woke from his nightmare to find he had nearly killed the person he loved most. And might have, if not for her father's quick response.

The fear in Mary's eyes was his undoing. *My God! What have I done?*

✚ ✚ ✚

The next day, Mary delivered an ultimatum. "I can't go on like this anymore. I want to support you, but you can't keep shutting me out. For the health of our marriage, you must tell me what's going on inside your head so I can help you move past it."

Ed hung his head in shame. *What's wrong with me? I can't describe it.*

Mary pounded the table. "You can't fake your way through this any longer. Something's wrong with you! You're not the same person I married."

Ed wanted to curl up and die. *I'm losing her. And I'm powerless to stop it.*

PART III

CHAPTER 68:
CLEVELAND, OHIO
MARCH 2013

MAGGIE CLICKED off the camera. They had been filming for about five hours with only a few short breaks, and both women were exhausted.

"You did good, Mary. I'm so proud of you, and I know Ed would be too." Maggie reached across the table and patted her friend on the hand. "Your hand is so cold! Are you feeling ok?"

"Oh yes, I'm fine," Mary lied. "My arm must have fallen asleep from being on the table for so long." She hadn't felt well the entire time they were filming but didn't want to worry Maggie. "Let's just get through this. It's way past our senior bedtime." Mary let out a weary chuckle.

"Just one second." Maggie lifted a blanket from the couch and laid it across Mary's lap. "You can put your hands underneath the blanket. You'll be warmer."

Mary did as instructed. "All snugly warm now. Thank you, Maggie."

"I'll start asking you the questions again." Maggie wheeled around to the other side of the table and was ready to hit the record button when Mary stopped her.

"Maggie, wait. Before we get started, I have something to tell you." Mary's eyes glistened with unshed tears.

Maggie's freckled cheeks lifted into a soft smile. "Mary, I know what's going on, and if you say it, we'll never finish."

Mary nodded and blinked hard a few times. Filled with determination to finish Ed's story, she rolled her shoulders, took a deep breath, and signaled she was ready. Maggie tapped the record button once more.

✦ ✦ ✦

"What happened next?" Maggie asked.

"Ed told me everything. About horrific battles, wounded soldiers on both sides, mistreated POWs, Jewish civilians who were rounded up and killed by the millions, bombed-out cities and desperate people whose homes and livelihoods were destroyed, trauma around every corner, and most of all, about second-guessing every life-or-death decision he was forced to make in the direst of circumstances. On the exterior, he looked like his ruggedly handsome self, at least to me anyway. But on the inside, he told me he felt weak for not being able to control his negative thoughts."

"What then?" Maggie asked, her voice barely audible.

"I told him he was anything but weak, that I believed he was the complete opposite. A strong person admits a problem and works to overcome it. A weak person blames others for their problems and never moves forward. I'm sure I didn't use those exact words, but something close to it."

Mary took a sip of water. "The death of Scott Rollins weighed heavily on his mind. Ed was filled with intense guilt over the entire incident, and he kept replaying it in his head." Mary looked out the window, and despite the hour a cardinal was perched on the sill. Its head was cocked to one side as if it were listening to their conversation. Mary smiled and turned toward Maggie. "After our talk, Ed contacted Robert Louis and Dean Cooper and the three of them paid a visit to Janice Rollins."

Maggie nodded and shifted her weight in the chair. "I bet that was difficult for them."

"All three of the survivors were filled with guilt, not just my Eddie. It had been three years since they'd seen Janice last, and they found her living with her parents and two-year-old son. After they were introduced to the toddler, the guys told the boy they were his uncles." Mary's voice cracked, but she pressed forward.

"When Ed returned home, I could tell a huge weight had been lifted off his shoulders. A few weeks later, he formed a small war group made up of guys he trusted. They met for breakfast each week and were able to get troubling thoughts off their chests instead of letting them fester. He came to understand other veterans were experiencing the same emotions, and that helped him to feel more normal."

"How were things with you and Ed after *the incident*." Maggie used air quotes.

Mary let out a raspy laugh. "I would say our love for each other grew stronger after *the incident*. We made a pledge to look forward and not look back at the things that couldn't be changed. Ed applied for the Veteran's Unemployment benefits and used the GI Bill to go to the Northwest Ohio Meat Cutting School to learn how to be a butcher and shopkeeper. He thought about college, but he was 28 years old and wanted to get into the workforce to earn money."

"What were you doing at the time?" Maggie stretched out a kink in her back.

"I purchased a sewing machine and started my own seamstress business. I worked from my parents' home until we bought our first house, and socially, I played the role of gate keeper."

Maggie's eyebrow lifted. "What do you mean gate keeper?"

"I vetted all our social activities. We hung out with people we trusted and avoided situations where Ed's time in the service would be the main topic of conversation."

"I see, "Maggie said, nodding. "Anything else you care to share?"

Mary turned her head away from the camera and looked skyward. "Yes, Ed really didn't want to talk or think about the war anymore. He asked me to get rid of his war memorabilia, pictures, letters, and journals." I'll never forget what he said: "Reading that stuff brings me back to a place I ache to forget. Burn it!"

"Burn it?" Maggie shook her head vigorously. "If he asked you to burn it, why do you still have all this stuff?"

Mary grimaced. "I didn't have the heart to destroy any of it. Our love letters to each other and pictures of our dear friends from that time were a huge part of our early life together. Not all of it was bad; much of it was beautiful. While I respected his need not to talk about the war years, I sealed everything in a box and stashed it away. I treated it like a buried time capsule."

"Do your kids know about this stuff?"

"I shared pictures with Peach and told her the good parts of the story. But none of my children were told of Ed's exploits during the war, or about what went on between us when he returned."

Maggie leaned forward. "Why not?"

"I kept my promise to my husband. And admittedly, I feared that if we shared his stories with our children, they might barrage him with questions and trigger his insidious thoughts. Or even worse, start to fear him."

"So why are you telling the story now?"

Mary had prepared for this question. "Shortly after the war, we received the nicest Christmas card from one of the officers that Ed had worked with during the war. His name was Capt. Weaver and he penned a note to Ed, but he also wrote to me directly."

The card had been preserved in a plastic bag for the past 68 years, it was dated December 3rd, 1945. Mary picked up the card from the table and read it out loud.

Hello Eddie.

I didn't get home until 7 November but am glad to be home now. I have your address and have had it for a long time, but I've lost some others. I wonder if you could happen to have Kacymarek's and O'Malley's and any others there abouts. I hope you are settled down to a job if there is one available and things break for you. If I can be of service, let me know.

Mary paused and looked straight at the camera. "And here's what he wrote to me."

Dear Mrs. Eddie-

This is merely to reiterate that fact which you already know, namely, that that husband of yours was the best platoon sgt (Sergeant) in the army and led the best platoon in the army. Only about 40 people know this, and I am glad to be one of those.

As Mary held the Christmas card in her hands, she thought about Charles Leibold, Dean Cooper, Scott Rollins, Robert Louis, Capt. Weaver and of course, her darling Eddie. All of them had since passed away, taking their war stories with them. She questioned if anyone would still care about the bravery these medics displayed in the most horrific of circumstances. But she cared, and that's all that mattered.

Mary spoke from heart, her pride for Ed bubbling forth. "These days, our country seems divided on so many different issues. Not too long ago, our generation of young people banded together to save the world from persecution and oppression. Sacrifice, compassion, and kindness held our country together during those difficult years. Most people are fascinated with Hitler, Mussolini, and Churchill and other famous leaders. But the war was fought and won by thousands of regular men. Men just like your brother, my husband, and his platoon. And some very brave women, too. It was excruciating for me when I didn't hear from Ed for long stretches at a time. Every time I learned that a young man we knew died in the war, a piece of me died, too. A day never went by that I didn't remind myself how lucky I was that my love came back home alive."

Mary put the card back on the table and picked up a portrait of her and Ed. "I'll never know how these old pictures made it through the war, and later, the flood. Maybe God put them in my possession so that Ed's story could be shared before it was lost forever, and that we never forget the best and worst parts of humanity."

Maggie dabbed her eyes with a tissue. "Anything else?"

Mary took a deep breath. "In conclusion, I'm proud to say my husband Edmund D. Kruszynski was a good son, brother, father, and family man. He served his country and did his level best to be a good leader for his platoon. He was a compassionate medic, and he and the forty men he led saved countless lives. Both allies and enemies."

Mary paused. Had she done Ed's story justice? Yes, she believed she had to the very best of her ability. Now she wondered how best to end the story. After a moment's reflection, she found what she wanted to say.

"I attest this to be a true account. My name is Mary Kruszynski.

And I am the Medic's Wife."

CHAPTER 69:
CLEVELAND, OHIO
MARCH 2013

THE DAY after filming, Mary fell ill. She was taken to the hospital and hospice was called. Only two days after recording Ed's story, she passed away peacefully. While her death was not totally unexpected, losing Mary was devastating for her children, grandchildren, and friends old and new. She gave love unconditionally and was cherished by all who knew her.

Ever thoughtful and forward-looking, Mary had pre-planned for her funeral arrangements. Her granddaughter, Peach, gave her eulogy, during which she talked about how close they became when Mary was her roommate in the months after the flood. "My grandmother was an exceptional person, a true bright light. We will all miss her greatly."

Mary was laid to rest in the Brecksville Cemetery. She was buried next to Ed. They were married for 58 years and remain together for eternity.

The day after the funeral, Peach, Dean, and Kory went to the Assisted Living Center to gather Mary's possessions and close out her account. The family came prepared with large plastic tubs and the three of them went through the room with a "fine tooth comb," to coin one of Mary's favorite phrases. At the end of their search, they discovered a few more $100 bills wadded up in some of Mary's hiding places. "More bingo money," Kory said with a sad smile.

They took one last scan of the room to see if they missed anything, and Peach instinctively looked under the bed. "I found something," she announced as she pulled out two books and a large shoe box. Opening them up, she cried, "Hey, these are Gram's photo albums that were damaged in the flood!" Kory and Dean walked over for a closer look.

"Gram tried to restore some of the damaged pictures when she lived with me. Each night, she showed me a few photos and told me the story behind them. I wish I could go back in time and ask her more questions."

"I feel the same way," Dean said.

Kory nodded in agreement. "Is there anything else in the box?"

Peach put the box on the bed. Inside, she was surprised to discover reel-to-reel tapes, VHS videos, and 8mm cassettes. Some were labeled and some weren't. "What's on those tapes?"

Kory glanced inside the box. "Those are family movies that Dean and I have seen a million times. Mom and Dad were big on filming birthdays, first communions, and the opening of Christmas presents."

"Is it okay if I take everything home?" Peach asked. "I'd love to see all those old pictures again. I can also take the home movies to a photography studio and see if they can digitize all these different formats and put them on a flash drive for us."

"That's a great idea," Kory said, her eyes brimming with tears.

"I agree," Dean said. "It's a smart move to get them converted before the tapes degrade any further."

When the three of them finished packing all of Mary's belongings, they met with Stephanie to close the account. Before they left, Kory said, "I knocked on Maggie's door when we first arrived and did again as we were leaving Mom's room. There was no answer either time. I walked the corridors hoping to bump into her but still no luck. I really wanted to say goodbye and thank her for being such a dear friend to our mom."

Stephanie smiled weakly and turned her head away. "I've been in this business a long time and never witnessed two people develop such a fast and enduring friendship. They made our jobs fun, and they pushed their friends to enjoy life to the fullest. Maggie came to us with stage four breast cancer. Her family told me she only had five to six months left. She beat the diagnosis by well over a year."

Kory covered her mouth with her hand and Peach dropped onto the nearest chair. Dean rubbed his forehead. "Mom never told us Maggie was sick," he murmured.

"Their generation was used to overcoming hardships. Your mom and Maggie were so resilient and full of life, and never spoke about their ailments to anyone." Stephanie swallowed hard. She steepled her fingers together in front of her and delivered the news they had all begun to expect. "Maggie got sick the day after your mom passed away. She fought the good fight but died in the hospital just a few days after Mary did."

Margaret (Maggie) O'Sullivan was 92 years old.

CHAPTER 70:
BRECKSVILLE, OHIO
JUNE 2014

THE BOX of videos had been collecting dust in Peach's home for over a year. She blamed work, but in all honestly, knew grief had prevented her from dealing with it. Finally, one sunny afternoon, Peach felt ready to open the box.

She grabbed a pair of scissors from the desk, opened the carton, and removed the tapes. As Peach swished her hand around the bottom of the box, she discovered something curious.

It was Mary's cellphone. Kory had purchased the smart phone for Mary so she could learn to text message, but she rarely used it. Peach figured Kory or Dean must have absentmindedly tossed the phone in the box with the rest of the cassettes. *Oh hell. There's no harm in looking at a few pictures.*

Peach knew the security code and typed G-R-A-M. Sure enough, the smartphone unlocked and the home page lit up. She went right to the photo icon on the device and found five blurry photographs of carpeting, a ceiling, a wall, and a window. Finding nothing of interest, she decided to check the video recordings. When she noticed the time stamp on the first video, she nearly fell out of her chair. *This was taken only a few days before Gram passed away!*

There were two short videos and five long segments. *What is this?*

Peach clicked on the first video and there was Mary sitting at a table. She was smartly dressed, wearing a lavender blouse with a matching purple and yellow scarf. Around her neck was a beautiful Camay necklace Ed had gifted her. Mary's face was made up like she was going to a wedding, complete with lipstick and eyeliner. She appeared thinner than Peach remembered, but still looked beautiful and vibrant on the screen.

Peach heard a familiar voice; the rich Irish brogue gave it away. *Maggie!*

She laughed out loud when she watched the ladies doing their "practice" videos. When Peach clicked on the first hour long segment, she quickly understood the treasure she'd discovered.

For the next five hours, Peach didn't move a muscle as she watched and listened to her grandmother's testimony.

My God, I never knew the entire story... none of us did.

EPILOGUE

The driving force in getting this story out was indeed Mary Kruszynski, the medic's wife. After the flood destroyed some of her and Ed's wartime correspondences, Mary preserved the remaining articles she had kept in her possession.

Incredibly, she managed to restore over 200 photographs taken between 1940–1945. She painstakingly cleaned each photo by hand.

Mary pieced together Ed's remarkable story from documented records, personal correspondences between her and Ed, newspaper articles, and from her own memory. We are all forever grateful that she videotaped the story for our family.

Mary was in her late eighties when she assembled and recorded these events. She enjoyed the rest of her long life and passed away at 94 years young.

I think she would be happy with the way her story has been shared.

Great job, Mom. Mission accomplished!

Mary Kruszynski
The Medic's Wife

PHOTOGRAPHS

Many of the following photographs were discovered inside of Mary's flood-soaked condominium. Later, they were digitally restored bringing them closer to their original condition. Other photographs are sourced from the U.S. National Archives and are marked as such.

Ed age 20, playing for team Camela. Circa 1937.

Mary, age 21, 1940.

Ed (22) and Mary (20) dating circa 1940.

*Ed receives a going away draft card from
the "Schoemberger's Gang" 1941.*

—— A BLOCK OF FIGHTING MEN ——

Neighborhood Pals Answer Call

Ninety-Six Families in Small Section Off Harvard Avenue Send 26 Sons
To Fight With U.S. Armed Forces on Far-Flung Fronts of the World

The Cleveland Press ran a story about how 96 families in a small
section off Harvard Avenue sent 26 sons to fight in the U.S.
armed forces. It was an unusual concentration of servicemen
coming from a small neighborhood. Ed is shown 3rd row,
3rd from left. Courtesy of the Cleveland News 7-23-1942.

1st row: Walter Luchka, Theodore Luchka, Carl Grossmeyer Jr., John
Edwards, Walter Pikus, James Green.2nd row: Joseph Gornick, Frank
Gornick, George Archer Jr.,
Frank Farren, Joseph Shimick, William Novak.

3rd row: Edmond Sliwinski, Stanley Koral, Edmund
Kruszynski, Curtis Clark, Steve Woicik, Mathew Zielinske.

4th row: Oliver Gault, Elgio A. Rogo, Gerard Kennedy, John
Papushak, George Papushak, William Rubick, George Rubick.

Ed right, Big Hand center, brother Harry left. Circa 1941

Ed's mother Stella. Circa 1941.

*The recruits work with instructors to learn the proper way to
rig up a one-man tent. Note the drill instructor, lower center on
bended knee with baton. Basic training, Ft. Oglethorpe GA 1941.*

Ed left, field training. Sometimes conditions are not ideal for setting up camp, 1941.

Ed's nose runs into the fist of a semi-pro boxer (Ed right). Fort Oglethorpe, GA. Circa 1941.

*Left, Ed sporting a new uniform. Right, showing off
his push-up honed physique. Circa 1941.*

Ed (left) promoted to Private. In field training with other members of the 65th medical regiment. Circa summer 1942.

Ed (center) working to reset a collapsed tent due to heavy rain. Field training circa 1942.

*Ed, center with sleeveless white shirt, standing inside
a no-frills mobile work tent. Circa 1942.*

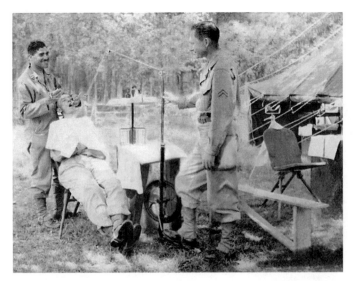

*65th Medical Regiment field dental clinic. Note the foot
pedal which powers the dentist's hand drill. Circa 1942.*

Weapons and communications training. Circa 1942.

Ed back on base. Circa 1942.

*Mary standing and Ed's two sisters, Helen and
Lottie, visiting Camp Forrest TN, 1942.*

*Mary, forth from left, visiting Ed (standing left) at Camp Forrest.
Ed's sister Lottie second from right. Army photographer far right.*

*Ed (on right) shortly after being promoted to
Sergeant. Camp Forrest. Summer 1943.*

Ed, left, in field training. Circa 1942.

*Mary and Ed, now married, and living off base
at Camp Forrest, TN. Winter 1943.*

President Franklin D. Roosevelt's motorcade stopped at Camp
Forrest as part of the President's war-time tour of camps.
Roosevelt was welcomed with an artillery salute from 35mm
howitzers as his motorcade rolled through the camp. Maj.
Gen. Horace McBride, Lt. Gen. Ben Lear, and TN Gov. Prentice
Cooper were among the other dignitaries in the car with
the President. Source: Roosevelt Library April 17th, 1943.

LITTER DIGEST
65 TH MED. REGT.

VOL. 2 NO. 13   CAMP FORREST, TENN.   AUGUST, 1943.

GAMES AND MUSICAL INSTRUMENT CONTEST

PRIZES FOR BOTH CONTESTS:
1st Prize: $5.00
2nd Prize: Two cartons of cigarettes
3rd Prize: One carton of cigarettes

This contest is being sponsored by the Regiment and conducted by the Special Service Officer. All entries are to be turned into the Special Service Office for judging. All entries must be in by Aug. 25th. Judges will be announced at a later date.

Here is a chance for all of you to profitably make use of some of your leisure time and get your imagination working. Maybe this will give you an idea. One of the oddest, but good, bands in North Africa is the Pill Rollers. The instrumentation consists of 3 tonettes, a fife, 2 ocarinas, 2 kazoos, 2 guitars, a mandolin and the following self-made instruments: 2 bamboo pipes, five jugs, 3 bottles, xylophone, string bass, washboard, tom-tom, drums, and zimbalon.

RULES FOR CONTEST:
1. Materials used must come from our regimental area.
2. Musical instruments can be any type of noise maker, rhythm, or pitch.
3. Performance on musical instrument not required.
4. Space required for games restricted to limited area such as concealed bivouac area or area available on boat.
5. No limit to number of players to participate in game.
6. Musical instrument entries must be tagged with name, grade, company, and explanation of how instrument is played.
7. All game entries are to be tagged with name, grade, and company with rules for playing game.

CO. "A" WINS CAMP FORREST SOFTBALL TOURNAMENT

Co "A" won the Camp Forrest softball tournament that is being sponsored by the Coca Cola Co throughout all the Army Camps in the nation.

In the final game played Mon. afternoon at the Sports Arena between Co "A" and 839th Ordnance, Co "A" won after a hard played game behind great pitching by Larry Wilson and the 839th Foeckler. They both allowed only four hits and it was Porteous' home run in the fourth inning and left fielder Comer's double in the fifth that sewed up the game for the 65th.

It was a great tournament all the way, nip and tuck down the stretch and Co "A" is deserving of all the credit for their great playing throughout the entire series. A trophy and medals are forthcoming.

Co "A" will represent Camp Forrest in a series of games to be played in Chattanooga in the very near future for at least the state championship in which the winning team goes to Detroit to compete for the National title.

The personnel of Co "A" team is: Mgr Cate, Wilson, Palicka, Porteous, Koener, Cowan, Kryzinski, Baronowski, Comer, Steele, Locck, LeFountain, Kilgore, Varian, Nichols, and Simpers.

839 ORD. 000001010
65 TH 00011 0X244

Private Jones had been courting a mountain girl in the vicinity of his camp. One night her father said, " "Jones you bin seeing our Nellie for nigh onto a year. What are your intentions—honorable or dishonorable?"

With an excited gleam in his eye, the GI asked, "Ya mean I got a choice?"

The Litter Digest was the official newsletter of the 65th Medical Regiment. Ed's team, Company A, won the Camp Forrest Softball Tournament. The team was headed to Chattanooga to play in the Army base regional championship round. 1943.

Ed was never far from his ball and glove, note the softball in left hand. His team (Company A) never got a chance to play in the regional tournament in Chattanooga. The 65th Medical Regiment was deployed to Europe two weeks before the scheduled games.

Photograph of Navy pilots playing basketball on the USS Monterey, ca. 6/1944. The jumper on the left has been identified as Gerald R. Ford. Ford served as the assistant navigator, Athletic Officer, and antiaircraft battery officer on board Monterey. U.S Archives.

William Patrick Hitler (left) was cleared to join the US Navy
after making a special request to President Roosevelt. He
served in the Naval Medical Corps, was wounded in action,
and received the Purple Heart. Source: US Navy.

Ed, standing upper left, with the 1st section of the
1st Platoon. Donhagadee Ireland, 1944.

Ed (left) with members of the 1st Platoon. Note the two schoolboys on the upper right hand corner sneaking into the picture. Winter 1944.

The 648th Medical Clearing Company train wearing protective gas masks. Spring 1944.

Sir Anthony Eden, England's War Secretary (center) accepts
a cigarette from a soldier from the 648th Medical Clearing
Company. Ed's handwriting "Mr. Eden" clearly visible on the
bottom of the photograph. Ditchley Park, England, 1944.

D-Day June 6th, 1944. U.S Archives.

Medics tend to wounded on the Normandy beaches. U.S. Archives.

Once filled with wounded, the LCTs would sail back to England or make a shorter trip out to sea and transfer the injured to large LSTs. U.S. Archives.

Hedgerow fighting. Normandy France June-July 1944. U.S. Archives.

*American infantry troops under enemy machine gun fire
near the city of Avranches France. 9 Sept 1944. U.S. Army.*

Members of the 1st Platoon bathing in a stream somewhere near Avranches, France. Ed on right. Circa fall 1944.

Surgical tent with the large red cross visible from the air (upper right). American ambulances and pup tents are camouflaged under a tree canopy (upper left). Near Avranches, France. Circa fall 1944.

Officer of the 648th in ankle deep water. Fall 1944.

Digging a slit trench. France, fall 1944.

Ed behind the wheel of a U.S. ambulance. France, fall 1944.

The 1st platoon unarmed and on patrol. Ed on far left. France or Belgium winter 1944–45.

The 1st platoon spent Christmas in Montmédy, France. The men signed a postcard which Ed kept throughout the war. Legible signatures include: Doc Caufman, "Foxhole Kid" Eddie, Howard R. Scott, Noel Riddle, Maurice Hart, Ray Moeri, Bud "Pard" Brinkley. December 1944.

*Inspecting a piece of abandoned artillery. Ed,
third from the right, standing behind the firing
mechanism. France or Belgium winter 1944–45.*

*Shot up WC54 ambulance near the outskirts of
Bastogne Belgium. January 1945. U.S. Archives.*

The 1st Platoon on foot in Bastogne, Belgium. Ed is pictured fourth person from the right. Note: The medics are weaponless. Winter 1944–45.

As the German army retreated deeper toward their border, they left behind a path of mass destruction. Part of the carnage was the slaughter of all livestock and service animals as the Germans fled past towns and villages. Here, the men find solace in seeing live horses which escaped the killings. Ed with hand on horse. Winter 1945.

*In a lighter moment the medics take aim with snowballs.
Citadel or blockhouse in the background. Ed standing
forth from left. Belgium, winter 1944–45.*

Skating down an icy street in Belgium. Winter 1944–45

Ed, right, standing in front of a citadel.
Belgium or France. Winter 1944–45.

Members of the 1st platoon enjoying a respite from
the war. Ed second from right. Belgium 1945.

The Army supplied venereal disease (VD) posters to prevent the spread of STD's but also to preserve valuable supplies of penicillin to treat battlefield related infections. US. Archives.

Smokescreens were used to camouflage troop and equipment movement. U.S. Archives.

Ed, second left, and his friends posing
outside a Nissan Hut. Spring 1945.

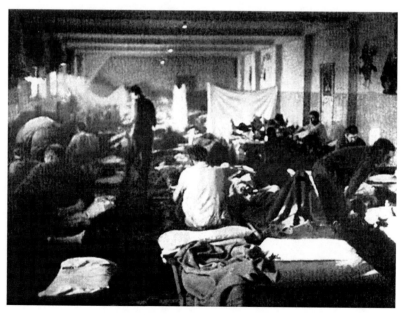

It was a luxury to find a safe place indoors to treat patients.
Note patient privacy section (upper right). Spring 1945.

Emaciated POWs found living in barracks.
Buchenwald Concentration Camp. (U.S. Archives)

A large pile of dead bodies at the Buchenwald concentration camp. The Nazis were unable to cremate the bodies before the camp was liberated. Members of the 648th medical clearing company entered the camp six days after its liberation. The undocumented soldiers in the photo above are S/Sgt Edmund Kruszynski (fourth from the left) and other medics from the 1st Platoon. Source: Jewish Virtual Library, photo taken by Sgt John Poulos MP in the 512th MP Battalion. Poulos was an early liberator of the camp. April 1945.

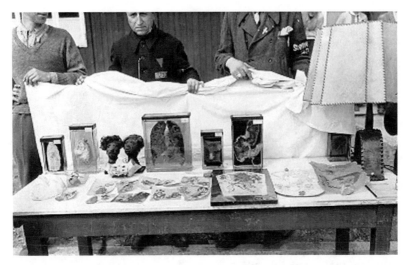

An exhibit of human remains and artifacts retrieved by the American Army from a pathology laboratory run by the SS in Buchenwald. Two shrunken heads from Polish prisoners who were recaptured and executed after escaping from camp. Tattoos allegedly extracted from prisoner's skin were made into lampshades and wallets and given as gifts to NAZI VIPs when they visited the camp. U.S. Archives.

Soon after liberation, child survivors pictured from Buchenwald's children's block 66. Germany. 11 April 1945. Source Jewish Virtual Library.

Ed sketched a map of his travels during his service in WWII.
Remarkably this map made it all the way through the
war. On the very bottom of the map he has a handwritten
notation which states "follow the red line with big dots.
It's our location and travels during the campaigns." His
final entry was Innsbruck Austria, likely June 1945.

Members of the 648th Medical Clearing Company.
Ed standing second from right. Summer 1945.

Edmund D Kruszynski, summer of 1945 in Munich Germany.

Staff Sergeant Edmund D Kruszynski, a WWII combat medic, participated in the following campaigns: Normandy, Northern France, Central Europe, Rhineland, and the Battle of the Bulge (Ardennes). He was awarded five bronze combat stars, the four stripes and slash on his left sleeve indicates the number of major battles (5) in which he fought.

His medals included the European, African, Middle Eastern Service medal with one silver service star, the American Defense Service medal and the Good Conduct Medal. His unit received the Meritorious Service Award for exemplary performance while in combat against an armed enemy.

Toward the end of the war S/Sgt Kruszynski treated allied and enemy POW's at the following Nazi concentration camps: Buchenwald, Ingolstadt, Schrobenhausen, Paffenhausen, and Dachau.

Ed and Mary received this Christmas Card from
Capt. Tom Weaver November 7th, 1945.

Dear Mrs. Eddie—
This is merely to reiterate that fact which you already know,
namely, that that husband of yours was the best platoon sgt
(Sergeant) in the army and led the best platoon in the army. Only
about 40 people know this, and I am glad to be one of those."

Ed and Mary on their 50th wedding anniversary.

AUTHOR'S COMMENTS

After my father convalesced from the war, he and my mother began to build their lives together. Ed used the GI bill to enroll in the Northwest School of Meat Cutting. He learned the craft of being a butcher and was taught the ins and outs of owning a meat market from his older brother (Mike) who owned a delicatessen.

Mary saved all the money she made working for Jack and Heinz and she and Ed bought their first grocery store in 1947. The first floor of the building was the market and my mother and father lived on the second floor. One year later, my sister was born and thirteen months later, my older brother came into the world. I'm the youngest, a decade younger than my brother.

As the years rolled on, my parents did well in business and upgraded their stores several times, providing good jobs for more people. Ed ran the stores and Mary kept the books.

Ed never again played baseball for Camela's, but he developed a love for golf and bowling, winning several amateur championships in both sports.

He and Mary loved dancing and joined various jitterbug and polka clubs, and later took up square dancing. They also enjoyed having season tickets to the Cleveland Browns football and Cleveland Barons hockey teams.

To my mother's amusement, the local senior citizen club created an "old man's" softball league. At age 70, Ed was the starting catcher for the team. Mary watched some of the games and coined the sport "slow motion" softball.

Mary and Ed attended almost every WWII reunion and loved sharing family updates with their friends from the Fort Oglethorpe and Camp Forrest days. Ed marched in Brecksville's annual Memorial Day parade and was a member of the local VFW club.

When Ed retired at age 65, he volunteered at the local Veteran's Administration Hospital. He counseled younger veterans who were experiencing PTSD and, in this way, was able to better understand and deal with his own periodic bouts.

On his 80th birthday, Mary hauled out Ed's Army jacket and made him try it on; remarkably, it still fit. He snapped off a crisp salute to his family and friends at the party.

U.S. Army S/Sgt Edmund D. Kruszynski (Krow) died in 2001 at age 83 and had a full military funeral. His casket was draped with an American flag and a bugler played "Taps," which made all of us tear up. An Army adjunct assigned to his funeral folded and presented Mary with the American flag that draped his coffin.

ACKNOWLEDGEMENTS

First, I would like to separate fact from fiction. *The Medic's Wife* is a WWII historical fiction memoir based on the true story of Staff Sergeant Edmund D. Kruszynski, his wife Mary, and a platoon of medics from the 648th Medical Clearing Company of the United States Army. To make this story more enjoyable and relatable, I used creative license to fill in gaps. I hope you enjoyed reading it as much as I enjoyed writing it.

The cities and travels of the 648th Medical Clearing company came from the United States Archives. I used actual unit histories and after-action reports, combined with my father's personal documents, to piece together the timelines and locations for the battlefield scenes described in the book. Other records such as WWII veteran oral histories, newsletters, and first-hand accounts of the battles were helpful in creating the combat scenes for various chapters. When there were discrepancies in the data, I used my best judgement to recreate the most likely scenario.

My father's journal entries and letters which appear throughout the novel are not the originals. Sadly, those treasures were lost or destroyed during the flood. Luckily, I was able to reconstruct many of them based on my mother's memories of her war time correspondences with my father. Understandably, with the passage of six decades, some of my mother's reminisces were incomplete. In those instances, I used oral histories of other veterans who were present at the time to augment the story. I believe these reconstructed entries reflect the essence of what my father was experiencing during wartime and enhance the authenticity of the story.

I used dialogue to provide characters with emotional depth, the scenes in which dialogue occurs between various characters was crafted using creative license but was underpinned by first-hand veteran testimonies and from Mary's own recollections. In some instances, I used aliases and/or changed the roles of certain characters out of respect for their deeply personal stories of tragedy, manner of death, or wish for privacy.

There were so many people who generously devoted their time and talents at various stages of the book's development. To each and every one, please accept my deep gratitude for the support you provided to me along the way. Your feedback made my father's story come to life, and for that, I most grateful.

First and foremost, I'd like to thank Tracy, my darling wife. She patiently listened to all my writing insecurities and kept encouraging me "to keep going" even when the task at hand felt so overwhelming. Finishing the book is much to her credit as it is mine.

My appreciation goes to my sister and brother (Doreen Bochmann and Dale Kay) for helping to identify people in the photographs, and for providing anecdotal history that supplemented the stories and scenes in the book. A special thank you to my brother-in-law, Carl Bochmann, for the support and love he extended to both Ed and Mary, especially toward the end of their long lives.

The story was enhanced via the photographic restoration work of Brigid Krane and Evan Ecklund from Artists Eleven. They are expert graphic artists and specialize in restoring damaged photographs. Each picture used in this book sustained water damaged on some level. Several of the photographs I thought were well beyond repair, only to be restored in stunning detail by Brigid and Evan. And thank you to Cherry Riddell for the use the Brecksville flood picture in Chapter 1.

Leslie Hertzenberg helped me decipher my father's handwriting. Especially when it came to analyzing the dates, combat campaigns, and locations which Krow scribbled down on his map in the heat of the moment.

Thank you to beta readers Tracy Kruszynski, Doreen and Carl Bochmann, Dale Kay, Brigid Krane, Evan Ecklund, Dr. Michelle Spina, Marci O'Neil, Cherry Riddell, Michael and Jeana Kruszynski, Austin and Rachel Kruszynski, and Richard and Nadine Edwards.

Mary's younger brother Ray Ratica and his wife Barbara were not only beta readers, but Ray also provided valuable recollections of when Ed returned home from the war. In a large part I crafted the "welcome home" scenes in the book based on Ray's boyhood memories.

I'd like to thank my developmental and copy editors who read the manuscript and provided valuable wisdom and advice on character development, pacing, closing loopholes, and how best to structure the chapters so they flowed nicely together. Those excellent editors are Audrey Beth Stein who coached me on character points of view, David Grandouiller who did the heavy lift on the initial development edit, and Laura Cooper whose deep knowledge of sentence and story structure brought this manuscript to life.

Special thank you to Bill Beigel WW2 Research Inc who located my father's service records, unit history, and after-action reports. The reports pinpointed actual locations, timelines, and the platoon's daily movements. They also contained a treasure trove of vivid military descriptions of the unit's combat campaigns which augmented the historical accuracy of the story.

Maj. General John A. Yingling, United States Army (Ret), and his wife, Ann, graciously welcomed me into their home and allowed me to explain the arc of the story to them. Maj. Gen Yingling shared how to best position the narrative to members of the armed forces, while Mrs. Yingling let me tap into her dual experiences as an Army wife and mother of a son who is currently serving on active duty in the United States Army.

Lastly, thank you to Hellgate Press for believing in the story, and publishing it nationwide.

ABOUT THE AUTHOR

EDMUND KRUSZYNSKI (Ed) was born in Cleveland, Ohio to second-generation Polish immigrants. He was the second in his family to finish college and spent the next thirty-two years as an executive in corporate America.

When he was younger, he craved to hear more about his father's service in WWII. But like many other veterans his father never spoke of the war, and when he died his father's role in the conflict may have been just another forgotten footnote in history.

But a small miracle occurred amid a catastrophic flood. A box was unearthed containing priceless correspondences between his father and mother during the war years. At first Ed thought he would create a nice family narrative to be passed down through the generations.

But his goals for the project changed when he got deeper into the research. While working on the project he discovered that his father, a WWII Army medic, witnessed the horrors of the Holocaust first-hand. With the recent wave of hostility and persecution in some parts of the world, Ed decided to take the story to a broader audience. "If we can't learn from history, how can we make the future a better place?"

Ed is married, has two grown sons, one grandchild, and a golden retriever named Lovey. He occasionally enjoys a glass of fine Kentucky Bourbon, which came in handy when he experienced a few creative lulls while working on this story. *The Medic's Wife* is his debut book.

We hope you enjoyed reading *The Medic's Wife*. To leave a review, just look up "The Medic's Wife" on Amazon.com. Thank you!

www.HellgatePress.com

Made in United States
North Haven, CT
08 July 2024

54520335R10187